Also by Portia MacIntosh:

Off The Record
Love on Tour
Drive Me Crazy
Truth or Date
It's Not You, It's Them
The Accidental Honeymoon
Never The Bride
Here Comes the Ex

Marram Bay series
Falling For You
Snow Love Lost
Met Your Match

Honeymoon For One
My Great Ex-Scape
The Plus One Pact
Stuck On You
One Night Only
Faking it
Life's a Beach
Will They, Won't They?
No Ex Before Marriage
The Meet Cute Method
Single All The Way
Just Date and See
Your Place or Mine?

Better Off Wed
Long Time No Sea
Fake It or Leave It
Trouble in Paradise
One Wild Night
Ex in the City
The Suite Life
It's All Sun and Games
One of the Boys
You Had Me at Château
Wish You Weren't Here
Too Hot To Handle

Praise for Portia MacIntosh:

'Smart, funny and always brilliantly entertaining, every book from Portia becomes my new favourite romcom.'
Shari Low

'I laughed, I cried – I loved it.'
Holly Martin

'The queen of romcom!'
Rebecca Raisin

'This book made me laugh and kept me turning the pages.'
Mandy Baggot

'A fun, fabulous 5-star romcom!'
Sandy Barker

'Loved the book, it's everything you expect from the force that is Portia! A must read'
Rachel Dove

'Fun and witty. Pure escapism!'
Laura Carter

'A heartwarming, fun story, perfect for several hours of pure escapism.'
Jessica Redland

PORTIA MACINTOSH is the bestselling author of over thirty romantic comedy novels. From disastrous dates to destination weddings, Portia's romcoms are the perfect way to escape from day-to-day life, visiting sunny beaches in the summer and snowy villages at Christmas time. Whether it's southern Italy or the Yorkshire coast, Portia's stories are the holiday you're craving, conveniently packed in between the pages.

Formerly a journalist, Portia has left the city, swapping the music biz for the moors, to live the (not so) quiet life with her husband and her dog in Yorkshire.

Website: portiamacintosh.com
Instagram: @portiamacintoshauthor

Always the Bridesmaid

PORTIA MACINTOSH

ONE PLACE. MANY STORIES

HQ
An imprint of HarperCollins*Publishers* Ltd
1 London Bridge Street
London SE1 9GF

www.harpercollins.co.uk

HarperCollins*Publishers*
Macken House, 39/40 Mayor Street Upper,
Dublin 1 D01 C9W8
This edition 2026

1

First published in Great Britain as *Bad Bridesmaid* by HQ,
an imprint of HarperCollins*Publishers* Ltd 2014

Copyright © Portia MacIntosh 2014

Portia MacIntosh asserts the moral right to be identified as the author of this work.
A catalogue record for this book is available from the British Library.

ISBN: 9780008802646

This novel is entirely a work of fiction. The names, characters
and incidents portrayed in it are the work of the author's
imagination. Any resemblance to actual persons, living or
dead, events or localities is entirely coincidental.

All rights reserved. No part of this publication may be reproduced,
stored in a retrieval system, or transmitted, in any form or by any means,
electronic, mechanical, photocopying, recording or otherwise,
without the prior permission of the publishers.

Without limiting the exclusive rights of any author, contributor or the
publisher of this publication, any unauthorized use of this publication to
train generative artificial intelligence (AI) technologies is expressly prohibited.
HarperCollins also exercise their rights under Article 4(3) of the Digital Single
Market Directive 2019/790 and expressly reserve this publication from the text
and data mining exception.

Printed and bound in the UK using 100%
Renewable Electricity at CPI Group (UK) Ltd

*For Kim,
my incredible mum*

Chapter 1

They say there is no such thing as bad sex. They lie.

After a couple of weeks of seriously steamy flirting with Zack Carson, I just knew that there would be fireworks when we finally got around to getting it on – but it's an uncomfortably hot Los Angeles night and, despite Zack's best efforts, the fireworks just aren't going off. Not even a sparkler. Not even a birthday cake candle. I'm too warm, I'm bored and my neck is starting to ache thanks to the overly ambitious position of Zack's choosing.

Did it occur to me that it might not be such a good idea to sleep with my boss's assistant? Of course it did, but one look into his sexy brown eyes combined with his jet-black crew cut and his chiselled, model-like good looks and I was never going to be able to resist – and that's before I realised he has a motorbike. Bikers are hot – especially tall, dark and handsome ones who are covered in tattoos like Zack is. Still, I've got nothing going on down there. I'm not sure how long we've been at it, but I'm ready for it to end.

I scoop together my long, honey-blonde coloured curls and twist them into a bun on top of my head. This does little to cool me down but I know that as soon as I break out my GCSE drama skills (I just about scraped a C grade) I can pull a Meg Ryan and put an end to this.

'That was awesome,' Zack says afterwards, in his strong Californian accent – one that never fails to fascinate me, no matter how many years I've been here.

I moved here when I was twenty-five, and in the four years I've been living and working here, I haven't lost my Kentish accent, not even a little. Everyone teases me for it; you wouldn't believe how many Mary Poppins jokes I have to endure on a daily basis. Despite being born and raised in Canterbury, my American friends can't distinguish between my accent and Dick Van Dyke's attempt at sounding Cockney, and so the soundtrack to my life here will forever be 'Chim Chim Cher-ee'.

I watch as Zack makes himself more comfortable on the sofa. As I anxiously nibble my middle fingernail, I wonder how quickly I'm going to be able to get him to leave.

'Could you fix me a drink?' he asks, flashing me a big, toothy grin. 'Whatever you've got.'

'Sure,' I reply reluctantly. 'Back in a sec.'

As I walk towards the sink I hear Zack call after me.

'This is a nice place you got here.'

'Thanks,' I reply. I'm not surprised he likes it; it was designed with someone like Zack in mind. The interior of my Beverly Hills apartment is everything you'd expect of a lad pad. It is ultra-modern, with clean white walls and huge floor-to-ceiling windows to make the most of the stunning view, perfect for the king of the castle. With its white walls, glass surfaces and the pretty LED lighting that runs around the room, the open-plan living area has the vibes of a fancy hotel lobby. I can change the colour theme depending on my mood, but unless I set the glow to pink (as I most often do) you could easily think this was still a bachelor pad.

The place came furnished (because the bachelor it belonged to met a girl, fell in love and decided he wanted to play house – sucks for him, great news for me) but the furnishings suit me just fine. The custom-made white leather sofa is a delight to sit on (it feels like Matthew McConaughey is hugging your bum), the kitchen has all the bells and whistles you could even begin to imagine (plus some I still haven't figured out) and the bathroom could rival certain spas we have back home.

You can tell the place used to belong to a movie star, because when I moved in there was a huge wall-mounted TV – which I have recently upgraded to an even bigger one – and I loved the way he had framed posters from his movies all over the walls, so much so that I did the same. I realise how vain that sounds, but it's not as bad in my case because my face isn't on the posters. I don't star in movies, I write them. Romantic comedies to be precise. I'm part of a small writing group called Pink Inc. and we've been responsible for all of the big hits in our genre over the past four years. I made a name for myself back in England when I was in my early twenties, writing for a girly TV drama called *Love Online*. The show was about a group of young women who decided to try and find love by meeting boys on the net. This was around the time social networks were becoming a 'must' among young people and the show turned out to be a huge success. So at least I have that to thank the MySpace generation for – that and the world embracing flattering, high-angle selfies. After that I went on to bigger and better things, before eventually moving here and joining a team of screenwriters.

My success can be a little off-putting for men – not because I am successful, but because of what I am successful for: writing love stories. When people know that you're responsible for these romantic movies they instantly think that you have unrealistic expectations about love. They expect you to be all lovey-dovey and mushy and on a quest to find a Prince Charming. For me this could not be further from the truth. I'm good at my job because I have a good understanding of the genre, not because I'm a soppy romantic.

I fill a glass with water and hand it to Zack.

'Is this vodka?' he asks with a puzzled look on his face.

'Water,' I reply bluntly.

'When I said a drink I meant something alcoholic. I need it after that,' he says with a wiggle of his eyebrows. I could do with a stiff drink too, but for me it would be to help me forget.

'Oh, sorry. It's just I've got to be up pretty early in the morning so …' So take the hint, Zack.

'Great. I'm tired too, and I love to spoon. Is that the bedroom over there?'

Whoa, stop right there, does he think he is staying over?

'Erm,' I start, unsure how to do this tactfully. This was only ever going to be a casual thing, and I thought Zack knew that. Sleeping together isn't ever going to happen – literally sleeping together, that is.

'You want me to go?' Zack asks.

'Well, yeah,' I reply. 'I'm just not great at sharing my bed. I'm a wiggler, I fling my arms around – it would be carnage.'

'It's three a.m.' Zack replies with a laugh. 'I'll take my chances.'

'Even so,' I reply, pausing to think of the right way to say this, 'I'd still rather you went home.'

'If I sleep here, I can give you a ride to work on my bike in the morning,' he negotiates, but I don't think you're allowed to side-saddle on motorbikes and a helmet would trash my hair.

'Even so,' I repeat myself, but before I have the chance to say anything else, Zack gets the message. He hops off the sofa and begins aggressively putting his clothes back on. I can tell that he is angry because even a simple task like putting his leg into his jeans isn't going very well.

'So this was just sex and now you want me out?' he asks angrily, but I don't give him an answer. 'I thought guys were supposed to do this to girls – use them for sex and then send them packing – not the other way around. Who do you think you are, huh?'

Still, I don't say anything. Well, what can I say? He's hit the nail on the head.

I stand by the door as I watch Zack get dressed. With his clothes on and his boots in his hand, Zack approaches me and places a hand on my shoulder.

'This is silly,' he says as he massages me. 'It's the middle of the night, we're going to the same place in the morning. You and I could be really good together.'

The fact he's even considering us having some kind of future together, after just one night, causes me to pull a face – an involuntary reaction I have to the idea of relationships, and one that I can't always mask.

'Let me guess,' Zack starts, 'Even so ...'

Again, I say nothing. Nail on the head.

'You're a fucking bitch, you know that?' Zack shouts as he storms out, slamming the door behind him.

'Yep,' I say quietly to myself before turning off the lights and climbing into my bed, alone, just the way I like it.

Chapter 2

Despite being late for work, I grabbed my usual skinny cinnamon latte from the coffee shop on the corner by my office before hurriedly making my way there.

'Hold the lift,' I call out, just in time to squash myself in with all the other people. And by lift, I mean elevator. There goes Dick Van Dyke again.

As we begin our ascent to the floor I work on, I finally get to take my first sip of coffee of the day. God, that feels good. I'd gasp with delight if there weren't so many people around who might find this odd. It is only as I examine my takeaway cup that I realise there is a phone number written on the side. I cast my mind back to the coffee shop. I was in a rush, but I definitely remember being served by a woman. Before I have a chance to consider what kind of vibes I'm giving off (I suppose I do flirt – for sport – with almost everyone) I remember the young bloke who handed me my coffee, the one with the gorgeous smile.

My new look seems to be a hit with the male population of LA, but it took a lot of work to achieve. Back in Kent I was Mia Harrison, a chubby brunette with very few men vying for her attention, and nothing much going on in life apart from work. I felt invisible, overlooked by everyone around me, and I'd had enough. When I moved to the States I decided it would be the perfect time to reinvent myself (what better place to fake it than LA?), so I slimmed down to a US size six (which is absolutely no fun to maintain), dyed my dull brown locks a sexy honey-blonde colour, and every morning I meticulously curl my long hair, squash myself into something sexy and step into a high pair of heels. I didn't do it for the people around me, I did it for myself. I didn't want to feel like I was blending into the background of my own life any more.

Now my name is Mia Valentina. I'm twenty-nine years old. I believe in taking good care of myself, eating a balanced diet and sticking to an ambitious exercise routine. OK, so I'm not really a female Patrick Bateman, but before I get dressed each day I do have a particular routine to make sure I can keep up my new look.

I'm not sure if adopting a fancy-sounding pen name and looking the part is helping my career at all, but I'm definitely not invitible to men any more. Men didn't look twice at Mia Harrison, but Mia Valentina ... she's a hit. I don't know why I'm referring to myself in the third person because that's me now. Mia Harrison is nothing but a distant memory. Even when I go home to visit (which, I have to admit, is not very often) no one from my past recognises me and my family all tell me how much I've changed – although not necessarily for the better. In fact, the new me isn't a hit with my family at all. I'm not talking about the way I look, more the way I am. I'm a different girl on the inside too. The old me had panic attacks. I was pushed around at work, messed around by men and, ever since the birth of my younger sister, even my family have made me feel like the second favourite child – do keep in mind that there are only two of us. Life before my sister Annabelle was born feels like a weird dream that didn't really happen, because ever since beautiful baby Belle bounced onto the scene, the attention has been fully on her. Sure, I achieved everything first, but Belle did it all better. It's a horrible thing to say, but I almost feel like I was the starter child, the practice run before Belle came along. I was five years old when Belle was born, so I've been second best for the majority of my life. That's why I love living out here, alone. No one knows the old me, I can totally be myself without worrying about the consequences – and believe me there are consequences, because these days my true self doesn't take things lying down.

'Good morning, Mia,' my assistant Dalia chimes brightly, despite it being past noon. That's the great thing about having an assistant, they go out of their way to assist you, even by making you feel like you're not incredibly late for work when you really are.

'Hey, Dalia, what's happening?'

'Well, the meeting started ten minutes ago, I tried to reach you on your cell.'

Oh, shit. I wish I could say that this was a one-off, but with great success comes a great ego. Even though I know that if I just got up a little earlier every morning, I could be on time for work, I still roll out of my bed when I feel like it and spend ages doing my hair when really I should be rushing to the office to make my meetings on time.

'Good morning,' I say cheerily as I burst my way through the doors to the meeting, grabbing an apple from the buffet table before taking a seat with the rest of the Pink Inc. team.

'It's not morning,' Molly informs me.

'OK,' I say, twirling my chair from side to side as I munch my apple.

'We were just talking about the script changes,' Savannah says, kindly bringing me up to date.

Between the three of us, we have the formula for making movies down to a fine art – although unlike me, Molly and Savannah are way into all the romantic junk that I have no time for in real life.

'Here,' Molly says, tapping the page of the open script on the table in front of me. 'We need to make some changes to this line.'

At the moment we're working on a movie called *Three's A*

Crowd, which tells the tale of two twenty-something best friends. Both party girls, their friendship comes under strain when one of them goes off on holiday and returns engaged.

'I wrote that line,' I say, almost offended. 'What's wrong with it?'

'I'm just struggling to believe that when Katie's best friend tells her she is engaged, she asks her if it's because she is pregnant. No one would do that.'

I have a little chuckle with myself because that's exactly what I said to my sister when she told me she was engaged.

'OK, so what were you thinking instead?' I ask.

'Perhaps it should be a sweet and sincere moment,' Savannah suggests.

We could try that. After all, we write romantic comedies, it needs as much romance as it does jokes.

'Sure, but what?' Molly asks.

We all sit in silence for a moment – well, almost silence. The unattractive sound of me crunching my apple can be heard all around the room.

'OK, let's try this,' I start with my mouth full. 'So, Emma tells Katie that she is engaged and Katie is shocked – she drops her cosmopolitan and spills it all over Emma's dress, just like we wrote originally. This time, instead of asking her if she's pregnant, the pair rush off to the toilets together to try and get the stain out of Emma's dress. For a moment no one says anything, they just both work together in silence, Emma holding the bottom of her dress taut as Katie carefully dabs at the stain with a wet paper towel. Now, the stain isn't as bad as it looks, and together they get it out. Then Emma leans on Katie while she dries it under the hand dryer.'

'I don't think any girl watching the movie is going to care so much about fashion that she'll want to watch them just removing a stain in silence,' Molly interrupts me.

'Let me finish then,' I say sharply. Another thing that changed when I became the new Mia was my tolerance for girls and their bitchiness. I don't really have any female friends here in the States, unless you count Dalia, but she's paid to be friendly to me and she doesn't try that hard. I have a sneaking suspicion she secretly hates me. Yesterday when I sent her out for condoms she looked at me like she wished I was dead.

Other than Dalia, the only other girls I have to deal with for lengthy amounts of time on a daily basis are Molly and Savannah. Savannah is a lovely, bubbly girl. We don't have much in common but we get along OK. When all else fails we can always have a girly chat together, about things like hair and shoes, because Savannah is a girly girl too. She has long, naturally curly brown hair and bright green eyes like me, which we bonded over the day we met because supposedly green eyes are quite rare. Whether it's true or not, it gave us something to talk about and thanks to that we've always got on well since.

Sadly, I never hit it off with Molly. We just don't seem to have anything in common apart from our girl parts. Molly is very tall and very slim. She's quite gothic looking, with her sharp black inverted bob and her heavy black makeup, but while she isn't particularly girly, she is still a romantic just like Savannah – and that is the one thing I don't have in common with either of them. The thing is, being a romcom writer, there's no way I can openly admit to my aversion to love. If people knew that I thought the stuff I wrote was slushy propaganda, cleverly designed to trick women into thinking they need a husband and a happy ever after – I'd be finished. The film industry may not benefit from you having a happy love life directly, but through the use of product placement they can helpfully suggest the kind of shoes you need to wear to do so, or the bag you need to carry, or the car you need to drive. Molly and Savannah believe that all you need is love, and making these movies is their way of showing you just how beautiful love is and how true love conquers all. Sadly, I don't believe a word I say. I know that every word I write comes from a dark and cynical place inside me, and the more I write, the less

I'm inclined to believe in romantic love as a thing. It's not a thing, it's a marketing tool. It's how you convince people to splash out on weddings and buy chocolate and flowers on Valentine's Day. Thankfully the people who watch the movies written by the Pink Inc. team don't feel the same as me, which keeps me in my flashy lad pad and my designer shoes.

Right, back to work. So Katie has just helped Emma clean the cocktail stain off her dress.

'So, they've cleaned the dress together in perfect silence, both just thinking about what has happened and how life as they know it is going to change. Katie is worried, not only because her best friend is about to have someone else equally as important in her life, but also because to an extent she's going to be left behind. Emma is going to be playing house, Katie is still going to be a single girl – only now she's doing it alone. She's scared. Anyway, Emma sees this. She takes her hand and she says: "Katie, you mean more to me than anyone in the world. I have known you all my life and just because I am getting married, it doesn't mean I won't want you around any more – I *need* you around. Look at the way you just helped me clean my dress – granted you were the one who spilt a drink down it – but even though you were upset you helped me, no questions asked. I lean on you, and not just when I need to dry my dress under a hand dryer. Yes, I have fallen in love, but it will never compare to the love I have for you, my best friend. It may not work out between me and this guy, but you and I will be friends forever. No one can change that."'

'Wow,' Savannah gushes. 'That's so beautiful.'

'Yeah,' Molly agrees. 'Really beautiful.'

For a moment my writing partners sit and think about what I have just said. What I want to do is roll my eyes, this friends forever crap makes me throw up in my mouth every time I even think about it. Instead I force a smile and jot down my idea before I forget it – well it's clearly an effective one. Is it hypocritical of me to write these loving and romantic tales if I don't believe them? Of course not, I write fiction. Fiction can be whatever you want it to be. If you haven't worked it out by now, I'm just really good at faking it.

Chapter 3

'Business or pleasure?' an LAX employee asks me as I awkwardly rummage around in my handbag to make sure I have everything I need to fly. I'm not sure if it's his job to ask me or if he's just making small talk, either way I answer.

'Neither,' I reply, although this answer obviously isn't a satisfactory one if I want to be allowed on an aeroplane. 'My sister is getting married,' I explain. 'I'm going home for the wedding.'

The man laughs and gives me a knowing smile, a smile that says: 'Family gatherings are hell. I feel your pain.'

It's not long until my flight now. While I wait, I suppose I should give you a little back story (as we call it in the movie-making business) so you can understand exactly why the business of my sister's wedding will not be a pleasure. Belle and I have never really been that close. I think we were when we were kids, but as we grew up we grew apart. While I was a shy, nerdy outcast at school, Belle was always an athletic, sporty member of the in-crowd. Her friends were all exactly like her – you know how they used to make the Bratz dolls look different, but at the end of the day they were all exactly the same – massive heads, tiny bodies and huge eyes, but with different coloured hair? Well that's what Belle and her mates were like. Despite being Belle's sister – and me being older than her and her friends – they didn't mind teasing me when they were all over at our house. I suppose it comes with the territory of being the uncool, 'unstylish' sister, but that doesn't mean it hurt any less. They don't pick on me any more, although I'm not sure if that comes with the territory of having loads of money and being able to get them tickets to movie premieres.

When Belle called me up to tell me she was getting married, I really did ask her if she was doing it because she was pregnant – and, yes, if I had been holding a cocktail I would have spilt it everywhere. I have only met Dan, the guy she is marrying, twice. He seemed OK, but at twenty-four years of age I think Belle is way too young to be tying the knot. Dan is twenty-four as well, and you've got to wonder about what's going on inside the head of a young lad who is so keen to put his fun single days behind him so soon in life.

The only thing that surprised me more than the fact that Belle was getting married, was when she asked me if I would be her chief bridesmaid. My sister knows all too well what the new Mia is like and that includes the way I feel about weddings. I haven't been a bridesmaid since I was a little kid so I don't really remember what it entails. Whatever it is, I know I am not the girl for the job. I asked her if I could think about it, and quicker than you could say 'I do', my mum called me up and informed me that I would be calling Belle back and accepting her kind offer. The thing that bugged me was the reason why Belle asked me. I mean, we're not close, so I can only imagine she is doing it for appearances; to have her successful sister by her side.

Even though it sounded like my idea of hell, I finally agreed to do it, safe in the knowledge I could pop home for a couple of days, do the wedding thing and then jump back on a plane and pretend it never happened. Well, it was a nice idea while it lasted, but shortly after I agreed, plans for the big day started being made – well, I say big day, it's actually more like *ten* big days. I haven't been fully briefed on the details yet, all I know is that the happy couple have rented a huge house on the beach in Cornwall so that most of the wedding party can stay there and celebrate with them. What I also know is that my boss hates me right now because we're really busy and I have had to book over a week off instead of four days. I'm not the employee of the month at the best of times, so I'm going to have to do some major butt-kissing when I get back.

While I am happy about not having to visit my hometown this time, I am not exactly jumping through hoops about the fact that I've got a twelve hour flight to London followed by a five hour train journey to the far side of Cornwall. I'm going to be knackered when I get there. Belle has planned my journey to the second, so at least I know when I arrive she and Dan will be waiting for me at the train station, ready to give me a lift to the party house so I can spend way too much time with the family I moved over five thousand miles to get away from. Oh joy.

***

'Is this your first time flying?'

'No,' I reply. 'Why would you ask that?'

The young man sitting next to me nods towards my hands. I hadn't even realised I was doing it, but I'm slowly but surely tearing up a sick bag into tiny pieces.

'Oh. My sister is getting married,' I say by way of an explanation.

'So you thought you'd, what, make extra confetti?' he teases.

I playfully throw a handful of shredded paper at the total stranger. Thankfully he takes my gesture as intended – as a joke – and doesn't have me manhandled off the plane by an air marshal.

'I'm heading home for my little sister's wedding. She's twenty-four. I'm twenty-nine and I'm single.' I stare at the stranger expectantly until he works out what is so wrong with that. It doesn't take him very long.

'Rather you than me,' the stranger says as he sweeps back his long fringe from over his eyes. 'You should have paid someone to be your date, get everyone off your back.'

'Oh, they would never believe I was a reformed character with a sudden respect for monogamy. It was only a couple of days ago I called my sis and told her she could come and stay with me if she wanted to call it all off. Anyway, it's too late now – unless you're not busy,' I jokily suggest with a wink.

'Honey, they'd be far more likely to believe you're a romantic than they would me being a straight guy.'

I can't help but laugh, although I'd never judge a book by its cover, this *is* LA after all.

'Anyway,' he continues, 'I'm going to London to try and meet a prince! I want to marry into royalty.'

'I'm not so up on current events back home,' I explain, 'but I'm fairly sure most of the royals are taken and/or straight.'

'Well aren't you a Debbie Downer,' he teases. 'I'm Ethan, by the way. I suppose we should do names.'

'Yes, we seem to have skipped that bit. A mere formality considering we're already plane pals. I'm Mia.'

'Plane pals!' Ethan squeaks jokily. 'We can share our lunch and go to the bathroom together.'

'I'm all for sharing but it might look like we're trying to join a different kind of club if we go to the loo together,' I laugh.

'Speaking of the not so exclusive Mile High Club – which I have been a proud member of since 2009 ...' we slap each other a high-five, '... that cute flight attendant is checking you out.'

'No! I thought he was looking at you ...'

'Nope. He's straight. I'm the authority on the matter and he is hot for you.'

I smile back at the tall, muscular flight attendant. His gorgeous smile and his dirty blonde hair would usually make for my type, but he's almost too pretty. Too polished and perfect. Of course, I can't tell Ethan that this gorgeous creature's teeth are too white.

That his face is too symmetrical. That his clothes are too neat. He looks like he'd want to snuggle afterwards and that's the last thing people do in aeroplane bathrooms.

'Not my type,' I insist to Ethan.

'Your type isn't gorgeous and crazy for you?'

'Nah,' I reply with a laugh. 'You might be into that weird stuff, but I'm not.'

'You like a bad boy?' Ethan asks.

'I do. I like them manly and dangerous looking. Rough and ready, heartbreakingly handsome, could have any girl they wanted – that's my type.'

'So you like the chase,' Ethan concludes. 'You reel them in and then you throw them back.'

'Well, you know, if we're sticking with the fish metaphor, you kill them when you catch them. What would I want with a dead fish? I just chuck them back, leave them for someone else to suffocate.'

'Mia, honey, you are a case study waiting to happen.'

'Why thank you,' I reply proudly.

After selecting the same movie, Ethan and I – or the plane pals as we're now known – both reach for our headphones. It's some weird animated movie and all the characters are things you would find in the bathroom. I watch Ethan recoil in horror as he watches a talking toilet brush chatting with a 'sexy' loofah with long eyelashes and lipstick.

'What the hell?' he asks me, his voice growing louder thanks to he headphones. 'Why don't they have anything with Ryan Gosling in' he yells to no one in particular. Most of the female passengers find this utterly charming (they're clearly Gosling fans) and applaud Ethan's bold move.

'Sir, if you'd like to sit down,' the sexy cabin crew guy insists firmly.

'Yeah, sit down,' I whisper to Ethan as I pull him back down by his arm. 'It's not worth getting wrestled off a plane for Ryan

Gosling – unless Ryan is the one doing the wrestling.'

'Aw, would you miss me, plane pal?' he teases me.

'I would actually, because for the first time in days you have managed to stop me stressing about having to go to this wedding.'

And now I've just reminded myself again …

***

As we touched down on English soil, everyone applauded the pilot for doing what he does every day of his working life. He's landed the plane, we're all alive, it's a miracle, applause, applause. In a new twist, Ethan started throwing the sick bag confetti in the air – something that landed us absolutely filthy looks from the crew as we left the plane. I did still get a wink from the cabin crew cutie though.

I know it's just a weird coincidence, but the more I tried to keep my mind off the wedding, the more things would crop up to remind me exactly what would be waiting for me when I got off the plane. The funniest of all was when the next movie Ethan chose turned out to be one of mine – and a wedding flick, no less. As Ethan gushed over the male lead, I decided it best not to tell him I had a hand in writing it, because I imagine it would take the shine off it a little.

After going through the usual airport motions without a hitch – which is surprising, considering Ethan told a hot policeman he had twenty grams of cocaine hidden in his rectum – I followed my sister's ridiculously detailed itinerary down to the letter and made it safely onto my Cornwall-bound train.

With four hours down and just one to go, I know it won't be long now until I arrive. My sister and her hubby-to-be will be waiting for me on the platform and then there really will be no turning back. I'll be in captivity and my sister will be my keeper – my sister who has told me that all wedding-based celebrations will not be optional.

To take my mind off where I am heading, I grab one of the trashy celebrity magazines I picked up at the train station. Unless their fame makes it across the pond, I don't know very much about what is going on in UK celeb culture, so reading about people from the likes of *The Only Way is Essex*, *Geordie Shore* and *Made in Chelsea* does little to hold my attention. Reality TV-inspired fashion is certainly a big hit here, though. I've only been home a few hours but I could play fashion bingo with the number of people I have seen replicating the styles these famous-for-being-famous people are sporting. I'll just tick each one off in this magazine as I spot it in real life. Huge false eyelashes, tick. Man-tans, tick. His and hers onesies, tick.

Looking at the current fashion here fills me with dread. I wonder what kind of bridesmaid dress my sister has lined up for me. They had the dress fittings ages ago, so I had to send Belle my measurements and hope she put them to good use. Even before my Hollywood makeover, my sister and I never had much in common when it came to fashion. Growing up one of the cool kids, Belle embraced any silly trend going. These days Belle no longer has her athletic figure and her dress sense has settled down to a comfortable style, think: function over fashion, comfort over style, etc. When I wasn't slim, my mum would make me feel like shit for even looking at a chocolate bar, but now that my sister is the one who has gained weight, my mum has put it down to her being a contented woman. Oh, and I'm dangerously thin and I don't eat enough. Even when the shoe is on the other foot, Annabelle is still perfect and I am still a huge letdown. It's almost like it doesn't actually matter, to anyone, what size anyone is. Belle will always be the favourite, and I'll always be the dissapointment.

It isn't fair to blame my mum for everything. Sadly, my dad is of a similar opinion, and I'm fairly certain my Auntie June hates my guts – she thinks I'm a bad influence on my cousins, who in turn love me for being a bad influence. My gran doesn't really 'get' me, but my granddad absolutely worships me. I'm so glad he's going to be there because he is always on my side, even when I know I'm in the wrong. That just leaves my Uncle Steve, and while he does like me, he is just too much. It's Auntie June and my mum who are sisters, so Steve treats me like we're mates, and he's always sucking up to me – I think he thinks I'll be able to land him a part in a movie or something. He's always trying a bit too hard to seem like a cool, young guy, which is bizarre. Still, it's nice to have another fan.

Hopefully, I'll be able to avoid having to spend too much time with anyone in particular, because so many other people will be there too – people who are not related to me and therefore might actually like me. I haven't met any of Dan's relatives, but I know there's going to be quite a few members of his family there. The rest of the guests are just friends of Belle and Dan, some that I don't know and some that I wish I didn't know.

After hours of travelling I can't help but let out a big yawn. Put it down to a combination of jetlag and tiredness, but I rub my sleepy eyes with my hands, smudging my heavy black eye makeup everywhere.

'Dammit,' I can't help but say to myself.

Grabbing my toilet bag, I head for the train toilets to smarten myself up. It won't be long before I arrive so I'd better go and apply my war paint.

Chapter 4

Ah, the great British Summer. Despite it being August, the sky is a thick blanket of cloud that is doing nothing to keep me warm. In fact, I am positively freezing. The weather back in Beverly Hills was supposed to be lovely these next few weeks, so a vacation from work to just chill out and enjoy the nice weather would have been welcomed. Instead I am here, in jolly old England, feeling the wrath of the hit-and-miss summer.

As I stand alone on the platform – under strict instruction from my sister, who couldn't stress enough that I should wait on the platform, lest I wander off and die – I give my outfit the once over. I check that my black and white bandage dress is straight and give it a quick brush-down with my hands. Safe in the knowledge that my hair and makeup look as best they can after a twelve-hour flight, a five-hour train, and countless hours waiting in between, I stand and wait for my sister.

Right on schedule, Belle and Dan appear out of nowhere and bound towards me like a couple of puppies would if I were holding a tennis ball made of meat.

'Hello,' I greet them with all the enthusiasm I can muster. It's clearly not enough though, because my sister and Dan simultaneously grab me and hug me.

'Wow, OK,' I can't help but blurt out. I'm not used to much affection these days – least of all group hugs.

'Don't let Gran see how thin you look,' my sister warns me when she finally lets me go. 'She'll flip.'

I could ask my sister – who is absolutely serious, by the way – how she proposes I hide my thinness from my gran, but I'm worried she might actually have a few suggestions. Whether it involves eating several Cornish pasties on the drive to the house or stuffing a pillow up my dress, I'm not really down for either.

'You're looking good too,' I tell her. 'You too, Dan.'

'Thanks,' he says, still as excited as a child at Christmas. 'We're so glad you could come, we were worried you might not show.'

'You really think I wouldn't show up to my own sister's wedding?' I gasp.

'Yes ... I mean no ... I mean, you're so busy with work all the time and—'

'Relax, Dan. I'm messing with you,' I assure him, but if I could have thought of a reason that wouldn't see me disowned by my entire family, believe me, I would have used it.

'Right.' Dan laughs nervously. 'Shall we get in the car?'

Dan, being the gent that he is, goes to pick up my suitcase by the handle.

'You might want to drag it,' I warn him. 'It's—'

Dan screams out in pain as he picks up my deceivingly heavy suitcase.

'—really heavy,' I rather pointlessly finish my sentence.

I stare at poor Dan who is doubled up in pain, his face turning purple, his eyes looking like they are about to pop right out of his head and bounce onto the train tracks ... but that's nothing compared to the angry shade of red my sister is turning.

'Prince, are you OK?' she asks, fussing around Dan, who seems to feel more pain every time she touches him.

'It's my back,' he tells me. 'I hurt it playing football when I was at school, ended my career before it started. If I overdo it, I put it out. Why is your suitcase so heavy?'

'Just clothes and shoes and stuff. I tried to warn you,' I reason.

'Mia,' my sister starts, and I just know that this is going to be all my fault, 'if you have broken my fiancé just in time for my wedding, I will *never* speak to you again.'

My eyes widen in response to the way my sister is overreacting.

'First of all, he's a man, not a toy,' I rant. 'Second of all, *I* didn't break him. He tried to lift my case before I could warn him it was heavy, it's not like I took a swing at him with a baseball bat.'

'I can't believe you're already trying to ruin my wedding,' my sister shouts.

'What the fuck?' I screech, but I don't get to say anything else before usually mild-mannered Dan interrupts us with an ever so slightly raised voice of his own.

'Enough,' he snaps. 'Let's just get in the car and head back to the house, it's not that bad and the house isn't far.'

'Are you sure, prince?' Belle asks in her sickliest voice.

'I'm sure, princess.'

Oh God, I'd forgotten about their soppy pet names for one another. Excuse me while I throw up.

Belle puts her arm around Dan and they slowly head for the car park.

'I'll just carry my own case, shall I?' I call after them.

'You should have done that in the first place,' Belle snaps back.

I drag my case to Dan's car before lifting it up and putting it on the back seat. It's not *that* heavy, but I suppose if the poor guy has a weak back there was no way it was going to end well. Belle and Dan are in the front, so I climb in the back with my case.

'Seatbelts,' Belle insists. 'We don't want any more accidents.'

As instructed, I strap myself in – as though I hadn't planned on doing it anyway. As soon as Belle has given us all the once-over she gives Dan the nod to set off.

I knew that I would end up having arguments with my little sister over the next week or so, but I hadn't expected the first one to be within minutes of seeing her. There's an awkward atmosphere in the car. I can just tell my sister is mentally planning the speech she's going to give me if Dan's back is anything less than one hundred per cent on their wedding day. I decide to try and quash the awkwardness by making small talk – and if there's one thing Belle loves talking about, it's Belle.

'So have all the guests arrived?' I ask.

'Would you believe you aren't the last person to arrive?' Belle says brightly, like that's supposed to make me feel like Sister of the Year. 'Dan's friend Leo and his mum aren't here yet because he's got work. He's a fireman.'

'That's hot,' I joke.

'Mia, no,' my sister says firmly.

'Oi, it was a joke,' I insist. Well, it was. Fire, hot, get it? My sense of humour is wasted on this audience. 'I'm a writer, I'm supposed to make crap jokes.'

'Anyway,' she continues, shrugging off my attempt at humour, 'our lot are here – Mum, Dad, Gran, Granddad, Auntie June, Uncle Steve, Hannah, Meg and Josh.'

Hannah, Meg and Josh are my cousins. They like me because they think I'm cool – much to their mother's disgust. I haven't seen them in a while, but I know that Hannah will be fifteen now, Meg is thirteen and Josh is ten.

'Are your family here, Dan?' I ask to keep the conversation going.

Dan opens his mouth to talk but my sister gets in there first.

'Of course they are,' she snaps. 'And we have our friends: Beth, Nancy, Jason, Heather.'

Belle says these names like they're supposed to mean something to me, but I have no idea who her friends are. Apart from Nancy, who has been my sister's BFF since she started school. I know her well because she spent a lot of time at our house, and because she relentlessly bullied me, despite being five years my junior. Belle wasn't always horrible to me, but when she was, you could guarantee she was doing it because Nancy was there. Whatever they though of how I looked, it was no excuse for bullying me.

As wedding parties go, it isn't massive, but Belle has been planning this wedding/mini holiday for everyone for a long time now. I wasn't doing the maths, but that sounds like an awful lot of people to be staying in one beach house.

'Where is everyone going to sleep?' I ask, curiosity getting the better of me.

'Oh, well, not everyone is staying at the house – only close family and important wedding people – and anyway, the house is massive,' Belle insists.

'Massive enough to sleep so many people?' I ask.

'See for yourself,' Dan says as he pulls into the driveway.

As I take in the stunning contemporary beach house that will not only be my home throughout my stay, but also the venue for my sister's wedding, my jaw literally drops. Not only is the house right on the beach, but it *is* massive. It looks like a hotel! This isn't any old beach house – you just know that one day an architect with endless money had this brilliant vision and the massive, brilliant white, funky-shaped property in front of us was what came of it. I have to admit, I'm impressed.

I am no sooner out of the car before my parents rush out of the front door to greet me.

'Hi Mum, hi Dad,' I say with a half-hearted wave. I must have used up the last of my enthusiasm at the train station.

'You're so thin!' my mum exclaims as soon as she gets a proper look at me. 'Don't let your gran see.'

Again, not sure how I'm supposed to do that, but it's a non-issue. You know when you're a teenager, and you have that voice in your head that is constantly telling you what's wrong with you and questioning whether youre good enough? Lucky me, I had my mum to say it out loud.

There's nothing wrong with how I look now, I swear, this lot just like to make me feel like I'm doing something wrong. Sometimes I wonder if it's punishment, for moving away, but if that were true you would think they would make me feel a little more welcome when I come back.

Judith Harrison isn't your typical overbearing mother, in fact she is quite the opposite with me. Both of my parents make a lovely fuss over Belle, but when it comes to me, it's like they can't quite be bothered. Sure, my mum will comment on how inappropriate my dresses are or how a combination of peroxide and LA sunshine will see me bald by the time I am forty, but they're not too bothered with how I live my life. It's not that they've given up trying now that they know I am a lost cause, I don't think they've ever had high hopes for me.

'Mia,' my dad says. That's his way of acknowledging my existence. The Harrison women may be noisy and bossy but my dad, Ted – the only Harrison man in our house – is very much the opposite, although that probably has something to do with living in a house with three noisy women for so long.

A middle-class couple in their late fifties, my parents are exactly as you would expect them to be: a little bit dull and a lot uptight – and I have no doubt that my sister is heading for a similar fate. In old photos of my parents in their twenties, my mum looks almost exactly like Belle does now – with the exception of the big hair, which I'm assured was the height of fashion back then. So unfortunately for my little sis, she will almost certainly grow up to look like our mum. My mum has her grey hair in, as I like to call it, a Nurse Ratched bob, and her personality is very much like that of the *One Flew Over The Cuckoo's Nest* character. I have always found my mum to be on the cold side. She always has to be in control, which makes her actions often seem mechanical, and she can be cruel sometimes – something I think she inherited from her mum. My dad is everything you'd expect of a fifty-nine-year-old henpecked husband. My mum would look young for her age if she were willing to colour her hair (she won't because she is dead against it for some reason), but there is no hope for my dad. He is almost entirely bald apart from a few tufts of white hair around the sides and back of his head, and he is embracing his impending old age by wearing trousers that are pulled far too high up.

'This is a nice place,' I say to no one in particular.

'I know, right?' my sister squeaks excitedly. 'There's a swimming pool, TVs, wi-fi, there's, like, a billion bedrooms, a games room … it's going to be so much fun.'

'Sounds expensive,' I can't help but say out loud.

'Nothing is too good for my little girl,' my dad says.

'We're just lucky you are the way you are, Mia,' my mum explains. 'We had saved up a wedding fund for two daughters, but with you, you know, not being the marrying kind, it made sense to use it all for your sister's wedding, make it really special for her.'

Everyone smiles like that is the sweetest thing in the world, but I'm upset.

'So you're using the money you had saved for my wedding to pay for Annabelle's?' I ask.

'Well, you're not getting married, are you?' my mum reasons.

'Yeah, but that's not the point,' I insist.

'Why can't you just be happy for me?' my sister asks me.

I massage my temples for a moment. Luckily I don't have any plans to get married, and even if I did I have plenty of money to pay for it myself, but that really isn't the issue here.

'I could do with a nap, could you show me to my room, please?' I ask.

'Of course,' Belle replies. 'Just let me introduce you to everyone.'

'I'd rather wait until I've had a nap and a bath if that's OK.'

'Don't be so selfish, Mia,' my mum snaps.

'Fine,' I give in, knowing that it's easier to just do it than try and fight it.

'Brilliant.' Belle claps her hands together. 'Mum, can you help

Dan inside, he's hurt his back.'

'How on earth did he do that?' I hear my mum ask as my sister drags me into the house.

'Mia did it,' my sister calls back.

Chapter 5

I thought the outside of the beach house was beautiful, but it's nothing compared to the interior. It's cool, it's modern and Belle is right, it seems like such a fun place to live. I may not get on with my family and the wedding stuff will probably suck, but at least I can watch movies on the big screen and chill out by the pool – that is when I'm not sunbathing on the beach.

Belle leads me into the huge sitting room, where two couples are sitting opposite each other on white leather corner sofas which make a square shape in the middle of the room. The four of them are drinking tea and chatting but as I walk into the room they stop abruptly and stare at me. The couple on the left are probably a little older than my parents (or perhaps they just look it), but if possible they look even more uptight. The lady is wearing a navy twinset and skirt and the man is dressed in a matching suit complete with cravat, making them look like they should be on a yacht. The other couple are elderly and, again, I'm going to hazard a guess that being cold and uptight runs in their family too.

'Everyone, this is my sister, Mia. She's just got in from America,' my sister announces to four unimpressed faces. 'Mia, this is Harriet and Peter, they're Dan's parents, and over here we have

Dan's grandparents.'

'Hello,' I say brightly, offering my hand for Dan's mum to shake first, as she is the closest to me.

'Charmed,' Harriet says coolly as she reluctantly shakes my hand.

I decide not to bother shaking hands with anyone else; they don't seem that bothered. It's awkward for a moment because we're just standing in front of them and they refuse to continue their conversation while we're standing there.

'Anyway,' a cheerful Belle starts, 'I'm just going to show Mia to her room so we'll see you for dinner later.'

I follow Belle from the living room to the kitchen where we find my gran, granddad and my Auntie June. My granddad rushes over to me with as much energy as his eighty-year-old legs will allow and gives me a big kiss and a cuddle.

'Kid, you're here,' he says, and for the first time, it feels like someone is actually pleased to see me.

'Of course,' I reply. 'I'm not going to leave you to suffer this lot on your own,' I joke, but my auntie doesn't find this funny and tuts loudly.

'Hello Gran,' I say as I walk over to where she is sitting. She offers me her cheek, which I dutifully kiss, before prodding me in the ribs.

'You're not eating, Mia,' she says angrily. 'I'm not letting you get back on that plane until you are a healthy weight.'

I roll my eyes at this but can't help but smile too, because I know that this is just my gran's way of loving me.

'Gran, in LA, this is a normal weight,' I point out.

If Belle looks like a younger version of my mum, then my mum looks like a younger version of Margret, my gran. Belle may still be bright, bubbly and sickly sweet – but I don't doubt for a second that she'll end up like my mum, my auntie and my gran – or the three witches as my granddad, Jack, jokingly calls them. My granddad is hilarious, constantly making jokes, winding up my gran and playing little pranks on people. I like to think that I take after my granddad, but I can't deny I have inherited a little coldness from my gran's side, especially when it comes to love. I have certainly inherited my granddad's sense of humour though and for that I am very grateful.

'Hi, Auntie June,' I say cheerily. I don't waste my time attempting to hug or kiss her.

'Mia,' she says, reinforcing my point that the women in this family are ice-cold.

I rack my brain for a topic of conversation that will fill the silence but I am saved from having to do so by my ten-year-old cousin, Josh.

'Mia, Mia,' he giddily shrieks as he runs towards me and throws his arms around me. Josh is member number two of my three-person fan club, so I feel almost invincible having both him and my granddad in the same room.

'Hey, turd,' I greet my favourite cousin. 'What's up?'

'Watch your language,' my Auntie June warns me. 'He's only ten.'

'Mum, I know the word "turd",' Josh whines.

'There, look, you've only been here a matter of minutes and you've corrupted my only son,' my auntie complains.

'Come on, June, he probably already knew that one,' my granddad says in my defence.

Belle looks put out by the fact that I am causing arguments already.

'Come on, Mia,' she insists. 'Let's get you to your room.'

'Please can I show Mia the games room?' Josh begs. 'Please.'

'Go on then,' Belle agrees. 'I'll wait here.'

Josh grabs me by the hand and drags me down a flight of stairs.

'The pool is through that door,' he explains before dragging me through a different door. 'This is the games room.'

The games room is packed full of funky furniture and fun things to do. There's a bar, a pool table, a huge television, pinball machines and a variety of chairs and beanbags to get comfortable on.

I notice my other cousins, Hannah and Meg, are both playing with their phones. They both say hello to me but seem far too engrossed in what they are doing to get into proper conversation.

'This is Max,' Josh says, introducing me to a young boy who is playing on the game console. 'He's Dan's cousin. He's ten, too.'

'That's awesome,' I say enthusiastically. 'Hey, Max.'

Max smiles nervously and gives me a wave.

'Well, I'd better get back up to Belle before she turns into Bridezilla and bites my head off,' I joke. Josh and Max laugh, and so do the two men who are playing pool behind us.

'OK, see you later, Mia,' Josh says as he grabs a controller off the table and gets back to his game with Max.

'Hello,' I say to the two men by the pool table. 'I'm Mia, Belle's sister.'

'Hi Mia, I'm Jason,' the younger man says. 'I'm Heather's husband.'

I shrug my shoulders. 'Oh right, I haven't met your wife yet.'

They must be Belle and Dan's dull couple friends, another pair of early twenty-somethings who thought it would be a brilliant idea to marry young.

The other guy at the pool table looks closer to my age. He's tall and skinny with spiked, dyed black hair and he's wearing a tatty jumper with a pair of baggy jeans. He looks stylish and handsome in a scruffy Robert Pattinson kind of way.

'I'm Mike,' he says, jokily grabbing my hand and kissing it. 'I'm Dan's much better-looking older brother. Did you say you were Belle's younger sister?'

'Very smooth,' I laugh. 'But no, on paper I am five years older than my sister.'

'But not married?' Mike asks.

'No,' I reply with an unimpressed look on my face.

'Hey, I don't care, I'm thirty and I'm not married either. I'm just letting you know what to expect because I'm getting loads of stick for it. We'll have to stick together.'

Mike flashes me a cheeky smile. He isn't my usual type but I can certainly imagine us spending a lot of time together while we're here, especially if we're both in the same boat.

'Well, I'd better get back to Belle,' I tell them. 'I'll see you both at dinner.'

Max, Jason and Mike all seem friendly enough, so at least I won't have to rely on my three-person fan club the whole time – I can have actual conversations with people outside my family.

'I'm back,' I announce as I enter the kitchen. Everyone is exactly as I left them and once again, only my granddad seems pleased to see me.

'Right, let's get you to your room,' Belle says. 'I don't have time for this.'

I grab my case and follow my sister up the staircase.

'I just met Max, he's a little cutie,' I tell my sister. 'And I met Jason. Oh, and I met Mike, Dan's brother.'

My sister stops dead in front of me, causing me to walk into her back and drop my suitcase. She turns around slowly.

'Mia, don't,' she pleads.

'Don't what?' I laugh.

'Mia. Don't. Don't even think about it.'

'Fucking hell, what do you think I am?' I ask, not wanting or expecting an answer.

'Mia,' my sister says firmly, 'don't you dare.'

'This looks intense,' a familiar male voice says from behind me.

'We're fine, Uncle Steve, I'm just showing Mia to her bedroom.'

'Here.' My uncle stops to pick up my suitcase. 'Allow me, that's too heavy for a young lady to carry.'

As he smiles at me my skin crawls.

'Cheers, Uncle Steve,' Belle says brightly. 'That's Mia's room over there. See you both at dinner – it will be ready at seven.'

Belle skips off back downstairs, safe in the knowledge she has warned me off Dan's brother and that my Uncle Steve will take good care of me.

'Shall we go to the bedroom?' Steve says with a wiggle of his eyebrows.

I reluctantly nod my head and follow his lead.

My uncle opens the door and allows me to walk in first. I am in a bit of a rubbish mood but it instantly vanishes when I see where I'll be sleeping. Everything in the room is lily-white, from the sheets on the king-size bed to the curtains that are blowing in the breeze coming in from the balcony. I walk across the room and step out onto the balcony where I take in the view. I have an ocean-facing room with a perfect view of the beach below and the sea which seems to go on for miles before meeting the skyline.

'Wow,' I say to myself.

'It's dope, isn't it?' says my uncle, who I hadn't realised had followed me. I was hoping he would just put my case down and piss off. 'Almost as dope as you.'

Lord, who taught this man the word 'dope'.

Before my makeover, my uncle – like my Auntie June – never really spoke to me. No one really bothered with me, I was far too plain and boring. He looks at me differently now. I'm obviously worthy of respect and attention now that I'm successful and I look a way that society deems vaulable. I know, I seem like part of the problem, by seemingly conforming, but I wanted to do it for myself. The problem is, now that I've got a decent job, and a cool life, it makes people think about what I could do for them. I think Uncle Steve wants to be buddies, to somehow get in with me in a way that benefits him, but I can't deal with him acting like some lad I've just met in a bar, rather than my actual uncle.

He's fifty-two, so it's not like we're going to have anything in common – other than an interest in my lifestyle, I guess. I think he forgets that he was never nice to me when I was a kid, and he looks on the 'new' Mia like a whole new person. I may look like a different person to him but, to me, he is boring old Uncle

Steve, the insurance salesman.

'Well, I'm going to get in bed,' I say, yawning for effect, but I am actually knackered so it didn't take much faking.

'But I want to hear all about life in LA,' he says, kicking off his shoes, flopping down on my bed. I think he's trying to seem young and hip but it just makes me cringe.

I hover around the doorway to the balcony, convinced my only option will be to try to jump off it if I can't get rid of him. Before I get around to it, my bedroom door is forcibly pushed open to reveal a very angry-looking Auntie June.

'What the hell is going on in here?' she bellows at the sight of her husband sprawled out across my bed.

For a few seconds no one says or does anything. No one moves, no one speaks, no one so much as breathes. Even if this doesn't look bad, it certainly looks weird.

'Well,' my auntie snaps. 'Explain yourselves.'

For some reason Auntie June is convinced that Uncle Steve is the kind of man women are going to want to steal – yeah, even me I guess – and it makes her come across as really intense, and it makes him act like a big baby.

'A spider,' my uncle blurts out. 'There was a spider in Mia's bed, and she's scared of them so I said I'd get rid of it for her.'

'Uncle of the Year,' I can't help but say sarcastically.

'So there was a spider on Mia's bed and you killed it?' my auntie repeats back to him, and it sounds even less believable the second time.

'Well, no. It got away.' My uncle shakes his fist at the pesky fictional spider.

'Right. Well I want to go for a walk before dinner, so come on,' my auntie says firmly. 'And Steve …'

'Yes dear?' my uncle says attentively, quickly jumping to his feet.

'Don't forget your shoes,' Auntie June says with a nod towards the floor.

My uncle nods sheepishly before grabbing his shoes and

scuffling out of the room.

'I'm watching you, Mia,' my auntie warns me.

I give her my friendliest smile as she leaves the room and closes the door behind her.

Finally alone, I pounce onto my bed in a way not too dissimilar to the way my uncle did, only my intentions are far purer. The plan is to have a quick nap, have a shower and then dress in something pretty for dinner, ready to make a good impression in front of the group.

Lying face down and horizontally across my bed, I struggle to find the energy to move. I need to though, if only to remove my dress and my face-full of makeup before I fall asleep on these white sheets. Just five more minutes and then I'll sort myself out.

Chapter 6

After hours of sitting still, first on a plane and then on a train, my entire body feels tense. I arch my back and stretch my arms and legs out as far I can but with no relief. I'll probably feel better when I get this dress off, and if I have a bath after my nap that will probably help to ease my stiff muscles too – that's if I have time.

Still face down on my bed, I grab my phone. I check the time to make sure I can fit in everything I have planned before the family dinner at seven o'clock, but something isn't right. I rub my weary eyes and look again – that can't be right. My phone seems to think it is quarter past seven already.

I jump to my feet with the intention of finding another clock, but I am halted by the state of my bed. Foundation, bronzer, black eye makeup and red lipstick stains are smeared all over the top of my previously beautiful white quilt cover.

I glance around the room for a clock, convinced something has screwed up my iPhone clock when it tried to change itself to UK time, but I can't find one. I step out onto the balcony and look for the sun, deluded in thinking I'll be able to figure out the time from its position in the sky. I humour the idea for about five seconds before accepting that I'm no Girl Scout. It is then that I spot a man walking his dog along the beach.

'Excuse me,' I call out at the top of my lungs.

'Yes?' the puzzled-looking man calls back.

'Do you have the time, please?'

The man, still confused, does as he is told and looks at his watch.

'It's twenty past seven,' he shouts.

'Is that in the p.m.?' I ask.

The man laughs at me and replies, 'Yes, that's in the p.m.'

I shout a quick thank you before running back into my bedroom and plucking up the courage to look in the mirror. My beautiful curls are all messy and flat, my dress appears to have twisted three hundred and sixty degrees around my body, and my makeup is so crazy and smudged all over my face it looks like I've been getting off with an evil clown.

I spend thirty seconds that I don't have trying to figure out what will make Belle the angriest: I could smarten myself up and be even later for dinner (that I was supposed to be down for twenty minutes ago) or I can hurry downstairs now, looking like this. There's only one thing for it – I grab my face wipes from my bag and begin taking off some of my makeup – but not all of it, because I won't have time to apply any more and there's no way I'm going down without it.

As I hurry down the stairs I try and fluff up my hair a little before yanking my dress back into place, just seconds before I burst into the dining room. As I enter the room everyone stops eating and stares at me in total silence.

'Hello,' I say cheerily.

'We thought you weren't coming so we started without you,' my mother informs me.

'Sorry, I must have fallen asleep,' I explain, although anyone with half a brain can probably figure that out just by looking at me.

'We were going to just shove you on the kids' table,' my sister says, like it's some kind of punishment. The truth is I would much rather sit with the kids than the adults. 'Anyway,' she continues, 'someone injured my fiancée's back and he's in bed indefinitely, so you can sit here next to me.'

While my sister didn't straight up announce to the room that it was me who broke her prince, judging by the unimpressed faces surrounding me, I can hazard a guess that she has already filled them in.

I take a seat at the table and begin eating the spaghetti bolognese that is laid out for me. Normally I'm not a big fan of meat, but now doesn't seem like the right kind of time for a conversation about it. I'll eat enough pasta to be polite and make sure I go out and buy plenty of things I do like as soon as I can get away.

'So you're the movie maker,' Dan's mum says, and judging by the tone of her voice, she is either seriously unimpressed with my line of work or she believes I intentionally tried to harm her son.

'I am. I write romantic comedies,' I admit, just in case anyone in the room doesn't know or believe that I am capable of such a thing.

'Anything we might have heard of?' a woman who I have not yet been introduced to asks.

'*The Unhappy Couple*, *Battle of the Bridesmaids*, *Nate from Next Door* ...' I start reeling off a list of the most well-known films I have worked on. 'I have a film in the cinema at the moment called *For Better, For Worse*.'

'Well, isn't that impressive,' Dan's mum says, not even sounding the slightest bit sincere.

I glance over at my parents to see what they're making of this conversation, but they hardly look up from their meal. It's not that I feel like I need their approval, it would just be nice to feel like they were proud of me.

'You'll have to write a movie based on my wedding,' Belle says excitedly. 'Just make sure you make my character much more attractive than me.'

This is one of those things that my sister says – but doesn't really mean – so that everyone in the room will shower her with compliments. As expected, everyone tells her how pretty she is and how slim she's looking.

'You used to be quite fat, didn't you, Mia?' Belle's best friend (and my former bully) Nancy announces to the whole room. 'If Belle wanted to feel more confident about her shape I'm sure you could offer invaluable advice … unless you do it the Hollywood way and stick your fingers down your throat.'

Everyone laughs at Nancy's charming little joke about eating disorders, because we all know eating disorders are *hilarious*.

'Well, my sister does look great,' Belle starts, 'and I just seem to be gaining weight all the time.'

My sister sounds glum that the over-dinner conversation is all about her weight, even though she essentially brought it up.

'Don't be so hard on yourself,' I say to try to make her feel better. 'I work in a place where people wrongly think that skinny and success go hand in hand, and that's just not true. And I'm sure that if I worked in a bakery, where people actually enjoy food, rather than fear it, I'd be much happier.'

'So you think I just eat cakes all day?' my sister asks me angrily.

'No, I didn't mean that,' I insist – because I didn't. 'All I'm trying to say is that people who make cakes don't generally look down their nose at people for eating them – you get shamed for eating a muffin in our office.'

'You think I eat too much and that's why I'm fat,' my sister concludes, pushing her plate away.

Once again, everyone's eyes are on me. I can tell, as they all watch me shovel a forkful of spaghetti into my mouth, that they all agree with Belle.

'Don't be foolish, Belle,' my grandma chimes. 'You don't want to be as thin as Mia, it's not healthy to be like she is.'

'You're perfect just the way you are,' my mum insists. It's funny, because when I was chubby not once did she tell me I was perfect as I was. 'You're so happy with your life that silly things like a few pounds here or there don't have any bearing on your happiness.'

Words that would have been music to my ears, when I was a teenager.

'It must be hard for you, Mia, to see your little sister getting married while you're still single,' Nancy says in a faux sympathetic voice.

'And writing all those romantic stories, but having no love in your life,' my auntie says, continuing Nancy's sentiment.

I shrug my shoulders.

'No, because Mia isn't romantic,' Belle says, and I'm not sure if it is in my defence or if she's joining in with the Mia-bashing. 'She thinks love is silly.'

'Surely she can't think that,' a girl about the same age as my sister chimes in. 'She wrote *Nate from Next Door* – which I love – and you can't write like that if you don't believe it.'

Everyone looks at me for an explanation as to how I can have little interest in love but write about it so convincingly.

'Does George Lucas believe that Ewoks are real?' I ask the room. 'Does Bram Stoker believe in vampires? Does even one person who works for Disney in any capacity believe that an old bloke can float his house to South America using nothing but a shit-load of balloons?'

I hear a few sniggers from the kids' table at my use of the S word, but the grown-ups are all staring at me like I'm some kind of monster.

'Well, that's depressing,' Nancy laughs.

'My favourite love story is a lie,' Belle's friend says solemnly.

'Oh, for God's sake,' I can't help but snap. 'It's fiction and fiction is made up. That's just the way it is.'

Everyone continues to eat in silence and I feel bad for ruining the atmosphere, but it wasn't my fault. Belle is getting married and she's happy, and that's great. Why can't people just be happy for her and stop obsessing over what her happiness means for me, her older sister who is still on the shelf? Don't they think I am happy with my life? I am ecstatic when I am back in LA, it's just being around this lot that makes me miserable.

Chapter 7

'Good morning,' I sing brightly as I enter the kitchen.

Like the rest of the house, the kitchen is all decked out in white. The chrome appliances are the closest thing this room has to offer in terms of colour, it's so white and clean it's giving off the creepy vibes of a hospital operating theatre. I watch as my sister chops up a plate of sausages before dousing it in ketchup and handing it to Josh – on second thoughts, it's more like a morgue than an operating theatre.

In contrast to all the horizontal lines created by the drawers, frameless cabinets and work surfaces, the vertical blinds cast shadows all around the room. Long, thick, dark shadows, creating prison cell type bars everywhere. These bars may be an optical illusion caused by nothing other than an obstruction of light, but they feel real. I feel like I'm in a prison.

'Morning, Mia,' my sister says as she fries bacon. 'We were just talking about how you can't get married, even if you want to.'

Forget what I just said. It's not like an operating theatre, it's not like a morgue and it's not like a prison – I'm right in the heart of the psych ward.

I glance around at the other people in the kitchen. Josh, my only ally in the room, left as soon as he got his breakfast, so that just leaves me with my sister, my gran, my mum and my auntie. Despite the warm weather outside it is positively frosty in here.

'I'm sorry, what?' I ask, because that made no sense to me at all.

'I've been reading up on wedding superstitions, you know, just so I have all bases covered,' my sister explains.

'That makes perfect sense,' I say sarcastically.

'Mia,' my gran interrupts, 'superstition is such a large part of getting married.'

'*And* being married, am I right?' I say as I give my auntie a playful nudge and wiggle my eyebrows. I thought she might be able to see the funny side of what happened yesterday by now, but the angry frown on her face confirms otherwise. 'So, what does that have to do with me?' I ask my sister.

'Three times a bridesmaid, never a bride,' my mum warns me – the same mum who bullied me into being my sister's bridesmaid even though she knew I had already been a bridesmaid twice when I was younger.

I stare at her blankly.

'Basically,' my sister begins, 'the whole idea of being a bridesmaid is so you can distract the evil spirits that try to ruin the wedding.'

'Like vodka?' I laugh, causing my gran to click her tongue at me. 'Like a stunt double then?' I ask, semi-seriously.

'Yes,' my sister says excitedly, clearly delighted that I get it. 'So the bridesmaid deals with the evil spirits that will be trying to stop the wedding from going ahead, but in doing so the bridesmaid catches a lot of bad luck – like being single and alone forever.'

'Mia is doing a good job of that so far,' my mum snorts.

'Oh, see before I just thought it was a silly tradition but now … I think you ladies are completely nuts.'

'Mia,' my sister squeaks, 'don't speak to Mum, Gran and Auntie June like that.'

'And you.' I point at my sister. 'You're the queen of crazy if you believe that. If you really did believe it, there's no way you would have asked me.'

My sister looks embarrassed.

'Wow, really?' I ask in disbelief. 'You believe this rubbish and you're still willing to let me take the risk?'

'Well, you're never going to get married, are you?' my sister reasons.

I look over at my mum for some kind of support.

'And we did spend your share of the wedding fund on your sister,' my mum half-jokes.

'Unbelievable,' I say as I shake my head. Thank God I really don't have plans to get married because my family are trying to make sure I'm fucked from the word go.

Belle wanders over to me sheepishly, spatula in hand.

'You're not mad are you, sis?' she asks.

'Of course I'm not,' I say, giving her a playful shove so she knows I mean it. 'You're right, I don't ever want to get married, I'm just messing with you.'

'Phew.' My sister breathes a sigh of relief and gets back to her bacon.

Am I stupid for being upset over everyone constantly reaffirming that I'm never going to get married? I know why I don't want to get married, but they don't understand the way I feel. I can only imagine they think that no one would even want to marry me in the first place.

I know this is only my first proper day here – but already I can't wait for this stupid wedding to be over, so I can get on the fastest flight back to lovely LA, relaxing in the knowledge that I've clocked enough family hours to last me at least a couple of years.

'Bacon sandwich?' my sister asks me.

'Oh, no thank you,' I say politely. 'I'm not really a bacon kind of person.'

'But you used to love bacon sandwiches,' my mum insists.

'I'm sure I used to love being breastfed, but I don't fancy that anymore either,' I insist.

I don't know why I expected to get a few laughs from the room, that joke was never going to go down well. My mum rolls her eyes, my gran tuts and my auntie looks repulsed.

'Mia, I'm not entirely happy about your foul mouth and your disgusting sense of humour being around my kids,' my auntie explains.

'Well, I'm quite fond of my foul mouth and my disgusting sense of humour – in fact, I'm literally attached to my foul mouth, so unless you want me to stay away from my cousins …'

'Could you? Thanks.' My auntie forces a fake smile. I told you, she just hates me.

'I could do you some sausage while the pan is still on,' my sister suggests in an attempt to diffuse the situation.

'I'm fine, honestly. I'll just grab a coffee, I'm not much of a morning person.'

'Well, there's a machine over there. None of us have any idea how to use it though,' my sister says with a shrug of her shoulders.

I glance over at the fancy, hi-tech coffee machine that no one has been able to figure out how to use. I'm a coffee junkie, so I have a similar machine at home – I'll be able to work this, no problem.

'When you're done, go and put some clothes on because we're all going to this fish and chip restaurant in the town. Well, everyone but Dan, he's still stuck in bed with a bad back,' my sister reminds me, like I might have forgotten.

'I am dressed,' I protest, glancing down at the hot pink beach dress I had deemed the most appropriate to wear around my family. 'Anyway, I'm really tired from all the travelling yesterday so I thought I might just chill out here today, make sure I'm ready to start celebrating tomorrow.'

I give my sister an overly enthusiastic thumbs-up. Hopefully by mentioning the thousands of miles I have travelled just to be with her on her big day she will be grateful enough not to force me into wedding-based celebrations just yet.

'That's fine,' my sister says, much to my surprise. 'Well, we'd rather not take the kids with us and Dan isn't exactly up to looking after them.'

Wow, that's twice today she's brought up the fact I injured her fiancé. As far as I'm concerned, Dan's bad back is not my fault, but I'm the only person in this house who doesn't blame me.

'You want *me* to look after kids?' I laugh. 'I'm sure they can take care of themselves.'

'Josh and Max are only ten.' My sister says this with such an alarmed squeak that you'd think I had just suggested we leave a toddler in the cutlery draw.

'Anyway, she doesn't want me near her kids,' I say with a nod towards June.

'*She's* the cat's mother,' my mum insists, reminding me of my manners – God forbid anyone should say anything that might be considered rude this morning.

'It will do you good to learn some responsibility,' my Auntie June insists.

'You mean it will do you good to dump your child on me while you go off and eat chips,' I reply.

'Mia, why can't you just do this?' Belle pleads.

'Because I'm not a child-friendly person,' I insist.

'You're not a bacon person, you not a morning person, you're not a child-friendly person – are you sure you're a person at all?' my mum snaps.

'OK, fine,' I say in submission. 'I'm going to go and do some work by the pool, just let me know when you need me.'

It's like I only need to be in a room for five minutes before everyone is pissed off and it's all thanks to me. I'm not sure what it is about me that my family seem to find so intolerable because, from where I'm standing, *they're* the ones with the flaws, not me. OK, so I may not be into love, marriage and babies, but I'm a nice person, I'm kind, generous and polite – all the things you're supposed to be – until people give me reason not to be. I'm not cold like my mum, I'm not a bully like my sister and I'm not horrible like my auntie. Perhaps I'm not as nice to my Auntie June as I could be, but this level of dislike comes after years and years of her actively despising me, and for no good reason.

The plan is to get comfortable by the pool, do a bit of work and then try and swim off the dinner I ate out of manners last night. I hadn't bargained on babysitting two young boys but they're good kids, I'm sure keeping an eye on them won't affect my plans.

Chapter 8

Finally connected to the beach house wi-fi, my phone springs back to life. After a day of peace and quiet from my best friend (who is also my calendar, camera, alarm clock, emailing device, web browser ... oh, and it can make calls too) normal service has been resumed. There are several emails from my assistant, Dalia, filling me in on every little thing that has happened in the office as well as a few from Savannah and Molly who already seem pretty stressed out trying to get on with our latest project without me. Molly hinted that my boss was unhappy with me taking vacation days (that I was owed, might I add) while we're in the middle of a new movie. If only they knew what a rubbish time I was having. I'd much rather be at work.

I have only just made myself comfortable next to the pool, but I know that I'll get my work done a lot easier if I type on my iPad instead of my phone. I drag myself to my feet and begin (what feels like) the long journey up to my room – then again, running up two flights of stairs will do me good, I feel so bloated from dinner last night.

When I finally reach my room I am a little taken aback to see my uncle already in there.

'Can I help you?' I ask bluntly.

'I was just …' My uncle's voice quickly changes from a hushed tone to an awkwardly loud one. '… making sure that spider hadn't come back.'

'What?' I ask, but as I notice him looking over my shoulder I turn around and see my Auntie June standing behind me.

'You're with Mia,' my auntie says, like I'm not even there. 'Again.'

'Spiders,' my uncle laughs with a shrug of his shoulders.

'You're *that* scared of spiders?' my auntie asks me in disbelief.

No, but my uncle is that scared of her.

I just shrug – well, what else can I say?

'Anyway, we're heading out now. You will take proper care of the children, won't you?' my auntie asks again.

'Yes, yes,' I reply. 'I thought I'd take a nap while they play in the sea. Sound good?'

My uncle laughs at my blatant attempt at humour, but Auntie June looks disturbed.

'Mia, you don't take your eyes off them,' she says sternly.

'I won't,' I reply sincerely.

'Come on, Steve,' my auntie instructs her husband before they leave my room together.

'Unbelievable,' I say to myself, before grabbing my iPad and heading back downstairs.

I am only back in my seat by the pool for a few minutes before my sister wanders in with Josh and Max.

'Now, be good for Mia,' my sister instructs the children. 'And you be good for the kids,' she warns me.

I find it funny that no one trusts me with these children, and yet they will leave them with me anyway because it suits them.

'Right, who fancies a cigarette?' I ask Josh and Max the second my sister has closed the door behind her. The boys laugh, which says it all about my sense of humour. 'But seriously, are you guys OK to amuse yourselves while I do some work?'

'Can we go in the pool?' Josh asks.

'Can you both swim?'

The boys nod.

'Are you sure?' I ask. 'Because your mums will like me even less if you die.'

Both Josh and Max simultaneously talk me through their swimming achievements to date.

'OK then, but only if you stay in the shallow end. I'll be sat right here so I'll notice if you wander into the deep end,' I warn them.

'Can you get us our swimming trunks?' Josh asks.

Not only do I not fancy rooting through other people's things to find swimwear for the boys, but that sounds like it will take a long time and I'm worried today will be my last chance to get some proper work done.

'You wear underwear, right?'

Josh and Max nod.

'Well, you're sorted. Go, have fun.'

The boys look at each other for a moment, unsure of whether or not I have the authority to let them go swimming in their underpants. They don't think it over for too long before running towards the pool, screaming with delight before dive-bombing into the beautiful blue water.

I only get to feel like the world's coolest babysitter for a moment before I realise that it is proving almost impossible to concentrate on my work with Josh and Max screaming and splashing each other. I can't exactly go and work in another room, not after the jokes I made about drowning them in the sea. Whether it's the sea *or* a swimming pool, if I kill these kids my sister will almost certainly have another reason to blame me for ruining her wedding – and I can't have that.

'Hey guys, do you want to watch a movie?' I ask.

'We've seen all the kids' movies they have here,' Max calls back.

'What about if I let you watch a grown-up movie?'

The boys both cheer with excitement as they climb out of the pool.

'Come on, this way.' I toss them each a towel and head for

the playroom.

'Right, let's see,' I say to myself as I examine the top shelf of the cupboard where the DVDs are kept. They actually have quite a good selection – I'm a total film buff and even I'm impressed. I quickly run my finger past any movie that I was involved in writing or any others of a similar genre, I don't want to fill their young, impressionable minds with any romantic junk. '*Pulp Fiction*,' I squeak with delight. 'Have you seen it?'

The boys shake their heads, it's like they haven't even heard of it.

'What? You haven't seen *Pulp Fiction*?' I ask in disbelief, putting to the back of my mind the fact that the boys are ten years old. I'm sure I was still at school when I watched it for the first time. 'It's a masterpiece.'

Maybe it's because I take my love of movies very seriously, maybe it's because I'm a Quentin Tarantino fan or maybe it's because I just want to go against my auntie's wishes, but I decide that this is the movie the boys should watch.

'Just don't tell your parents, OK?'

They nod eagerly.

I pop the DVD in the machine and sit myself down on the sofa with Josh and Max. I'll stick around for a few minutes, just to make sure they're enjoying it, and then I'll head back into the pool room and do my work.

As the opening scene in the diner plays out, Josh and Max's eyes are glued to the big screen. Ah, that look of wonder, that mesmerised stare – I remember when I watched my first Tarantino movie, they're going to love it.

'Well, I'm going to leave you guys to enjoy this,' I say as I head for the door, but it falls on deaf ears.

I grab a couple of beanbags, one to hold the door to the games room open and one to do the same with the door to the pool, that way I'll be able to hear them if they need me. As I put the second beanbag in place, I overhear an especially swearword-heavy line of dialogue. For a moment it occurs to me that maybe this isn't the best film to put on for a couple of kids whose parents have sheltered them from bad language and inappropriate behaviour their entire lives, but that's exactly the reason they should see it. This movie is a work of art, everyone needs to see it ... although probably not when they're ten years old. Well, Josh and Max are clearly enjoying it and that leaves me to get on with some work. What's the worst that can happen?

***

Perhaps it has something to do with the water – the way it reflects on the walls and the gentle sounds it makes as it laps against the sides of the pool when there aren't any noisy children splashing around in it – or the fact that jetlag is still screwing with me a little, but it wasn't long after I sat back down by the pool when I fell asleep. So much for getting some work done before the adults get back ... oh my God, the kids!

I jump up from my seat and dash into the games room, only to find Josh and Max exactly as I left them, their eyes still glued to the screen as Samuel L. Jackson finishes delivering that epic speech from the final scene of the movie.

The boys, who are not even aware I have re-entered the room, both blink at the screen, their facial expressions giving nothing away. I wonder if they have even spoken to one another during the film.

'So, what do you think?' I ask them as the credits roll.

'That was *so* cool,' Josh enthuses.

'I didn't want it to end,' Max adds.

'Well, there's plenty more where that came from,' I tell them, proud to have introduced them to a cinematic genius. 'Just don't tell your parents.'

'When can we watch another?' Josh asks excitedly. 'Do you think you can make everyone go out again tomorrow? What are we watching next?'

'Hold your horses,' I chuckle. 'I'll do my best.'

Right on cue I hear the sound of footsteps on the stairs. I quickly remove *Pulp Fiction* from the DVD player and put it back on the shelf, just as Auntie June walks in.

'Did everyone behave?' she asks, not wasting a second on pleasantries.

'Of course,' I reply. 'They're little angels.'

'I was talking to them,' my auntie informs me.

I roll my eyes at my auntie as Tarantino's two newest fans nod their heads.

I grab a bottle of water from the mini-fridge and take a swig, safe in the knowledge I have passed myself off as a capable babysitter.

'Wait a second,' my auntie starts, puzzled. 'Why are you two in your underpants?'

Caught off guard, I spray the big gulp of water I had taken out of my mouth. I cough and splutter for a moment (much to the amusement of Josh and Max) before trying to explain.

'It's not what it looks like,' I start, but my auntie cuts me off.

'What *does* it look like?'

I hesitate for a moment.

'I don't know, but the boys wanted to swim and I didn't think you'd appreciate me going in your room to find shorts.'

My auntie looks at the boys for confirmation and they dutifully nod. I think my auntie is picking up on the fact that we are all behaving very shiftily, but that's only because I let the boys watch a movie with an 'eighteen' rating, not because I held an impromptu orgy and decided my ten-year-old cousin and his mate could attend if they adhered to the dress code.

Auntie June sniffs her son suspiciously.

'You two, go and shower,' she instructs them, having obviously smelt the unmistakable whiff of chlorine on their skin, even though they're dry because they've been watching the movie for the past few hours.

'You're welcome,' I say victoriously. I may not have wanted to babysit today but I successfully kept the boys alive – something no one thought for a second that I could do, and yet they still left them with me. Never underestimate the lure of chips.

My auntie follows the boys back upstairs, eyeballing me cautiously as she leaves the room.

I don't waste my time wondering why June hates me these days, she just does and I'm weirdly OK with it. You would think I'd be distraught by the fact that pretty much every member of my family doesn't really like me but I'm OK with that too. I have a few theories going, most of which involve me being born to a sexy celebrity couple and ending up getting swapped in the hospital, but I made peace with them emotionally exiling me a long time ago.

I suppose I should go and do some work. As I head back to my poolside workstation I glance over the DVDs again, making a mental note that the boys should watch *Reservoir Dogs* next – as part of their film education, it's called Media Studies, I promise.

Chapter 9

Despite promising to keep working while I'm away, I didn't get very much done today. I tried, but I was only on a roll for about ten minutes before Belle called me for dinner, and all group activities are not optional – unless they need a babysitter.

'Bangers and mash,' my sister informs me cheerily as I enter the dining room. Oh boy, more meat. Still, my sister will take it personally if I don't participate, so I suppose I'll eat the vegetables and push the sausages around my plate to create the illusion that I am eating them.

'Yummy,' I say enthusiastically.

Soon enough everyone is seated at the two tables, the grown-ups on the main table and everyone under sixteen at the kids' table next to us. Even though not everyone is staying at the beach house, we seem to be spending a lot of time together and eating all our meals together – thanks to Bridezilla's ridiculously strict scheduling.

This evening I am sitting between my grandma and a hard face … my Auntie June. I was expecting to be in a horrible position, with shit being flung at me from both sides, but they're not giving me a hard time at all tonight. My gran has always had moments of indifference towards me, but my auntie is usually unrelenting.

Not tonight though.

'I hear you did a good job with the kids,' my dad says to me from across the table. 'Well done.'

This comment catches me off guard as I am eating a mouthful of peas, causing me to swallow the wrong way and cough a little.

'Yeah.' I sip my water. 'Well, they're good kids. I had fun.'

'Maybe you do have maternal instincts,' my mum says warmly.

I glance around the table and see that everyone is smiling at me.

'Maybe,' I reply, knowing full well that I am about as maternal as a shoe. Still, if people are going to be nicer to me for showcasing these 'normal' feelings then I'm all for it. Whatever makes my stay here more tolerable.

'You did do a good job,' a voice that sounds exactly like my auntie's says, but it can't be her, can it?

I look to my right to see my Auntie June smiling at me. Yes, smiling at me, and it's not forced or smug, it's genuine.

'You've clearly done some growing up, Mia,' she adds.

Belle, visibly annoyed that I am getting more attention than her, attempts to put me back in my place.

'Mia, why aren't you eating your dinner?' she asks angrily.

'The vegetables are delicious,' I say, deflecting.

'Well, it's your show business diet, isn't it,' my mum chimes in. 'It's a tough business. Things like that matter.'

My eyes widen. First my dad compliments me, then my auntie is nice to me and now my mum is defending me – and everyone is still smiling. I must be dreaming.

Perhaps now everyone is seeing me in a better light, this wedding might not be so bad – I might even have fun.

'So, you're refusing to eat my sausages?' Belle persists.

'I don't really eat pork,' I reason. My sister looks angry but everyone else in the room seems fine with me until …

'I don't really eat pork,' a voice echoes my own. Everyone looks towards the end of the table, where the kids' table is. Josh is grinning widely.

'Excuse me?' my auntie says to her son.

'I don't really eat pork,' he continues as he eats, much to Max's amusement. This time I notice the accent he's putting on.

When I let Josh and Max watch *Pulp Fiction* I didn't think that they wouldn't tell their parents about it, but there's one thing I didn't anticipate happening – something that is inevitable when you watch a Tarantino flick – they've caught the quoting bug.

I glance down the table at them, pleading at them with my eyes not to take this any further, but they're not looking at me, they're having too much fun.

'Why not?' my uncle asks his son curiously.

'I don't want to eat dirty animals,' Josh replies.

He's butchering the lines – no pun intended – but it's obvious what he's doing.

Everyone in the room is still baffled, apart from Dan's older brother Mike who is chuckling to himself – he's clearly a fan of the movie. If this situation wasn't all my fault I might find it funny too. It's true what they say, children have minds like sponges.

'They're covered in *shit*,' Josh elaborates, clearly having the time of his life. '*That's* dirty.'

On hearing her ten-year-old son say shit, my auntie snaps her head to the right at an impressive speed. The smile is immediately wiped from Josh's face when he realises how angry his mum is, and just how much trouble he's in.

'Where did you hear that?' his mum asks him.

'I don't know,' he replies, fooling no one.

'Max?' my auntie asks her son's partner in crime, but he's frozen still and completely silent.

'Josh, tell us where you heard that,' my uncle demands, sounding angrier and angrier as he says each word.

Just keep your mouth shut, Josh. This will all blow over.

'It's *Pulp Fiction*,' Mike says in an attempt to diffuse the situation. Little does he know, he has just sealed my fate.

'Where have you seen …' my auntie's voice trails off as she turns to face me, this time her movements are slow and sinister. 'You!'

My auntie points at me with her knife, and whether she just happens to have it in her hand or she's actually planning to stab me, I decide not to take any chances and jump up from my seat. I move around the table as I try and explain.

'You let my son watch a "fifteen" rated film?' she shrieks, as she tries to chase me around the table.

'I think it's an "eighteen",' Mike unhelpfully chimes in, which only makes my auntie angrier.

I'm too busy trying not to get stabbed to notice what everyone else in the room is making of this, but I know for sure that no one is doing anything to intervene.

'It's a classic,' I say by way of an explanation.

'A classic that's full of swearing,' my auntie yells.

'It isn't gratuitous swearing, it's all in context,' I insist.

'Actually, I think it features over two hundred and sixty uses of the F word,' Mike muses.

'Mike, my God, you're killing me, give me a break,' I plead.

Everyone at the table just stares at me. They're probably thinking this is just classic me – and they're not impressed. Everyone has a face like thunder. Well, everyone but Belle that is, who looks delighted that universal balance has been restored. Everyone hates me again.

Chapter 10

'I'm not saying you're not likeable,' my sister explains as she examines her underwear-clad body in my bedroom mirror. 'Just that you need to try harder to make people like you.'

I lie back on my bed and exhale deeply. Dan's back is still bad so he's still stuck in bed. I assumed that was why Belle asked me if she could try on her bridal underwear in my bedroom, so he didn't see it. In actual fact, this is her not so subtle way of telling me that I need to try harder to 'make people like me' – which, in my opinion, is as good as telling me that I am not likeable.

'What do you think of the shoes?' Belle asks. OK, so I'm here for a lecture *and* to watch my sister prance around in her underwear and a pair of white ballet pumps.

'They're nice,' I reply. Personally, I would have gone for something with a heel, but with my sister usually opting for ugly, clumsy, flat mules no matter what the weather, I'm lucky she isn't forcing a pair on me to go with my bridesmaid dress. The wedding ceremony is taking place on the beach, so the outfits have been tweaked accordingly.

'I can't wait to see what my dress looks like with the shoes and the veil,' she says to herself as she wiggles her hips in front of the mirror with a level of narcissism not unlike that of Patrick

Bateman when he's shagging those hookers in *American Psycho*. 'The clothes should have been delivered by now.'

Right on cue there is a knock on the door.

'Come in,' Belle calls out, still admiring her figure.

Uncle Steve walks into room with an armful of garment bags.

'Here's the first lot,' he starts, before clapping eyes on a nearly naked Belle and stopping in his tracks. And then there's me, in my pink nightie.

He quickly averts his gaze to the ceiling.

'Thanks, Uncle Steve,' she squeaks as she takes the clothes from him. As Belle dumps the clothes down on the floor and begins ripping into them, my uncle sidles over to me.

'Trying on your dresses?' he asks enthusiastically.

'No,' I say with a laugh. 'Well, not with an audience.'

'You should, I can give you a male perspective, from someone with a keen eye for style.'

'Aw, thanks, uncle,' Belle interrupts. 'Can you go get the rest of the clothes first?'

'Yeah, okay,' he replies helpfully.

'Right, if you want me to try anything on we're doing it now, before he gets back, because I'm not standing around in my underwear,' I say, hurrying my sister.

'Well, it probably covers more than your bikini, but anyway, *I'm* the bride, me first,' Belle complains. 'Not everything is about you.'

I exhale deeply. There's no reasoning with Belle at the moment
Belle finds her dress, hops into it and demands I zip her up.

'Wow,' I exclaim.

'I know, right?' my sister replies as she twirls around in front of the mirror.

Lucky for me, Belle took my exclamation as one of delight rather than one of horror. Make no mistake though, I am horrified.

In addition to her white stockings and white ballet pumps, my sister has slipped on a strapless, white tutu dress. She looks like a little girl about to perform Swan Lake with the rest of her ballet class, but if I tell her as much she will no doubt act as moody and stubborn as a bratty little diva.

'Do you like it?' she asks.

'It's ...' I pause to think carefully about what I'm going to say. 'Is it a bit short for a bridal gown?'

And that's me saying that!

'I'm getting married on the beach – duh! It has to be short or it will get covered in sand. All the outfits are short, even the men's trousers. We're going for a sort of casual formal look.'

As my brain tries to process exactly what a casual formal look is, I feel a headache coming on.

'So, what's my dress like?' I ask, suddenly terrified.

'All in good time,' my sister says. 'I'm trying to figure out how this veil goes on.'

I take the sparkly white birdcage veil from my sister and begin fixing it in place on her head.

'Here, it's easy.'

My sister takes a long hard look at her outfit in the mirror. A single tear rolls down her cheek and for a moment I am touched by her sweetness – that is until that beautiful single tear turns into an eruption of wailing and a flood of tears. I may not be an expert on the emotions of your typical bride, but I'm fairly sure this is not a display of happiness.

'Belle, what's wrong?' I ask.

'My wedding is ruined,' she cries. 'My wedding is ruined and my marriage is going to fail. And it's all *your* fault,' she adds.

'What? How is it my fault?' I'm confused.

'Because ... because ... because ... because ... because ...'

As my sister struggles to say what she wants to say because she is so upset, it occurs to me that this would be an inappropriate time to start singing 'We're Off To See The Wizard' at her, so I don't.

My mum comes bursting into the room.

'Oh, Belle, darling, what's wrong?'

'Mia did it,' Belle wails.

'Mia, what have you done now?' my mother asks me angrily.

'I really don't know,' I reply honestly.

Soon enough we are joined by my grandma, who must have heard the commotion too.

'What's going on?' she asks as she joins my mum in comforting Belle.

'Mia has upset Belle,' my mum tells her.

My gran, who doesn't look the least bit surprised, rolls her eyes.

'You tell us what she did, Belle,' my gran demands.

I wait patiently to find out what I have said or done that is so horrible while my mum and gran fuss around my sister, drying her eyes and rubbing her shoulders.

'She … she … she put my veil on me,' Belle sobs.

My mum and gran both stare at me.

'I did,' I reply timidly. I was only trying to help her out, did she want to do it herself or something?

'Oh, Mia, how could you?' my gran cries.

'It's because she knows she's never going to be a bride because I made her my bridesmaid and she wants to take it out on me by ruining my wedding and my marriage and my life,' my sister sobs without pausing for breath – and at such a speed that I'm still not sure what she's talking about.

'Can someone who doesn't need to blow their nose explain the problem to me?' I ask, annoyed that I'm being made out to be some kind of wedding saboteur.

'It's bad luck for a bride to wear her entire outfit before the big day,' my mum explains.

'And you put my veil on me,' Belle sobs. 'It tempts fate.'

'Oh! Shit, Belle, I'm sorry.'

I had forgotten about her silly wedding superstitions, but surely she realises I was only trying to help her, and they are only silly superstitions after all, nothing is done and dusted.

'So, what do we do?' I ask. 'Walk backwards? Throw some salt around?'

'Mia,' Mum snaps. 'Take this seriously.'

I thought I was.

'Ask her to leave,' Belle sobs.

'Mia–' my mum starts, but I cut her off.

'I can hear her! It's fine, I'll go.'

As I walk towards the door my uncle comes charging in with more garment bags.

'Sorry,' he says breathlessly, 'I couldn't get rid of the delivery man. Did I miss anything?'

Belle stops crying and for a moment everyone stares at him, wondering what he means.

'I mean, did I forget anything? Or is this it?'

'Just Mia, ruining everything again,' Belle sobs.

I sigh. Well, what else can I say at this point?

Chapter 11

Today, I am officially persona non grata. With my sister crying hysterically in my bedroom, and nowhere else in the house for me to go without being treated like a shit in a swimming pool, I have ventured outside for a walk on the beach. The only problem is that, because I was thrown out of my bedroom, I couldn't get any shoes to put on – not much of a problem walking on the beach, but I'm fairly sure my little nightdress is not an ideal outfit for taking a stroll. What choice do I have, though? I'm not allowed in my room, my auntie doesn't want me going anywhere near the kids, none of Dan's family or friends want anything to do with me and if I stayed in the house Uncle Sleaze would only stalk me from room to room, drooling.

So, a walk alone on the beach it is. It's a lovely day today – nice and warm luckily, and the sun is shining bright in the sky. If I wasn't so unprepared I could have kicked back here and done some work, or just topped up my LA tan that is fading by the day.

As I walk I think about my sister and why she is upset. I do feel bad about what happened today but I didn't intend to upset her or jinx her or whatever she seems to think I had in mind when I put that veil on her head. If Belle wasn't upset about this she would still be banging on about me giving Dan a bad back, or upsetting the family by teaching the kids inappropriate language. There must be a bigger issue deep down somewhere because what I see as silly little mistakes my sister sees as me being on a one-woman quest to ruin her wedding.

'Hello again,' a strong Australian accent snaps me from my thoughts.

I turn around to see a big, buff blonde dude walking out of the sea, not unlike that scene in *Casino Royale* where Daniel Craig emerges from the water in his little blue trunks. A soaking wet golden retriever with a tennis ball in its mouth follows him closely.

I glance behind me to see if he's talking to someone else – certain I have never met this man before in my life – but there's no one there.

'Hi,' I say cautiously.

'How are you?' he asks, flashing me his perfectly white teeth as he smiles. I may not have a clue who he is, but he's gorgeous.

'I'm OK. You?'

'I'm great … you don't remember me, do you?'

I shake my head. This man is convinced he knows me but this is the first time I have left the house since I got here and I don't know when or where else we could have possibly met.

'We've met?'

'Yes,' he says confidently. 'You're from the big house.'

The handsome Aussie points towards the beach house behind me.

I stare at him thoughtfully as I run my hand through my hair and rack my brains, but I still don't have any idea who he is.

The handsome Aussie laughs.

'A couple of days ago you asked me for the time. From your balcony,' he laughs.

'Oh! That was you?' I ask. 'Were you Australian then, too?'

I don't remember that man being so handsome or having an accent of note, then again, I had just woken up and I had a lot on my mind.

'Nah, this is just something I'm trying out today to pull chicks,' he jokes. 'Yes, of course I was Australian then.'

'Well, you never know,' I tease. 'After all, it says "lifeguard" on your shorts, doesn't mean you are one.'

'So, you're looking at my shorts, huh?' he replies with a wiggle of his eyebrows. 'I am a genuine lifeguard though. Genuine Australian, genuine lifeguard.'

'Oh. Sorry,' I giggle awkwardly.

'At least I'm wearing shorts,' he teases, nodding towards my outfit.

'It's a long story.' I sigh. 'Sometimes I wear clothes.'

'Only sometimes, huh?'

At this stage in our flirting his dog grows tired of waiting and drops the ball at his master's feet. Just in case he doesn't take the hint, the dog barks.

'Just a second, Jay,' the man says to his dog. 'Well, maybe next time you have clothes on, if you want to–'

Jay barks again impatiently, quashing any chance the lifeguard had of being smooth.

'I work just down the beach, there's a café there. I'll buy you a—'

Jay barks again, only louder and more aggressively this time. I can't believe I'm getting cockblocked by a dog.

'I'll leave you boys to play fetch,' I tell him as I wander off.

'Wait,' the sexy lifeguard calls after me. 'I don't even know your name.'

I shrug my shoulders.

'If you tell me yours I'll tell you mine,' he jokes, but he's starting to sound the tiniest little bit desperate now.

'You'll figure it out,' I call back.

As I stroll back to towards the house it seems like my luck might be changing. A sexy new friend will certainly make my stay here a lot more fun.

When I set out for my walk I didn't think for a moment that a hot, Australian lifeguard was going to emerge from the sea. One thing is for sure though, I won't be throwing this fish back just yet.

***

'Hello,' I say nervously as I walk into my bedroom, worried Bridezilla might be waiting for me so that she can bite my head off.

I spy Belle sitting on the floor. She seems a lot calmer now, and is unwrapping more clothes.

'Belle, I'm really sorry about before,' I tell her sincerely. 'I didn't know about that superstition, or I would have never done that. I thought I was helping.'

'It's OK,' my sister says calmly. 'You weren't to know, you're not wedding minded.'

I don't know what 'wedding minded' is, but I imagine it's something my mother told her I was not, so that she would forgive me for my faux pas.

'Well, if you still want me to try my dress on, I may as well do it now before I get dressed.'

'OK.' My sister jumps to her feet excitedly and unzips one of the garment bags. 'Ta-da,' she sings as she holds my dress up in front of me.

Not unlike my sister's dress, my bridesmaid dress is also a strapless tutu dress, only mine is in bright orange. Without saying a word I slip off my nightdress and step into the dress before my sister zips it up for me.

'Do you love it?' she asks as I step in front of the mirror. My God, it's disgusting. I would never accuse my sister of intentionally making me look bad so that she looked better ... but ... no, on second thoughts, I would totally accuse her of that.

'I look like something from *Toddlers & Tiaras*,' I say blankly.

'That reminds me,' Belle chirps excitedly as she rummages around in a box before presenting me with a sparkly, gold tiara. 'Here you go.'

I obligingly pop the tiara on top of my head and it takes all my strength not to laugh or cry, because this is what I am going to have to wear on her wedding day – her wedding day where people will be taking photographs that will haunt me for the rest of my life.

'How come the other dresses are coral and mine is bright orange?' I ask my sister as I watch her take out the other bridesmaids' dresses, which are equally as tacky but a much nicer shade.

'Because you're chief bridesmaid,' she says brightly. 'Your dress is special, just for you.'

Bullshit. She's made mine extra disgusting on purpose, just to piss me off. Why would she get me an orange dress? No one likes or suits orange. Even oranges don't suit orange, it's a horrible colour.

I am just about to say something I will regret, when I notice my sister is on the verge of another meltdown.

'Oh God, what now?' I ask.

'The men's trousers, they're not shortened,' she explains. 'They need to be shortened so they don't get covered in sand.'

'Well, can't they just roll them up?'

'Mia, don't be stupid,' my sister snaps. 'They were supposed to be shortened. The theme is casual formal. Short trousers, untucked shirts and unfastened bowties, that's what I wanted. This is your fault.'

'Go on then, how is this my fault?' I ask angrily, interested to know how I could have had anything to do with this problem.

'When you put that veil on my head you sealed my fate. My wedding is ruined. The trousers are wrong, Dan is injured—'

I cut my sister's sentence short by slapping her across the face. Not too hard, but hard enough to stop her hyperventilating and to get her attention.

'And you slapped me across the face,' she yells, adding yet another thing to the list.

'Because you're being hysterical,' I explain. 'Listen to me. Dan got hurt days ago, and the trousers were already wrong *before* I put the veil on your head. They were already in the room and they were already wrong. The karma fairy didn't sneak in and lengthen the trousers just to ruin your wedding, I promise.'

Belle takes deep breaths, puffing her cheeks out as she exhales.

'OK,' she says calmly.

'This is what we'll do. You and I can pop into town and find a tailor, and they can make the changes to the length, OK?'

'OK.'

'And I'll even buy you an ice cream or something,' I tell her, because I've just heard about this café on the beach, not too far from where the hottest lifeguard works …

Chapter 12

Shell's Café is the cutest little café I have ever seen, and Shell herself is a lovely lady. From the moment Belle and I arrived she has treated us like royalty – she even offered us cupcakes on the house, but as delicious as they looked with their piped-on pink buttercream, chocolate sprinkles and dash of glitter, I had to say no. Belle, who actually bakes cakes for a living, didn't hesitate in saying yes to one of the delicious looking cakes.

'This is lovely,' Belle announces after she takes her first bite. When it comes to cakes Belle is somewhat of a snob, so it says a lot about Shell's cakes that my sister is praising them.

Growing up, it was a shared love of baking that brought my sister and me together on those rare occasions we could actually tolerate spending time together. Whenever it was a family member's birthday, we would team up and bake them a cake or some cupcakes, and we were actually quite good at it. Sure, we'd argue the entire time, but we actually made a pretty good team. As we got older we kept up the tradition, but we would complain even louder each time about having to spend time together (although, if I'm being honest, it felt kind of nice to spend time together – well, maybe not nice, but it certainly felt more normal than hating each other) until one day we just decided to stop, but my sister went on to make a career out of it, working for a cupcake café back in Canterbury.

'Well, I'm glad you like it,' Shell says brightly before turning to me and opening her mouth, but my sister starts talking before Shell has a chance to say anything else.

'Dan, my fiancé, said that there was no way he was going to let me make my own wedding cake, even though I offered, so he arranged a surprise cake for me. I told him I like the ones from Le Papillon bakery in Paris, you know the one from that TV show with the amazing cakes? So, he's ordered me one from there!'

'That's nice,' Shell replies politely. 'Mia, I want to hear more about your movies.'

'What do you want to know?' I ask, aware of the evil looks my sister is shooting me for hogging the attention. It's not like I'm doing it on purpose, is it? After all, it was Belle who brought up working in a bakery that prompted Shell to ask me what I did for a living.

'Do you have anything in the cinema at the moment?' she asks excitedly. 'I love to go to the cinema.'

'I do, it's a wedding film actually.' One of my many wedding films, which is hilarious considering I hate weddings. 'It's called *For Better, For Worse*.'

Shell, who is probably in her forties and seems to love the colour pink almost as much as I do, squeaks like an excited teenage girl.

'I saw the trailer for that, it looks so good. Are you working on anything at the moment, my love?'

'I am, but we're in the very early stages.'

'You should set a scene here,' Shell suggests. With the cream walls, pretty pink cushions and curtains and the dollhouse-esque furniture – not to mention the fact it is situated overlooking the sea – Shell's Café would actually make a pretty good setting for a romcom … not that I'll be setting any movies in Cornwall any time soon.

'Definitely,' I lie.

Whenever the door opens, a little bell rings to alert Shell that customers have arrived, and as I hear the familiar tinkle again my eyes dart towards the door and then back to looking at my sister.

Shell excuses herself so that she can go and serve her customers.

'Wow, it really is *The Mia Show* and we're all just guest stars in it,' Belle says, unimpressed.

'I can't help it if people want to know about my job.'

I hear the tinkle again and I feel my eyes pulled in the direction of the door – it's an elderly couple.

'Just like you can't help looking at the door – don't think I haven't noticed. Who are you looking for?' my sister asks.

Before I have a chance to make something up, the door tinkles again. This time we both look, and this time it's my fit lifeguard who walks inside.

As soon as he sees me he waves and heads towards us.

'Suddenly it's all so clear,' my sister sighs.

As he approaches our table in nothing but a pair of red shorts I notice my sister look him up and down.

'And now it's clearer,' she adds.

'Hello ladies,' the fit lifeguard says in that gorgeous Australian accent of his.

'Oh, and now it's crystal clear,' my sister says, much to his confusion.

My sister knows all about my no strings attatched attitude when it comes to men – and it's much to her disgust. My sister is a proper romantic and she finds my approach to dating positively revolting. Belle just doesn't understand that even though marriage and babies are what she wants from life, for me it's all about having fun and never getting too serious with anyone. For Belle marriage is a commitment, for me it's a death sentence – neither of us is wrong, it's just that different people want different things from life.

'Hello again,' I say.

'Hi,' he replies coolly.

'This is my sister, Belle. The one I was telling you about,' I lie, to try and score myself some brownie points with my sis. 'The one who is getting married.'

'Congratulations,' he says, rubbing my sister's shoulder. Belle, who may not be into flings, is still temporarily disarmed by a little attention from a hot guy.

'Usual is it, Chris?' Shell calls over.

'Please,' he calls back.

'So, *Chris*,' I say, showing off the fact that I know his name now. 'How is work?'

'Work is slow,' he replies, 'but that's a good thing in this game.'

I smile and nod as he waits expectantly for me to tell him my name, but I'm not giving it up that easily.

'What's with the tennis ball?' my sister asks, breaking the silence as she clocks the ball in Chris's hand.

'It's my dog's,' Chris explains. 'He loves balls.'

I snigger.

'Oh my God.' My sister looks mortified. 'Mia, I'm going to wait outside.'

We wait in silence as Belle leaves the café. Once she's outside, Chris sits down at the table opposite me.

'So, it's Mia, is it?' he asks, and I nod my head. 'Well, Mia, what are you doing tonight?'

'I'm not sure what my sister has planned for me, why?'

'We could meet up later tonight, play a little ball or whatever,' Chris jokes.

'That sounds like fun,' I reply.

We make arrangements to meet later so I say goodbye to Shell before heading outside to find my sister.

I find Belle sitting on a bench, under the safety of the white, lacy parasol she insisted on bringing with us. She looks like she's about to burst into 'Supercalifragilisticexpialidocious' any second.

'So, what's happening with you and Neil Buchanan?' my sister asks as I approach her.

'I don't get it,' I admit as I sit down on the bench.

'The Baywatch guy,' she explains with a roll of her eyes.

'You mean Mitch Buchannon.' I give my sister a playful nudge. 'Neil Buchanan was the guy from *Art Attack*.'

'He died, you know,' she says solemnly.

'I think that was a hoax,' I explain. 'He's still alive.'

'No, he had a heart attack,' she insists.

'Belle, that sounds like the punch line to a bad joke.'

My sister thinks about this for a moment.

'Whatever. What's happening with you and that guy?' she asks.

'We're meeting up later tonight – don't tell anyone,' I warn her. I may be a grown woman, but I don't think the family will be too impressed by me going on a date with a guy I have just met, and the last thing they need is another reason to look down their noses at me.

'Fine,' my sister snaps. 'Go out with this guy who could be a rapist or a murderer. See if I care. Just make sure you let me know if you're dead so I can change the seating plan for my wedding.'

'I suppose saving lives by day would be a great way to hide the fact he kills women by night – that would make a great plot for a movie,' I think out loud, not that it's the kind of movie I'd be allowed to make.

My sister shuffles angrily in her seat, accidentally jabbing my head with her parasol.

'I can't believe you're carrying that thing,' I laugh.

'If I don't I'll get sunburned and look awful in my wedding pictures,' she snaps. 'You'd love that wouldn't you, me looking all red?'

'Red is better than orange,' I say, instantly wishing I hadn't.

'You have a problem with your dress I suppose,' my sister starts, but I decide it best to nip this one in the bud.

'I'm kidding, I'm kidding. I just don't think you need that much protection from the sun, it's not that warm. Just put some sun cream on.'

'You're the one who needs to take protection more seriously,' my sister says as she stands up, 'because that lifeguard probably has sex with every trampy tourist who comes by here.'

Meow. Sweet, innocent little Belle just got her claws out.

Chapter 13

Considering this was all last-minute, my date with Chris the lifeguard has been positively romantic – well, on paper at least. When I turned up, Chris was waiting for me on the beach. He had laid out a blanket and two glasses of wine, so we could chill out and watch the sun go down over the ocean. I know this scene well, I have written this scene a thousand times, and if we were romantically inclined people then it would be beautiful and romantic ... but I'm not a romantic, and I don't think Chris is either. Still, we had a few glasses of wine, a nice chat and now we're strolling along the beach back towards the beach house.

'I would have invited you back to my place, but we have a rule: no guests at night. My flatmates work shifts so ...' Chris' voice trails off, he sounds so disappointed.

'Don't worry about it. I'd ask you in for a drink, but you saw how my sister reacted when we flirted in front of her. I come from a family of prudes.'

We're walking quite close to the sea and I can feel the tide splashing around my feet as we walk hand in hand. Thankfully I'm wearing a pair of barefoot sandals, so nothing that I mind getting wet, and my dress is so short I would need to be in an Olympic-size swimming pool to get it damp. Chris turned up for our date in his red lifeguard shorts – so he's either technically working or he thought I was really into them – and he still isn't wearing a shirt, but I'm not about to complain about that.

'That's a real shame,' he says, and he sounds like he means it.

'Well, you're the local, is there somewhere quiet we can go hang out?' I ask.

Chris stops suddenly, and because I am holding his hand this brings me to a halt too. He looks left, he looks right, and then he smiles at me widely.

'Here?' I squeak, trying to feign at least a little shock. The truth is, I've wanted to rip those shorts off him since the first time I laid eyes on him – well, the second time I laid eyes on him, the first time I was preoccupied.

Chris wiggles his eyebrows, as if to ask: 'What do you say?'

I glance around to weigh up the likelihood of us getting caught with our pants down. The beach is quiet, in fact I haven't noticed any other people around for quite some time now.

'Why not?' I give in – not that I took much persuading in the first place. It turns out my lust for Chris is way stronger than my common sense right now.

Before I have a chance to give it much thought, Chris literally sweeps me off my feet and lays me down on the sand, pouncing on top of me.

'You could have taken me on dry land,' I laugh as I feel the tide splashing over us.

'No, this will be hot. It will be like *Pirates of the Caribbean* and I'll be Captain Jack Sparrow, mate,' he says, doing what I imagine is his best impression of Johnny Depp's legendary character.

'You know how I know you're not faking that Australian accent?' I say as Chris kisses my neck. 'Because that sounded nothing like Jack Sparrow – you're terrible at accents.'

'Do you mind,' Chris laughs. 'You making fun of me isn't exactly keeping the wind in my sails.'

'OK, sorry. Weigh anchor.'

'All hands on dick,' he jokes as he presses his body down against mine and kisses me on the lips, breaking only to ask: 'How do you feel about the poop deck?'

I can't help but laugh before grabbing a handful of his messy blonde hair to pull his mouth back to mine. The last time I had sex was that snooze-fest back in the States with Zack from work, so obviously anything was going to be better than that, but not only is Chris smoking hot, he's also so much fun.

As our kissing gets more passionate I feel Chris gently run his hand up my dress and remove my knickers with the skill of someone who does this all the time. Well, I do this all the time too, and begin pulling down Chris' shorts with my toes.

'Oh my God,' I hear a familiar voice call out. It's quite dark where we are, but as I glance back I can just about make out three figures running towards us. 'Mia, what the hell?' Belle shrieks as she stands over us with Josh and Max by her side.

'Whoa,' Josh says excitedly. 'Mia, were you drowning?'

'Erm, yes,' Chris says, still on top of me. Thankfully, despite the subtle removal of my underwear, I am still wearing my dress, so my modesty is just about protected and the kids have no idea what is going on. Thank God Belle made herself known when she did, because even though we were only kissing, I can't guarantee we wouldn't have been getting up to worse, minutes later.

'Did you have to give her the kiss of life?' Max asks.

'Yep, that's what that was,' I say quickly. It's one thing to let the kids watch an 'eighteen' rated movie, but if my auntie found out they'd seen me rolling around in the sand with a man, she would murder me for sure.

As we lie there in the water, Chris still on top of me, I don't think it could be possible for my sister to glare at me with any more anger ... that is until the tide washes my red thong right on top of her barefoot.

'Ew, gross,' Max shouts as he notices. 'Where did that come from?'

'Mermaids,' Chris says with a nod of his head.

'He's a ten-year-old boy, not a six-year-old girl,' I whisper. I can't pretend I'm not amused by this – at least the kids have no idea what is going on, even if Belle does.

Max frowns, clearly not buying it.

'What it is, boys, sometimes bad people visit the beach too, that's why I brought you out for a walk tonight, it's not safe on your own,' Belle explains.

'Bad people like pirates?' Josh asks.

'Yo ho!' Max yells.

At this point I can't keep my face straight for a second longer and splutter out a laugh. As everyone looks at me to see what the matter is, I quickly disguise my laughing as coughing – well, I was just drowning after all.

'Well, we'd better get Mia back inside,' my sister reasons, raising her eyebrows at me expectantly.

'Yeah, give me a minute,' Chris says awkwardly. 'You know, to make sure she's OK.'

'I'm going to go and tell everyone what happened to Mia,' Josh yells as he runs towards the house.

'No, I am,' Max insists as he follows him, leaving us alone with my sister.

When the kids are finally gone, Chris and I burst out laughing, but Belle looks furious.

'Well I suppose you'd better help me get her inside the house,' Belle says angrily. 'It will look weird if you don't.'

'Sure,' Chris says willingly. 'But I really am going to need a minute.'

'You people are disgusting,' my sister mutters as she walks back towards the house.

'Here we go,' I say as we climb to our feet. 'I hope you act better than you do accents.'

Chapter 14

The drowning cover story may not have been my idea – in fact, it was kind of thrust upon me if you'll pardon the pun – but it's actually won me some sympathy because everyone in the house is fussing around me and praising Chris.

'Thank you for saving my daughter,' my dad says sincerely to Chris as he puts a brandy in his left hand and shakes his right.

'I was just doing my job,' Chris says seriously. 'No need to thank me.'

'Yeah, there's no need,' Belle echoes angrily.

'Nonsense,' my mum says as she rubs the towel that is around my shoulders. 'Mia, you're soaking wet.'

I look over at Chris and I can practically see the corners of his mouth twitching as he fights off a smile.

'Listen, I know it's not much for saving my daughter's life,' my dad starts, 'but my other daughter is getting married next week and we'd love you to be a guest at the wedding.'

I watch as my sister's eyes widen with horror.

'You can't invite people to *my* wedding,' she says angrily.

'Belle, Mia could have died,' my gran snaps.

I know it's wrong and that I shouldn't have to rely on stunts like this to get attention, but suddenly people aren't being quite so horrible to me. Well, everyone but my sister and my auntie, who is staring at me at the moment – God knows what is going through her mind, she probably wishes Chris had left me to die.

'I'd love to, if that's OK with you,' Chris says to Belle. He smiles sweetly at her and everyone in the room buys it. My mum gives my sister an encouraging nudge.

'OK, fine,' Belle gives in. 'But just the party, not the service.'

'Excellent,' my dad says with a clap of his hands. 'Judith, let's walk the hero out.'

'Belle, be a love and help your sister to her bedroom. Put her in a nice warm bath, I'll be up in a moment,' my mum says before following my dad, much to my sister's disgust.

As people begin leaving the living room, heading off in different directions now that the drama is over, my auntie wanders over to me for a quiet word.

'I had to take you swimming enough times when you were a kid to know that there's no way you could get into difficulty in water that shallow,' my auntie says suspiciously. 'I'm watching you, Mia.'

I smile at her. Well, what can I say? She's not as daft as she looks.

'Right, come on,' my sister says, not even trying to hide her annoyance.

I climb to my feet slowly and weakly, keen to milk my near-death experience for as long as possible. I know that it isn't right, but my parents are being nice to me – to *me*. I have to make the most of this.

My sister grabs me by the wrist and drags me upstairs. I wait until we are in the privacy of my en suite before setting about some sort of apology.

'Belle, I am so sorry about that,' I tell her honestly as I watch her run my bath.

'Mia, I don't care if you want to have sex with every guy you meet,' my sister starts as she pours bubble bath into the water. 'If you want to get every disease under the sun, that's up to you.'

Charming.

'You have to understand something though,' Belle continues as she forcefully yanks my dress over my head, 'this is *my* wedding. *I'm* supposed to be the centre of attention. If you're not banging on about your movies then you're pretending to drown, and all to steal the attention from me.'

I face-palm so hard my hand nearly comes out the back of my head.

'Belle, seriously, I am not trying to steal the attention from you,' I explain as I cross my legs self-consciously, suddenly remembering I lost my knickers earlier.

My sister unhooks my bra, turns my body to face the bath and gives me an encouraging shove towards it.

'Just wash,' she insists. 'See if you can make yourself any less dirty.'

And with that, my sister storms out of the bathroom. Well, that's me told.

As I climb into the bath and sink down into the lovely warm bubbles, I think about what my sister has accused me of. I would never go out of my way to try and ruin her wedding – and if she really knew me then she would know that. She's the self-absorbed one, not me. Just look how far I have travelled to be a part of this stupid wedding – risking my job by taking time off when we are in the middle of a project, putting my life on hold to come and be a part of hers. So, I messed up a little tonight, no harm done though, crisis averted.

I am snapped from my thoughts by my uncle charging through the bathroom door.

'Mia, thank God you're alive. I was asleep, I didn't know about your accident. Are you OK?'

'Yes,' I reply, grateful for all the bubbles that are protecting my modesty, 'but could you give me some privacy, please. Before—'

'Before what?' June asks as she walks into the bathroom.

'Is there someone at my bedroom door selling tickets for this?' I ask no one in particular.

'Steve, what are you doing here?' my auntie asks him.

'Checking on Mia, she could have died,' he explains.

He actually sounds really worried about me.

'So, what do you care?' she asks.

'What do *I* care? I'm her uncle! Don't *you* care?'

My auntie shrugs her shoulders.

'She's fine, now come on,' June snaps, as she drags my uncle out of the bathroom.

'Close the door, please,' I call after them, but neither oblige.

I lie back and dip my sea-soaked, sandy hair under the water. After running my hands through it a few times I sit back up – only to find my mum sitting next to the bath.

'Oh my God, does everyone have to see me naked tonight?' I complain.

'Young lady, I have seen you naked more times than everyone else in the world combined.'

Debatable.

'What's up?' I ask, because there's no way my mum will be going anywhere until she has said what she wants to say.

'Are you happy?' she asks me.

'I'm happier when I get to bathe in private, but otherwise I'm not too bad,' I joke as I reach for the shampoo. 'Why?'

My mum grabs the shampoo, which is closer to her, and passes it to me.

'I'm just going to come right out and say it.' My mum takes a deep breath. 'Did you try to kill yourself tonight?'

I can't help but burst out laughing, but she is being completely serious.

'Mum, of course not,' I reply as I rub the shampoo into my long, blonde locks. 'Why would you think that?'

'Well, your sister is getting married, she's got everything she wants in life. It's only natural to feel jealous.'

'You think I'm jealous?' I squeak. 'Mum, Belle has everything *she* wants in life; the things I want are very different. You think

I don't have anything?'

'Well, what do you have?' my mum asks, and I feel my jaw drop.

'Mum, I have more money than I can actually spend. I have a great job in an exciting industry. I get to hang out with movie stars. I have an awesome home where the weather is amazing ... you think that's me not having anything?'

'Well, not really,' my mum replies, and she's totally serious. 'What good is it all if you have no one to share it with?'

'Mum, I'm going to rinse my hair now. If you're not gone by the time my head is out of the water I think I might just go back under and stay there.'

'Why are you being like this?' she asks. 'I'm just worried about you.'

'Well I'm fine, OK?'

My mum nods her head before leaving the room, closing the door behind her.

I can't believe what she just said to me. I have achieved so much, and yet my mum is more impressed by my sister for finding a bloke stupid enough to marry her at twenty-four years of age – surely anyone can do that? I could do that if I wanted to, but I don't. People are just going to have to accept that.

Chapter 15

After my bath last night, I was far too tired to dry my hair so I went to bed with it wet, which means I woke up with damp pillows. What you can't see can't get you in trouble with your sister though, so I flipped the pillows upside down, just like I did with the quilt my first night here to disguise the fact that it is covered in makeup – still not sure what I'm going to do about that one.

I quickly blow-dried my hair before slipping on a pair of denim shorts and a white off-the-shoulder T-shirt. I covered my face in makeup and then headed downstairs ready to face everyone. The plan is to look smart, act bright and just generally show people that I am glad to be alive – that ought to quash any rumours regarding my failed suicide attempt.

'Good morning,' I say cheerily as I enter the kitchen. 'What a beautiful day it is today.'

Hmm, perhaps I should take it down a notch.

My auntie is sitting at the table. There is a cup of tea in front of her but she is just staring into space as Josh and Max run around the table. They have their hands shaped like guns as they chase each other, taking fake shots as they exchange lines of dialogue inspired by their new favourite movie.

'Look! I shot him right in his face,' Max yells.

Some of the quotes aren't so bad ...

'That's fucked-up,' Josh replies.

... but some of them are much worse.

Auntie June doesn't even flinch at the dirty words that just left her ten-year-old son's mouth. I make myself a coffee before sitting down opposite her.

'Listen, I'm really sorry about letting the kids watch that film,' I tell her sincerely. 'I had no idea they were going to ...' I rack my brain for the right words, '... embrace it like they have.'

'You look like a bitch,' Josh shouts at Max.

'What's done is done,' my auntie says flippantly.

'A bitch!' Josh yells again. 'A bitch!'

'I know,' I continue. 'I'm just really sorry.'

I look over at Josh as he points a loaded hand at Max's face. It's weirdly cute, but I cringe. I really didn't think this was going to happen.

'I'm going for some air,' my auntie says, as calmly as she can, before heading out the back door.

'Hey, Vincent, Jules,' I call the boys over once we're alone. 'Listen, can you tone it down a bit with the movie quotes? You're going to get me in trouble.'

'Is it true you tried to kill yourself last night?' Josh asks me curiously.

'No. Where did you hear that?' I ask.

'Everyone is saying it,' Max informs me.

'Everyone, huh?'

The boys nod their heads.

'Listen, I promise you that it isn't true. Don't listen to what the old people are saying, they're all going senile.'

'What's senile?' Josh asks. If there's one thing I'm learning about kids, it is that they ask a lot of questions and that they remember everything you tell them. 'Will I go senile?'

'It's a sort of crazy that only old people can go. You're fine.'

The boys both look visibly relieved.

'So, less *Pulp Fiction* quotes around the adults, and I didn't try to kill myself. That concludes our lessons for today, now go play video games or something.'

'Well, at least you're being honest with some people,' I hear my sister say angrily as the boys run off.

As I turn to face her, I realise that she has been crying again.

'Belle, listen, I didn't tell anyone I tried to kill myself. Mum just decided that, and I tried to put her straight but she didn't listen.'

'You think I care about that? God, not everything is about you, Mia,' she snaps.

I bite my bottom lip to stop myself from saying something in temper.

Belle drops a white folder covered in pictures of confetti, rings and champagne glasses, and quotes like 'happily ever after' and 'YOLO: You only love once' plastered across it, down on the table. As she sits down and places her head in her hands I realise I have two choices: I can leave as fast as my legs will allow me before she has the chance to say anything else, or I can ask her what the matter is and face the consequences of whatever that may be. As much as I want to do the former, I can't leave her here like this.

'What's wrong, Belle?' I ask, rubbing Bridezilla's shoulder without getting too close.

'The florist doing the flowers for the wedding,' I know what a florist is ... 'they've cancelled. Something about a death in the family. Well I hope they can't get flowers for the funeral,' she yells. Yikes, she's in full-on crazy mode.

'Come on, calm down. We can fix this,' I assure her, but she's having none of it.

'My wedding is cursed,' Belle insists. 'Even if we sort this, something else will just go wrong.'

'Well, whatever goes wrong, we'll fix it. Your wedding is *not* cursed,' I insist. 'Good luck and bad luck aren't real, if you believe you have bad luck then you will. It's like: is the glass half-full or half-empty? It just depends how you look at it.'

'What glass? What are you talking about?' my sister snaps, clearly annoyed by my attempt to make her feel better.

'What I'm saying is that you need to stop thinking your wedding is cursed or it will be. Let's just fix this problem.'

'How?' she sobs.

'We'll find a new florist. Let me go get my iPad, I'll find you one.'

'You'd do that for me?' my sister asks, baffled by my kindness.

'Yeah. Well I am head bridesmaid, aren't I?'

'A nice one though? Not a horrible one to make me look stupid?'

I grit my teeth as I head up to my room to grab my iPad. She's lucky I'm not the person she thinks I am or she'd definitely end up with disgusting flowers after planting that seed in my brain.

***

'Hey Hannah,' I say as I pass my fifteen-year-old cousin on the corridor outside my bedroom.

'Wow, what are those on your feet?' she asks.

'Oh, you like them? They're barefoot sandals. They're great for the beach because they're not like wearing shoes, but they look awesome.'

'I love them! Do you have any more?'

'Yeah, of course. Do you want to borrow some?' I offer happily.

Hannah nods excitedly.

Hannah Edwards is exactly the kind of girl who would have bullied me if we went to school together. Lucky for me I'm her older cousin with the awesome clothes and the movie star best friends, which means I am useful to her every now and then. She is tall with an athletic figure – which makes sense, being a popular kid and being good at PE kind of go hand in hand – and I don't think I've ever seen her without her long brown hair tied up in a sporty but oh-so-cool ponytail. Like any teenager today, she forever has her phone in her hand, not that anyone knows what she's doing on it.

As I rifle around in the suitcase I never truly unpacked (just in case I need to run for my life) Hannah sits down on my bed.

'Can I ask you something?' Hannah says quietly.

'Of course,' I reply, as I search through my things that are now all over the floor.

'When you were my age, could you talk to your mum?'

'Could I talk to my mum? I could hardly look at her,' I laugh. 'But seriously, no. Not really. We're not big on talking in this family, are we?'

Hannah shakes her head. She seems quiet, like maybe there's something on her mind.

'Are you OK, Hannah?'

'What if I had a secret?' she starts cautiously. 'But I couldn't talk to my mum about it?'

I think for a moment. If Hannah were to confide in me and her mum were to find out, I really would be in big trouble.

'Han, I'm sure you can talk to your mum about anything. Try her, she might surprise you. If not, well, you know where I am, right?'

Hannah looks unconvinced.

'Here you go.' I present her with a pair of pink crocheted barefoot sandals, which she gleefully slips on. 'You can keep those if you like.'

'Wow, really? Thanks, Mia,' she chirps as we leave my room. We head downstairs together, bumping into Auntie June by the front door.

'What on earth are you wearing?' she says as she spies her daughter's new footwear.

'Aren't they awesome?' Hannah moves her feet so her mum can get a good look.

'You look like a prostitute,' my auntie says, unimpressed.

'I'm fairly sure they wear shoes,' I chime in, offended because they were mine after all. "Usually really nice ones.'

'Well, that's all they wear,' my auntie says smugly, like she has one-upped me.

I shrug my shoulders. 'I'm not their union leader. I don't care.' I laugh, and Hannah joins in. This makes June furious.

'Hannah, go and find your dad, see if he's ready to head out,' she insists. Hannah does as she is told.

'Mia, I want you to stay away from my kids,' my auntie says sternly as soon as we're alone. 'You are a bad influence.'

'I'll stay away from your kids,' I promise her. 'But I can't guarantee they'll stay away from me.'

As my auntie storms off upstairs, I head for the kitchen. Now to try and find my sister some flowers.

***

After helping Belle make a list of potential florists, I mixed myself a margarita, slipped on an itsy bitsy teeny weeny pink polka dot bikini, grabbed my iPad and snuck off to the beach to catch some rays and get some much-needed work done. I did offer to go and help my sister check out the florists on our shortlist but she muttered something about sabotage so I stopped listening, lest I take offence and punch her in the face.

I take a big sip of my drink, push my oversized sunglasses further up my nose and lie back on my sun lounger. I'll have a quick brainstorming session inside my head before I start tapping away on my iPad.

I only get a few seconds of peace before I notice a dark shadow over me – surely the sun hasn't gone behind a cloud already, typical when I've only just made myself comfy.

'For God's sake, Mia, you're practically naked,' my sister moans. So, it was a little rain cloud after all, here to rain on my parade no doubt.

'I'm on the beach, I'm wearing a bikini. You're the only one with the problem,' I remind her.

'There are plenty of people on this beach with a problem,' she insists.

I look up and see Belle giving filthy looks to a group of onlookers I didn't realise we had attracted.

'They're probably watching you, kicking off. Anway, something you wanted?' I ask impatiently, keen to get rid of her.

'Pretty much everyone has gone out – apart from Dan, who is still bedridden.' She just loves reminding me of that. 'I'm thinking maybe you should come to the florists with me.'

'As kind as your offer is,' I start sarcastically, 'I'm going to stay here and work.'

'The only thing you're working on is your tan,' Belle insists.

'That's the good thing about my work, I can do it anywhere.' I wave my iPad at her before taking another sip of my drink.

'Is that alcohol?' she squeaks, sounding thoroughly appalled that I am drinking when it isn't quite the p.m. yet.

'It's happy hour somewhere,' I say as I raise my glass to her.

'So, you're not coming?'

'You'll do a much better job without me,' I conclude, still a little pissed off about her not wanting me to go when I first offered.

I give my sister a wave as she storms off back towards the house. I just want a little time to myself, is that so much to ask?

Chapter 16

I was so wound up when Belle left me that I didn't get a second of work done. Something strange happened while I was lying on the beach. I pride myself on being a free spirit. I don't do anything that I don't want to (family weddings aside), I don't go anywhere that I don't want to (family weddings aside), I don't wear anything that I don't want to (bridesmaid dresses aside), but most importantly of all I don't worry about a thing. After a few very stressful years as a stressed out, insecure teenager, I learned that there is no point in worrying – if you can do something about the thing you are worrying about, then do it and your problem is solved, and if you can't do anything, then what's the point in worrying about it? Problem also solved … and yet today I find myself worrying, just like I used to. I'm anxious. I can feel my heart pounding in my chest, my head is spinning and my stomach is gurgling. I'm panicking and it's being trapped here around my family that is doing it to me. OK, so the beach house is a pretty sweet cage to be trapped in, but if I don't stretch my wings soon I really will throw myself at the mercy of the sea.

I can't stand being constantly blamed for everything that goes wrong, and it's only going to get worse. Had my sister hired a professional to plan her wedding and oversee everything from the early stages right up until the end of the reception, then everything would probably be fine, but because Belle has been overly ambitious without the wedding planning skills to pull it off, shit is going wrong, and rather than deal with it she's pinning the blame on me – the evil sister who cursed her wedding.

I need to calm down. I am currently climbing the stairs to the beach house and as fit as I am, I can hardly catch my breath. The plan is to slip off my bikini, hop into the shower, fix myself another stiff drink and then slob out in front of the TV. Maybe if I watch a violent movie or shoot some zombies I'll start feeling more like myself again.

As I stroll along the corridor towards my bedroom, I begin to loosen my bikini top with one hand, safe in the knowledge that the house is empty apart from Dan who is stuck in his bed. My iPad and towel prove too much for my other hand to hold and as they fall towards the floor my priority switches from keeping my top on to catching my iPad before it smashes. I clap my hands together, catching it seconds before it hits the ground but the same can't be said for my bikini top – which lands on my feet.

For a second I giggle to myself, because I know how bad this would look if my sister were to come home right now – I'd no doubt be in trouble for going topless in a public part of the house, even though Dan is stuck in bed and couldn't possibly see me. My amusement is cut short because, as I am crouched down on the floor, I hear someone moving around behind me.

'Hello,' I hear an amused and unfamiliar man's voice say.

'Hi,' I say cautiously, still staring straight ahead. I have never felt more topless in my life.

'Mia, I presume,' the man behind me chuckles.

'My reputation precedes me.'

For a moment, there is silence. The stranger doesn't say anything, and while I am no stranger to being topless in front of men, I am not about to flash some random man.

'Do you need any help?' he asks. The fact that he has a Kent accent is encouraging, it suggests that he is meant to be here and not a burglar or something.

'If you could grab my iPad that would be great, thank you.' I'm too scared to try and put my top on, lest I flash a little sideboob at this perfect stranger. Instead I cup my boobs in my hands before slowly standing up. 'And my top,' I add as I turn around to face him.

For a moment I just stare at the stranger, because he's not just any stranger … he's the most jaw-droppingly gorgeous stranger I have ever laid eyes on. Standing in front of me, smiling widely, is a tall, dark and handsome man. He's probably about my age, and I can tell by his posture alone that he is effortlessly cool. The blue jeans and skinny-fit navy T-shirt that he is wearing don't leave much to the imagination about his figure – the boy is buff, and if he's got more than fifteen per cent body fat I'll eat my bikini. His dark brown hair is blown back in a way not unlike I saw the TOWIE boys rocking in the copy of *Starstruck* magazine I read on the train, and his eyes … wow! Like me, the handsome stranger has green eyes. They're honest eyes but with a touch of mischief … I can't help but stare deep into them.

'I'm Leo,' he says, offering me a hand to shake. 'Dan's best man.'

Before I go to shake his hand it occurs to me that my hand bra is the only thing protecting my modesty right now, and cheeky Leo knows this.

'Nice try,' I laugh. 'And you're right, I am Mia.'

Leo laughs, only making his smile even more irresistible.

'How come I haven't met you before?' he asks.

'I could say the same.' Full-on flirting mode: activated.

'I'm a fireman,' he offers by way of an explanation.

'Well I tend to avoid fires, so mystery solved,' I reply before he has the chance to elaborate.

Leo walks over to me slowly, bends over and picks up my

bikini top from my feet. He ties it around my neck before turning his back to me.

'I suppose I should let you put that back on,' he says cheekily, so while his back is turned I do as instructed.

'Thank you,' I reply when I'm done.

'So,' Leo opens his bedroom door, 'do you want to hang out for a bit? Catch me up on what has been going on? Dan is sleeping and I probably shouldn't wake the patient up, and my mum has gone to her room for a snooze. I'm bored already. Weddings,' he muses.

We have so much in common already.

'Don't think that just because you wear a sexy uniform for a living that I will forget about stranger danger,' I tease.

'I'll wear it,' he jokes with a wink.

'Deal.'

I follow Leo into his bedroom and take a seat on his bed. As he tidies up the things he has unpacked so far I can't help but stare at him. If I were writing a movie I couldn't write Leo any more perfect – he even has a sexy job, but he looks more like a stripper version of a fireman than an actual fireman, which makes him even better.

'So, you're the one who writes love stories,' Leo teases.

'Yes, but don't be under any illusions, I'm not very romantic.'

'Neither am I,' he admits. 'No boyfriend then?'

Leo takes a seat next to me on the bed.

'Nope. I'm not really a boyfriend kind of girl. Do you have a girlfriend?'

'No, no girlfriend,' Leo admits. 'I'm too busy, what with saving people's lives for a living.'

'Subtle,' I laugh.

I have only known Leo a matter of minutes but I can tell that we're going to get on just fine – like a house on fire, if you'll pardon the pun. It sounds like we have a lot in common: he puts his job before silly weddings, he isn't committed to a girlfriend

– just my type on paper. This is exactly what I need to get me through the next few days – someone just like me who has to endure all this wedding crap too.

For a moment, we just stare into each other's green eyes. Perhaps Leo is thinking the same as me, thanking the weddings gods for providing him with an ally.

Before I have a chance to break the silence, Leo takes my chin in between his thumb and index finger and brings my mouth to his for a kiss. It is only a brief kiss, but as our lips part it feels like a magnet is trying to pull my face back towards his.

'I've never kissed a fireman before,' I tell him in my sexiest tone of voice.

'Neither have I,' he replies. 'How was it?'

'Hot.'

Leo smiles at my fire pun.

'So, can I do it again?'

'OK,' I reply. 'But like you mean it this time.'

Luscious Leo the fireman doesn't need telling twice. He grabs me by my hips and sits me on his lap with the ease of someone who boasts the same muscle mass as Superman. This time we're kissing passionately, and we're not stopping any time soon.

With my date with Chris the lifeguard not going exactly to plan, I knew that I was going to have to find something to get me through this trip without losing my mind. What I hadn't bargained on was someone as gorgeous as Leo falling into my lap, or rather, me falling onto his.

Leo runs a hand gently up my back and unties the bikini that only ten minutes ago I was trying so hard to keep on. I reach down and fidget with Leo's belt as we kiss but it's a tough one to get off, especially without looking. Not wanting to waste a second, Leo takes matters into his own hands, whips off his belt and unbuttons his jeans, and just in case I might struggle with his T-shirt too he pulls it over his head, throws it across the room and gets straight back to kissing me. In the few seconds I had to look at his body I was more than impressed. Let's just say he makes Chris the lifeguard look like a beached whale.

Lifeguards, firemen, it's all saving lives, isn't it? And that's exactly what I need right now – I am on suicide watch, after all.

Chapter 17

You know what? I'm actually proud of myself for finally taking my role as bridesmaid seriously. Well, by taking it seriously I mean I have had sex with the best man – that's practically a wedding tradition. At least that's how I'll explain it to Belle if she finds out. That girl seems more concerned with my sex life than I am, which can only lead me to think that whatever she has going on between the sheets with Dan is underwhelming. It's funny, because with Dan being stuck between the sheets for the past few days I had almost forgotten he was here – and it's *his* wedding.

Dan isn't a bad-looking lad. He's isn't exactly the fittest person I have ever seen (Leo is, just in case you were wondering how he compares to the buffed up actors and Muscle Beach regulars I'm used to associating with) but he isn't exactly out of shape. Dan has very short dark hair – I imagine he goes to one of those barbers where they only offer one style – and his dress sense is a mixture of Adidas, Nike and Puma.

A little pillow talk (well, bedroom floor talk) with Leo taught me that he and Dan grew up on the same street together and have been friends for as long as he can remember. I learned that Leo is twenty-eight years old, that he has only just arrived because he had to work up until yesterday, and that he has come with his mum, Maria, who is a friend of Dan's family.

My little hook-up with Leo has left me with a smile on my face that will take a long time to wear off – something I'm hoping will serve me well because it's dinner time and, according to the boys, everyone still thinks I tried to throw myself in the sea in a fit of envy.

'Hello everyone,' I chirp as I enter the dining room. Once again, I am the last person to take my seat at the table.

As I sit down between my granddad and Mum, I notice that everyone else already has their food in front of them – pasta with ham and peas. Luckily I don't need to say anything because Belle is walking towards me with my plate.

'Mia, I know you're watching your weight so I made you a version without the carbs,' she announces loudly so the whole room can hear all about her grand gesture. She places the plate down in front of me.

'Oh, thank you,' I say, the enthusiasm in my voice fading as I realise she has presented me with a plate of chopped ham and peas.

I mean, what I actually said was that I didn't like to eat much meat, so presenting me with a huge plate of ham isn't exactly a step in the right direction. I would have preferd just the pasta.

Belle smiles triumphantly as she sits down – I suppose this is to teach me some sort of lesson. Well, she's not going to win this one. I pick up my fork and begin happily munching away, much to my sister's annoyance.

'Mia, you missed the introductions because you were late for dinner – again.' My sister pulls an unimpressed face. 'This is Maria, she is a friend of Dan's family.'

I say hello and wave to a little lady with short, dark, curly hair. Unlike most of the people from Dan's side, Maria seems friendly.

'And this is her son, Leo. He's Dan's best man,' Belle informs me. It's probably best I play along rather than admit we have already met.

'Hello Leo,' I say coolly.

'Hi,' he replies.

For a moment we exchange knowing looks, but not long enough for anyone else to notice. This is our private joke, and if it stays that way then things will run much smoother while I'm marooned on this beach with no one but my family and perfect strangers to keep me company.

'Let's all do something fun tomorrow,' Dan's older brother Mike says to everyone. 'Let's go to the beach and play games or something.'

'Everyone but your brother,' Belle reminds him. 'He is stuck in bed, after all.'

There you go, she's mentioned it again.

'Come on, future sister-in-law,' Mike starts. 'The kids will love it and it's better than us all sitting down for a screening of *Pulp Fiction*.'

All the adults in the room stare at me as they are reminded of my little error in judgement, but Josh takes this as his cue to do his best Christopher Walken impression – the bit where he talks about hiding a watch up his ass, and although it isn't word-perfect, it's actually a pretty good impression – this kid has a future in performing arts.

Leo and his mum look confused by Josh's sudden outburst.

'Mia put on a movie with adult themes for the children,' Dan's mum explains, bringing them up to speed.

'Hey, that makes it sound much worse than it was,' I can't help but complain. I turn to Leo and his mum to clarify. 'We watched *Pulp Fiction*, and they really liked it. It's not that bad.'

'Young lady,' Dan's mum starts, and I can tell already that I am not going to get off lightly here, 'the day your nephew calls you a "motherfucker" is the day you can have an opinion on what is not that bad when it comes to children.'

Everyone is taken aback by Dan's prim little mum saying 'motherfucker', but I can't help but find it hilarious, and the more I laugh the more others feel it is OK for them to laugh too. Mike starts laughing at his mum, all the kids join in and Leo appears to be stifling a chuckle too.

'Mia,' my sister snaps. 'Respect your elders.'

'Sorry.' I go back to eating my ham and peas.

'Everyone knows how to play rounders, right?' Mike persists. 'It will be fun.'

Mike flashes me a cheeky smile, and I flash him one back for changing the topic of conversation to something much less hostile. As we break eye contact I notice that our little exchange of looks did not go unnoticed by Leo.

'Rounders it is,' my granddad says, also keen to diffuse the situation.

As people begin chatting amongst themselves I can feel Dan's mum's eyes burning into me. Boy, does she look angry. This is my first proper interaction with Harriet Ryan, if you don't count our first meeting when she reluctantly shook my hand – but I hadn't expected her to so keenly join the club of women who hate me. Still, my sister, mum, auntie and gran will be pleased to have a new member.

Chapter 18

It's another beautiful day today, perfect for the family game of rounders I absolutely do not want to play.

Belle is frying breakfast for almost everyone, apart from Leo who is working out on the beach, so I decide to pop out and see him, a man after my own (very healthy) heart.

'Good morning,' I call over at Leo, who is all sweaty from running.

'Hello,' he replies, sitting down on the sand and patting the spot next to him inviting me to join him. 'I won't kiss you because I stink.'

'Not to worry, I'll get you later,' I laugh. 'I was actually looking for you last night, I wanted to explain what all that was about at the dinner table.'

Leo smiles as he stares at me expectantly. I just need to put the situation with my family into simple terms and he won't think I'm weird.

'Everybody hates me,' I explain. So much for not sounding weird, I feel like a dorky teenager again.

'It's OK,' Leo laughs, and I feel instantly relieved. 'I'm an only child so I've been spoilt stupid my whole life, but it's obvious to an outsider that your parents worship your sister. Not that I'm saying they don't love you – I mean, it's her wedding, people are bound to be fussing around her more.'

'It's fine, you don't need to try to make me feel better.' I smile, touched by Leo's words. 'But honestly, everyone here hates me.'

'Well, I don't hate you,' he replies as he rubs my knee fondly. 'I really like you.'

I smile for a moment, but then it hits me. He really likes me – what does that mean? When he said he didn't have time for a girlfriend, and then put the moves on me within minutes of meeting me, I assumed he was like me, not looking for a commitment, never getting too close to anyone ... *I* would never tell anyone that I really liked them, not even my family – although I suppose that is because I don't like them at all.

'Listen.' I quickly move my knee from under Leo's hand. 'You're a great guy and everything, and I really enjoyed yesterday. I'm just not looking for anything more than a bit of fun,' I explain. In my head this makes perfect sense but when I say it out loud it always sounds bad.

'Oh, I was just trying to make you feel better about everyone in that house hating you,' Leo laughs. 'I don't want anything more than your body, promise.'

He's sort of joking, but it's a big relief.

'You promise me you don't want me for my mind?' I tease.

'I promise,' he laughs. 'I won't respect you afterwards, not even a little.'

I plant a kiss on his sweaty cheek.

'Good,' I reply. 'Well, I'll leave you to your exercise. See you at the big rounders game.' I give Leo a faux enthusiastic double thumbs-up.

Before I get to the house I turn around and watch Leo doing press-ups. Rather than go inside and have people question my life choices over breakfast, I think I'll stay out here, you know, just to spot Leo while he works out. What are friends (with benefits) for?

Chapter 19

'You're up, Nancy,' Mike calls out.

'Stupid game,' Nancy mutters to herself as she picks up a bat ready for her turn.

I wait patiently to bowl as Nancy does a few stalling stretches.

Mike could only manage to talk the under-thirties into playing today (except for Dan, who is stuck in bed – in case you hadn't heard), but luckily that made twelve of us, which is perfect for a game of rounders.

Bridezilla got to pick the teams, deciding it should be boys against girls. The only problem was that there are seven girls and five boys, so Belle decided that, as the most 'boy-like', I should be on the boys' team. She was probably trying to insult me, but I'm delighted to be with the guys instead of the girls. So, it's me, Mike, Leo, Josh, Max and Jason against Belle, Hannah, Meg, Beth, Nancy and Heather. Well, it was supposed to be, but as the sun came out Belle retired to the tent she has pitched on the beach so that she can hide from the dangerous rays that are hell-bent on burning her before the big day.

'OK, ready,' Nancy moans reluctantly.

I bowl her a good ball but it goes straight past her and into Mike's hands.

'No-ball,' she calls out.

'Just because you miss it, doesn't make it a no-ball,' Mike informs her.

'That was a no-ball,' she insists. 'Throw it again. I play by English rules, I'm not changing the way I play just because Mia is here.'

'What are you talking about? You missed,' I tell her sharply.

'The teams aren't even fair, there are six of you and only five of us,' she whines.

'Not that that could've had anything to do with you missing the ball,' I start, 'but you're only a player down because Belle is hiding in her tent.'

'Well, I'm not playing until the teams are fair,' she says stubbornly, sitting down on the sand.

Mike shrugs his shoulders and no one else has anything else to say on the matter.

'Fine,' I say as I storm off towards the tent, where I find my sister reading a copy of *Fifty Shades of Grey*.

'Wow, really?' I can't help but blurt out. She's a prude as far as my behaviour is concerned, but she's happy to read a bit of filth.

'What do you want?' Belle asks, far too engrossed in her book to look up.

'Can you please come and join in, or tell Nancy grow up or something, she's ruining the game.'

'I told you, I can't play because of the sun,' my sister insists, her nose still in her book.

'I'll smother you in sun cream,' I promise. 'You must have some in that bag.'

Despite only being a matter of feet away from the house, my sister is carrying around a huge bag full of all sorts of things – everything from first aid stuff to insect repellent.

'Come on, we're having so much fun,' I lie. 'You need to de-stress, this will be perfect.'

I watch as my sister thinks carefully about what she should do.

'OK, but only for ten minutes, and I will need a lot of sun cream first.'

'Great.' I clap my hands. 'I'll go and tell the others.'

I leave the tent to give my sister a little privacy while she douses herself in factor fifty.

'She's coming out,' I shout to the group. Everyone looks bored and hot, and they seem relieved that we're going to get back on with the game. It was a nice idea to start with, but now everyone just wants it to be over.

I can't help but stare as a shirtless Leo takes a seat on the sand, lying back with his hands behind his head – in fact, I'm not the only one who has noticed this, all the women seem to be captivated.

'Come on, Belle,' an impatient Mike calls out, possibly something to do with the fact we're all ogling Leo.

As Belle emerges from the tent we all cheer her as she walks over, that is until we realise what she's wearing. My dear sister is covered from head to toe, protecting her skin with a variety of clothing, a headscarf and a pair of long socks. Now, don't get me wrong, it *is* hot today – but it's England hot, not Ethiopia hot.

'Belle, you're going to melt—' I start, but she doesn't let me finish.

'Yeah, you'd like that, wouldn't you,' she snaps back.

'OK,' I say slowly. 'Well, let's play.'

I look over at Nancy who is still waiting for me to bowl her a 'good' ball and I decide it's simpler to throw her an easy one than to argue with her. You know what they say about arguing with an idiot: don't do it because they will bring you down to their level and beat you with experience.

'Here we go,' I say, as I throw the ball ever so gently. Nancy squeals with delight as she hits the ball but it comes flying back towards me and practically lands in my hands.

'Out,' Mike calls before Nancy has even reached the first base.

Nancy points at me menacingly with her bat before she hands

it to Belle.

'You blokes are too competitive,' she says, and yes, that means me.

'Come on then, Annabelle. Channel your old PE days,' I tease as she makes her way to bat. My sister brandishes her bat like she means business, I bowl her the ball and she hits it a little better than Nancy did, but once again it comes towards me. The ball lands at my feet so I pick it up and throw it to Josh who is manning the first base, but as Belle scrambles to get there first she trips (probably because she's dressed like Lawrence of Arabia) and as she falls to the ground, in what seems like super-slow motion, her face blocks the path of the ball, and they both land together on the sand.

'It's still in, Belle,' Josh helpfully calls out to his cousin, who is face down on the floor. 'Keep running.'

Mike and I exchange worried looks as Nancy runs over to her BFF to see if she's OK. As she rolls Belle onto her back I can't help but slap my hand over my mouth with horror – look at all that blood! We all rush over to Belle, forming a circle around her.

'Don't worry, I'm trained in first aid,' Leo says as he runs over.

I bite my own lip anxiously as Leo assesses the damage.

'It's just a burst lip,' he tells Belle. 'Nothing to worry about, you won't need stitches.'

'Just a burst lip?' my sister yells, spitting blood all over him. 'I'm getting married in a matter of days. How long will this take to heal?'

'A few days,' Leo replies patiently. 'Three, five maybe.'

'Mia Valentina strikes again,' my sister screams at me. 'You really are determined to ruin my wedding, aren't you? Why don't you just do the job properly, shave my head, burn the beach house down …'

'I'll go get you some wipes,' I say softly to Leo as my sister continues her rant.

I head for the tent and begin looking in Belle's bag of tricks for something to make Leo look less like an extra from The Walking Dead with all that blood splattered all over his body.

'You know, for someone who isn't trying to ruin her sister's wedding, you're doing a great job at it,' I hear Leo laugh behind me.

'Don't,' I plead as I hand him the wipes. 'I'm going to be in so much trouble for this. I really didn't mean to.'

'Hey, I know that,' Leo insists as he removes the blood as best he can. 'Come here.'

As luscious Leo wraps his arms around me, I can feel myself relaxing in his embrace. I exhale deeply as I feel all my tense muscles slowly going back to normal as he holds me close and rubs my back.

'You OK?' he asks.

'I will be,' I reply. 'It's just this situation and this lot. I'll be glad when I can go home.'

'LA is home?'

'It is,' I reply. 'I thought you knew that.'

'I just think that's cool,' Leo explains. 'You'll have to let me visit.'

I wiggle free from his arms a little and look into his eyes. I'm not sure I have ever been so attracted to anyone before. Usually the physically attractive guys are absolute pigs but not Leo – Leo is lovely.

'Do you want to do something?' he asks.

'Oh, I want to do something all right,' I say, grabbing his face and kissing him passionately. I'm not sure what just happened but he instantly made me feel better, so I'm showing my gratitude the only way I can think of.

Leo sweeps me off my feet with his big, strong, fire-fighting arms and lays me down on the tent floor. His body has only just met mine when we are interrupted.

'Oh my God,' squeaks the unmistakable (but slightly muffled) voice of my sister. 'Is there anyone you don't plan on screwing on this beach? Should I warn Dan's family that you might try and lure Max down here, or Dan's dad or his granddad!'

I can't help but roll my eyes as Belle rants, still holding a tissue over her bloody lip. I can see that her comment about me screwing people on the beach registered with Leo, so I'm going to have to explain that one later. Awesome.

'We were just—' Leo starts, but Belle interrupts him.

'Don't worry, Leo, I'm not mad at you. This is just what Mia does. She sleeps with everyone, she tries to steal the attention and she ruins weddings.'

'In my defence, ruining weddings isn't exactly my thing, I haven't ruined anyone else's wedding,' I insist. Well, I haven't, but I suppose now isn't the time to bring that up.

'I came on to Mia, I promise,' Leo insists.

'Literally,' I joke, but this type of humour is wasted on my prudish little sis.

'Can you give us a minute, please?' Belle asks Leo, who obliges. Brilliant, no witnesses, and I'm trapped in a tent with Bridezilla.

My sister sits down next to me, grabs a compact mirror from her bag and examines the damage to her face for a moment. It does look nasty, but the bleeding seems to have stopped and with a bit of luck it will clear up before the wedding – even if it's just enough for us to hide it with makeup.

Belle snaps the mirror shut and looks me dead in the eyes.

'Please don't ruin my wedding,' she pleads.

'Belle, I promise you I'm not trying to ruin your wedding, this was just an accident.'

'And promise me you won't ruin Leo's life.'

'What?' I can't help but laugh. 'Why would you think I'd try to ruin Leo's life?'

'I don't think you'll *try* to do it, but you will do it if you keep this up,' Belle insists, and she's being completely serious. 'Leo is a good man. He's sweet and kind. You're going to hurt him if you involve him in your silly, slutty sex games.'

'First of all, I'd just like to get it on record that I find that really fucking offensive. Secondly, I don't think Leo is the kind of guy that you think he is. He really did come on to me first, I had no intention of going there until he made the first move. Not only that, but when I told him I wasn't looking for anything serious he told me he felt exactly the same. This is a holiday fling, nothing more.'

I don't get an apology, but Belle nods in recognition of what I have just said.

'OK then, so you won't mind doing me a favour,' she says confidently.

'Go on.'

'No matter who or what is to blame, I feel like my wedding is doomed. I need to do everything to make sure things go to plan, and if you really don't have any feelings for Leo then you won't mind doing this for me.'

I look at my sister expectantly as I wait for her to spit out what this big favour is.

'A sex ban,' she announces proudly, like this will be the answer to all her problems.

'What do you mean?' I ask.

'You, not having sex until after the wedding. When you start thinking with your tuppence, things just start going wrong for everyone.'

I take a very brief break from being offended to grin widely.

'Did you just say tuppence?' I laugh.

'Oh, and what do you refer to it as? Something sexual you heard in a porn film no doubt,' she snaps.

I'm still laughing, only now my jaw has physically dropped too.

'Why don't you just say vagina?' I ask.

'Because that's a dirty word,' she replies seriously.

'No, it's not. That's what it's called.'

'Well I'm not saying it,' she insists.

'Say vagina.'

'Mia, stop it,' my sister demands.

'Just say vagina and I'll stop,' I laugh.

'Mia,' Belle snaps, only far angrier this time. 'I know you'll probably find it difficult but just do this for me. Please.'

I'm not sure my sister is smart enough to work a little reverse psychology on me, but it's working. As much as I hate being told what to do, I hate the fact that she thinks I can't go a few days without sex even more. At least if I do as she asks, she'll have one less reason to blame me for things going wrong.

'I shouldn't have to do this,' I start, 'but I will. Happy now?'

'Oh I'm so happy,' she snorts sarcastically. 'Dan can't walk, my face is pouring with blood and I have to worry about you keeping your knickers on.'

There's just no pleasing some people.

Chapter 20

After taking an abstinence pledge just to please my sister, I didn't much feel like going back to the house to play happy families. Everyone either hates me or feels sorry for me because they think I'm so miserable I tried to throw myself in the sea, and then there's Leo who I'm going to have to explain all of this to. To be honest, if I hadn't already slept with him I'd probably find it easier to tell him that I had herpes than explain why my sister has made me promise to swear off sex for the forseeable.

It is for that reason that I decided to take a stroll along the beach before popping in to see Shell for a cup of coffee (on the house, because she's such a lovely lady) and to inhale one of her cupcakes. We chatted the afternoon away, and at first I didn't feel too awkward in my bikini because people were coming in from the beach, but as the evening approached I felt more and more naked – I've got to stop wandering off without proper clothes on.

So, here I am, wandering along the beach, alone, in my bikini, and not only is it getting dark but it's getting pretty chilly too. I really don't want to go back to the beach house, but I'm running out of options.

Just when I think I'm totally screwed, a familiar face runs over to me and starts licking my toes.

'Hello, Jay,' I say brightly as I rub his head, something I instantly regret because he's all soggy from playing in the sea.

'Look at that, I think he likes you. Usually he hates the women I …' Chris's voice trails off. 'I mean, usually he just isn't very nice to women.'

'You mean I wasn't your first?' I gasp in a faux surprised voice.

'Technically we didn't actually do anything, so my number remains the same.'

'It sounds like that's a good thing,' I laugh.

As Chris walks closer to me and puts his hands on my waist, it's almost as though I can read his mind. I know exactly what he wants.

'I see you're out without clothes again,' he says. 'Some might say you're asking for attention.'

'And you're going to give it to me, I suppose?' I smile.

Chris shrugs his shoulders.

'Well, no one is around,' he says. 'Except Jay, but he's fine as long as you let him watch.'

I laugh, but the truth is that as easy as it would be to get with Chris right now (and there's the added bonus that my sister wouldn't find out) I just can't stop thinking about Leo. I can't quite make sense of the way I'm feeling, but I suppose it's only fair, isn't it? If I can't sleep with Leo, then it isn't fair to sleep with Chris … no, I don't know what I'm talking about either. I've never felt like this before, but then again I've never been put in this position before.

'The thing is,' I begin to explain, and I can see Chris's smile drop almost straight away, 'this is going to sound stupid, but I promised my sister that I wouldn't have sex until after her wedding.'

Chris looks at me, visibly confused by what I have said.

'Why would she do that?' he asks.

'Basically, she thinks my vajayjay will be the end of her. She also doesn't think I can do it, so the urge to prove her right, sibling rivalry and so on …'

'I can appreciate that, I had a bit of that going on with my little brother back home – of course it was mainly to do with surfing.'

We laugh together at the silly situation, but I'm glad that he understands.

'Well, there's only one thing for it,' Chris starts. 'Want to get drunk?'

'Ah, alcohol – the next best thing after sex. I'm in.'

Well, I certainly don't want to go back to the beach house, but if I have to it may as well be when I am very drunk and everyone else is asleep.

'I thought girls thought chocolate was the next best thing after sex?' Chris asks, puzzled.

'It depends when you ask,' I tell him. 'Right now I need a cocktail more than I do a bar of chocolate.'

'Well, I'll get both, just in case.'

I smile.

'There's a shop not too far from here,' he tells me. 'I'll go in and get us something strong. You can wait outside with Jay – no shirt, no pants, no service,' he teases.

I give him a playful slap across the chops.

'I'd give you some money, but I don't have any on me. No pockets,' I laugh.

'That's OK,' he replies. 'I won't get the good stuff.'

As we stroll along the beach I feel happy that I have a friend here, but at the same time I feel strange, like I'm being disloyal to Leo. But what is Leo to me? Nothing. Hardly even what you'd call a friend.

Anyway, alcohol. That will make everything better.

***

I am drunk and it feels good. Drunk Mia is way smarter than sober Mia; drunk Mia has it all together and figured out.

Chris and I sat on the beach, drank the cheapest vodka mixed with coke and chatted about everything. He had some very helpful suggestions about how I can better survive my sex ban, although I'm fairly sure that having sex with myself probably still counts because if Belle caught me doing it she would probably beat fifty shades out of me.

Like the gent that he is – and not the tourist sexual predator my sister thinks he is – Chris walked me back to the beach house to make sure I got there safely. Halfway through the night he gave me a T-shirt because I was starting to get really cold and he wasn't wearing it. I forgot to give it back before he left, and can't help but laugh as I look at my reflection in the huge hallway mirror. The top is black and across the chest is an arrow pointing to each arm along with the caption 'I don't need a licence for these guns' – hilarious considering how scrawny my arms are.

As I creep up the stairs I do so in perfect silence. Luck is on my side because there are no creaky floorboards, nothing for me to knock over and I'm doing an excellent job of staying on my feet.

As I make my way along the corridor my bedroom is in my sights. Just a few more feet to creep and I'll save myself a bollocking for waking everyone up.

As I open my bedroom door it allows just enough light into the room for me to see that there is a man in my bed. Shit, Leo must be waiting for me to finish what we started earlier. Poor guy, he isn't going to understand this sex ban, it's going to seem like I'm rejecting him.

I quietly close the door behind me. As I make my way towards the bed, pulling off my T-shirt as I tiptoe across the pitch-black room, I feel a cheeky smile spread across my face. My sister told me I couldn't have sex, but she didn't tell me that I couldn't involve myself in sexual activities. I've found a loophole and I plan to exploit it – at least tonight, you know, so that Leo doesn't take it personally when I explain why I can't go all the way.

I climb in bed slowly and quietly before slipping my hand under the covers and trying to get into his pyjama pants – this will be a wake up he'll never forget.

Leo starts moaning immediately – I've not even started yet. The noises he is making are getting louder and louder. I take this as my cue to rip the covers off and get theatrical, but I soon realise that these are not noises of pleasure he's making, they are noises of pain, and they're really loud now. Actually, they're much louder than I realised because before I know it people are rushing into the room to see what's wrong.

'What's the matter, darling?' my sister asks anxiously as she flicks the light on. Oh crap, she's going to see me bending the rules – and why would she call me darling?

Put it down to my reflexes being slower thanks to all the alcohol, but it is only as I see my sister and Leo both standing in the doorway that I quickly remove my hand from the waistband of the person next to me. Please, God, don't let it be Dan that I am in bed with.

My sister looks like she is about to explode with anger and Leo is just staring blankly at me. I'm not sure I need confirmation, but I look to my right and sure enough, a surprised and hurting Dan is looking back at me.

For a moment no one says anything, until …

'Are you touching my fiancé?' Belle asks calmly. 'On the … on the …'

'Princess, I swear I didn't ask her to,' Dan starts babbling, the little grass.

'Shut up,' she snaps. 'I'm talking to Mia. Well, did you?'

I think about my words carefully for a moment because I wouldn't want to not explain it properly and get thrown off the balcony by Bridezilla, but waiting only makes her look even angrier.

'Mia,' Leo prompts me.

'I thought it was you,' I blurt out to him. 'I thought you were waiting for me to finish what we started earlier. It's *my* bed.'

'Well that sex ban didn't last long, did it?' Belle snorts.

'I wasn't strictly aiming for sex.' I laugh awkwardly, but my sister is *not* amused. 'What is Dan doing in my bed anyway?'

'He was uncomfortable and stopping me from sleeping so I said he could have your bed,' Belle explains. 'I left you a note.'

My sister nods at my bedside table and sure enough there is a note there waiting for me. I pick it up and read it out loud.

'Mia, I'm giving Dan your bed, you can sleep on one of the sofas in the living room. Annabelle.'

I look up at Belle who is *glaring* at me.

'So, let me get this straight, I'm supposed to sleep on a sofa from now on?' I ask angrily.

'Hardly as bad as having your fiancé sexually abused by your sister,' she reasons. I imagine it would be a waste of my time to explain that she had already demoted me to the sofa before I attempted to inappropriately touch Dan.

'Belle, listen, I'm really sorry,' I tell her sincerely, because there's no way I ever would have done this intentionally. 'I didn't turn the light on before I got in bed, so I didn't see your note.'

'Just grab what you need and go to the sofa,' she demands as she picks up the T-shirt from my bedroom floor. As she holds it up in front of her she reads the caption out loud. 'Whose shirt is this?' she asks angrily.

'It's mine,' I insist. 'I sleep in it. Usually,' I add.

'Mia, it stinks of aftershave, so unless you've started sleeping in that too …'

'Belle—' I start, but she doesn't let me finish.

'Just go and sleep on the sofa and I'll listen to your excuses when I feel less like killing you,' she says quietly.

'She can sleep in my bed,' Leo, who has been quietly taking everything in until now, chimes in. 'I'll sleep on the floor.'

'She doesn't deserve your kindness,' Belle says as she places a hand on Leo's face. 'I am so angry and so disgusted. I'll deal with you tomorrow,' she tells Dan before she goes off back to bed.

Poor Dan. Obviously I didn't mean to do this, it was a horrible drunken lapse of judgement, but Dan really is entirely blameless. I didn't even really touch him but I think I might have hurt his back and if that gets any worse I'll be in even more trouble.

'Come on' Leo says, nodding towards the door. I nod my head sheepishly. 'Sweet dreams,' he says to Dan before leaving the room.

'Goodnight, Dan,' I say awkwardly. 'Sorry again.'

Leo and I make the very short journey to his bedroom in silence.

'I feel like I should explain but I'm not sure how,' I say as I close the door behind me.

'You don't have to explain anything,' Leo replies. 'You take the bed, I'll take the floor.'

I glance over at the king-size bed.

'You can't sleep on the floor,' I insist. 'We're both adults, right? We can just share the bed.'

Leo looks at the bed thoughtfully before looking back at me.

'I promise not to feel you up,' I insist with a nervous laugh.

Just when I think I might have finally convinced him to join everyone else in hating me, Leo's straight face dissolves into an amused smile.

'I can't believe that happened,' he laughs. 'How *did* that happen?'

I shrug my shoulders. I don't have much drama in my life back in the States, I'm pretty laid back and – I like to think – effortlessly cool, but for some reason I am the worst possible version of myself when I am around my family – especially around Leo. I am incapable of being cool or sexy in his presence; I'm like a female porno Mr Bean.

'I thought Dan was you,' I insist again.

'Don't worry,' Leo assures me. 'Belle and I were actually having a chat about you when we heard the screams.'

'It's all lies,' I joke as I take a seat on the bed. The worst thing is that the things she has said are probably mostly true. 'I should have known she'd sit you down and try to put you off me.'

Leo takes a seat next to me.

'Actually, I asked her if we could talk about you.'

I look at Leo for an explanation.

'Before dinner your youngest cousin called me a bitch and then he told me that you tried to kill yourself.'

'Josh,' I say with a nod. 'You know, I didn't—'

'I know, Belle already told me it was a misunderstanding. She also told me she'd slapped you with a sex ban, and do you know what? I thought she was being ridiculous, I couldn't understand why she would feel the need to do that ... *now* I understand why,' he laughs.

'I *am* going to do as she asks,' I tell him honestly. 'I'm not sure it's entirely necessary, but I want to show Belle that I'm not trying to make her life difficult – so I'm going to do it.'

'Good for you,' Leo replies, followed by a few seconds of awkward silence, the two of us just sitting on the bed facing forwards.

Maybe I'm still drunk, but whether I meant to do it or not I have upset my sister and I need to put that right. If that means not having sex until I am back home then so be it. It's not like it's going to be difficult, is it?

Right on cue, Leo pulls off his shirt revealing that rock-hard fireman's body I've been trying to forget he has.

'I didn't bring any pyjamas,' Leo informs me.

'My nightwear is in my room, but if I go and get it I'm worried Belle might think I've gone back for seconds.'

'What about that T-shirt.' Leo nods towards Chris's top that is still in my hand.

'Not mine,' I reply, hoping that will be that. I could have pretended that it *is* mine, that I wear it as a joke, but it stinks of sweat and there is no conversation that will be more awkward than what would happen if I were to get in bed with Leo wearing a top that smells like man sweat and seawater.

'Is it your lifeguard's?' he asks. I wasn't expecting that, then again, he did say that Belle had filled him in. It's a good job I've sworn off sex, because there's no way Leo would want to touch me again if he thinks I'm after every man on the beach.

'He's just a friend,' I insist, not that it matters.

'Just a friend but you ended the night wearing his shirt?' Leo asks, sounding ever so slightly bothered.

'The last time you saw me earlier, what was I wearing?' I ask, ready to prove a point.

'A bikini.'

'And what am I wearing now?'

'OK, point taken, but you're telling me he didn't even try anything?'

'He might have tried, but I'm banned from sex, remember?'

Leo smiles and raises his eyebrows. I wish I could tell what he was thinking. He asks a lot of strange questions for a one night stand.

'You're sure you don't mind sharing a bed with me?' he asks.

'Leo, I should be asking you that. This is *your* bed.'

'I'm fine with it,' he replies, pulling off his shorts and getting under the covers.

I glance down at my bikini, unsure whether or not it will stay fastened through the night. Then again, I don't have much choice.

'We could always make a barrier down the middle of the bed,' I joke as I get in next to him. 'If we were in a rom-com, that's what we'd do.'

'We'll be fine. Life isn't a romcom,' he laughs.

'And don't I know it,' I reply.

We're both lying on our sides, staring into each other's eyes. For a moment neither of us makes a sound, we just stare.

'Are you going to get the light?' I ask.

Leo stares at me a few seconds longer before he speaks.

'Tell you what.' Leo grabs his pillow and places it at the foot of the bed. 'Just to make this easier, I'll sleep at the other end.'

'You don't have to do that,' I insist, but he turns the light off and does it anyway.

'Not many men could handle sleeping in a bed with a girl in nothing but a bikini,' Leo whispers, 'especially when they already know she's great in bed. You're lucky I'm a gentleman.'

'Just my luck,' I reply. 'Sweet dreams.'

Chapter 21

I wake up to find that my bikini has survived the night, my modesty is saved – OK, perhaps that's a stretch. Another thing I have noticed is that Leo isn't here.

I climb out of bed and head for the door. I have no idea what time it is but I'm going to need a shower and some clean clothes, and there's no time like the present. I also need a strong cup of coffee to try and appease the hangover gods.

I grab the stinky T-shirt Chris leant me before tiptoeing out of the room. Still on the balls of my feet, I try to close the door behind me as silently as possible, but it's all in vain.

'Whose bedroom is that?' a familiar voice asks.

'Good morning, Uncle Steve,' I say brightly as I adjust my bikini to make sure all bases are covered.

'Whose bedroom is that?' he asks again.

'Leo's.'

My uncle shrugs his shoulders.

'The best man,' I remind him.

'Oh boy,' he says, his jaw dropped. 'Is this one of those hook-ups?'

Before I have the chance to reply – not that I am entirely sure what to say – my auntie appears behind him and begins her own line of questioning.

'What has she done now?' she asks.

'She slept with the best man,' he tells her.

'Mia, you slept with the best man?' my auntie echoes.

I open my mouth to speak but my cousin Hannah gets there first.

'What did Mia do?' she asks curiously.

'She slept with the best man,' my auntie and uncle inform her in unison.

'I don't blame her, he's fit,' Hannah replies as she walks off, tapping away on her phone.

'You don't mean that,' my auntie calls after her before turning back to me. 'She doesn't mean that. You're a bad influence on her. Sleeping with the best man, for God's sake.'

'Who slept with the best man?' I hear a male voice ask. We all look down the corridor to see Mike and Belle approaching.

'Mia did,' my auntie tells them, and you can tell she's enjoying every second of this, she isn't even trying to hide it.

'You could have put some clothes on after,' Belle complains.

'Where to begin?' I ask myself. 'Belle, you kicked me out of my bedroom. Leo let me sleep in his room – literally sleep in his room,' I say directly to my auntie and uncle. 'I can't get at my clothes, they're in with Dan.'

'Come with me now, I'll escort you,' Belle replies.

I love that she thinks I need an escort. I don't say anything, I just follow her to what used to be my room.

Belle opens the bedroom door and we both step inside. Dan is still fast asleep in my bed.

'Grab your things, and try not to rape him as you pass him,' she snaps.

'I'm going to pretend you said "wake him" and we can still be friends,' I whisper back. I grab my case, which thankfully I still haven't unpacked, and my makeup bag from the bathroom, before making my way back towards the door.

'Listen, I'm really sorry. Last night really was a terrible accident,' I tell her sincerely. 'I'll do whatever you want. No more sex, promise.'

'Are you done?' she asks without even looking at me.

'Yep.'

'Then get out.'

I am no sooner out the door when my sister slams it closed behind me. I start dragging my things across the hall when I realise Mike is still hanging around. Without saying anything he comes and takes my case from me.

'I hear you tried to wank off my brother,' he says with a cheeky grin plastered across his face.

'It was an accident,' I tell him. I realise that isn't a very good explanation for what happened but I don't have a better one and I really couldn't care less right now.

'You and I have a lot in common, you know,' he replies.

'Why, have you tried to wank off your brother too?' I ask, totally straight-faced.

Mike laughs as he places my suitcase down on Leo's bed.

'No, I just mean that we're similar people,' he explains. 'We don't go in for this wedding shit. We're people-people. We don't want to settle down and do all the shit we're supposed to want to do as we hit thirty.'

I wish this fucker would stop reminding me that I am nearly thirty.

'You think you've got me all figured out, huh?' I suppose he has, but it sounds kind of sad put into those words.

'Team Single,' he says with enthusiasm, offering me a fist to bump.

'I'll fist bump your face if you start the "forever alone" shit,' I warn him, and he soon backs down.

'Anyway, we're going to watch a film—'

'Who is "we"?' I interrupt.

'Me, Belle, a couple of her mates … Anyway, we're going to

watch whichever film gets the most votes and I'm counting on your support for *Django Unchained*.'

'I'm not sure I'm in the mood for a movie,' I reply, before quickly adding 'but thanks for asking.'

'It might be a good chance for you to build bridges with Belle,' he says to try and persuade me. 'She knows you didn't mean to do what you did, she's just angry you're getting more action than she is.'

Mike laughs, and I can't help but laugh too.

'OK, fine, just let me get washed and dressed and I'll be there to make sure we watch something good.'

'Team Tarantino?' Mike suggests, offering me his fist again.

'Team Tarantino,' I echo, bumping his fist with my own.

'Fuck it, come here,' Mike says, wrapping his arms around me and lifting me into the air. Standing way over six-foot-tall, Mike shakes me up and down like a cross between a child with a toy and someone performing a sort of reverse Heimlich manoeuvre.

'Am I interrupting something?' I hear Leo ask from behind us – I hadn't even realised he'd entered the room.

'Just Team Forever Alone having a meeting,' I joke as Mike puts me down.

'So, I'll see you downstairs?' Mike asks as he heads for the door.

'Sure,' I reply.

Before he closes it behind him, Mike slaps his hand on the door making a loud noise which neither I nor Leo were expecting.

'See you,' he shouts out in what I imagine is supposed to be a strong Mississippi accent. 'Downstairs. For an exceptional movie.'

'Very good,' I reply in response to his Leonardo DiCaprio impression, which only reminds me to make sure that Josh and Max do *not* watch this one – the last thing they need is another quotable movie to add to their repertoire.

'You two seem close,' Leo says as soon as Mike has disappeared.

'Oh, don't you start,' I warn him. 'The rumours about you and me are only just beginning, don't throw anything else into the mix.'

'Rumours about us?' he asks.

'People are saying we slept together,' I tell him.

'We did.'

'Yeah, but they think we had sex.'

'Again, we did,' he laughs.

'Yes, but not last night …' my voice trails off. 'Let's not complicate things, the official statement is that nothing happened. Got it?'

'Got it,' he replies with a cheeky salute.

'Good. Are you watching the movie with us?'

'Can't,' Leo replies. 'Promised my mum I'd take her to lunch.'

'That's sweet,' I reply. 'I wish I had that kind of relationship with my mum.'

'Well, we're all each other has. I'm sure your mum loves you, though.'

'Give it a couple more days, you'll soon realise you're wrong,' I laugh.

I grab a change of clothes and a towel and head for the bathroom.

'We could do something together this afternoon if you like?' Leo calls after me.

'I'd like that,' I reply. 'See you then.'

'Perfect.' Leo grabs his wallet from next to the bed before heading towards the door. 'See you later.'

As he passes me he plants a kiss on my cheek before disappearing, leaving me with nothing but the delicious smell of his aftershave in my nostrils and questions in my mind. Speaking of perfect, the more perfect he seems to be, the more I'm wondering what could possibly be wrong with him … there's always something.

Chapter 22

I enter the room to find Mike singing a rendition of Luis Bacalov's 'Django'. When he spots me he drops to my feet and serenades me with his out of tune singing.

'OK, we get it,' Nancy snaps from where she is sitting. 'You want to watch that crap. But we agreed we'd put it to a vote.'

I glance around the room, considering who is here and what the outcome of the vote is likely to be. At the moment it's just the four of us: me, Mike, Belle and Nancy.

'So, Mike, what do you want to watch?' Nancy asks him, like she doesn't already know the answer.

'*Django!*' he bellows, but she stops him before he can start singing again.

'Thank you. Belle?'

'*Dirty Dancing*,' she says excitedly.

'I want to watch *Dirty Dancing* too,' Nancy agrees. 'So *Dirty Dancing* it is.'

'Erm, excuse me,' I chime in, 'you didn't ask me.'

Nancy looks puzzled.

'Well, you're a girl, so …'

'So, what?' I ask her. 'I'd rather watch *Django Unchained*.'

Nancy and Belle stare at each other for a moment, utterly

disgusted looks plastered across their faces.

'You're not a real girl,' Nancy concludes. I think she thinks that is going to be the end of it, but I'm not the insecure teen she used to bully once upon a time.

'You know, just because I don't like *Dirty Dancing*, doesn't mean there's something wrong with my vagina. I'm still a girl.'

'My God,' Belle shrieks, 'you're obsessed with … that.'

'Another thing we have in common,' Mike jokes to me under his breath.

'Why won't you say vagina?' I laugh at my sister, which is risky business considering she's still so mad at me over the events of last night. 'Nancy, you're not scared to say it, are you?'

'I prefer to call it my flower,' she tells me seriously.

'Ergh!' I can't help but cry out. 'No, thanks. Honestly, guys *hate* to hear girls saying cringey things like that.'

Belle clicks her tongue at me.

'I suppose you have a rude word for it,' she says.

'I just say vagina, or vulva, depending on which bit I'm talking about, like a grown woman,' I point out.

'Wait, they're different things?' Mike asks, his face contorted into an uncomfortable confusion.

'I'll draw you a diagram,' I tell him.

'So, *we're* doing things that guys hate, but you're the permanently single one,' Nancy reminds me smugly.

'Single by choice,' I reply.

'Yeah, you keep telling yourself that,' she laughs.

'OK.' Mike jumps to his feet. 'I think we should just all agree to disagree. Nancy, Mia is single by choice and there is nothing wrong with her vagina. Mia, if Nancy wants to call it her flower, that's up to her. Now can we just watch the fucking film, please? I've had my fill of fanny chat for the day.'

I giggle at his choice of words, but the 'real' girls hiss and boo him.

'You're just as disgusting as she is,' Belle insists.

'Anyway, we could always ask Leo if there's anything wrong with Mia's flower,' Nancy starts. 'We've all heard the rumours.'

'Leave Leo out of this,' I snap, surprising myself a little. 'Treat me how you want to treat me, but leave him out of this.'

'Touchy subject,' Belle adds with a smirk.

Mike jumps to his feet and looks at his watch.

'Well, it's nearly midday, who wants to start drinking?'

I raise my hand.

'I'm going to get the drinks, you'd all better be done with this shit when I get back,' he warns us. You don't know how nice it is for me having other people around who swear freely, even if it is just Mike and Leo – oh, and the kids, but that's a touchy subject still.

As soon as Mike leaves the room, Nancy continues.

'Well, if nothing is going on with Leo, you won't mind me having a go.'

'I thought you had a boyfriend,' I remind her.

'I'm always looking for an upgrade.'

I look over at my sister who doesn't seem bothered by this at all.

'This is your best friend,' I remind her.

'I know,' Belle replies. 'Wouldn't it be great if my best friend and Dan's best friend got together? Just think of all the couples' stuff we could do with Heather and Jason.'

'Like swinging?' I joke, but we've already established that my kind of humour is wasted on this lot.

Belle and Nancy chat while we wait for Mike to return. I stare at them as they come up with a plan to bag Leo for Nancy. I'm not sure why I'm so bothered by this, but I absolutely am. It's probably because Leo is such a nice person, and Nancy is absolutely not. He deserves better than being an 'upgrade' Nancy is considering to make her dull gang of friends complete. It's not I'm jealous or anything, I just don't want to see Leo get used by her.

'Look who I found,' Mike sings as he enters the room with Heather and Jason.

'Brilliant, now we can vote again and see if we have a winning movie,' Nancy says excitedly.

'Well, not really,' Mike replies. 'It's still three for the boy film and three for the girl film – no offence, Mia.'

'None taken,' I laugh.

'I think you might be wrong, actually,' Nancy says. 'Yes, Heather will pick *Dirty Dancing*, but let's ask Jason what he wants to watch.'

Everyone looks at Jason, including his wife Heather who shoots him a look, a look that I imagine is supposed to terrify him into siding with her.

'Actually, I quite like *Dirty Dancing*,' Jason insists.

'Where's your fucking balls, man?' Mike asks angrily.

'Really, he does,' Heather insists. 'We performed "I've Had the Time Of My Life" in a couples' talent show and we won!'

Upon hearing the words 'couples' talent show' I throw up in my mouth.

'That's not real, is it?' I ask, my jaw practically on the floor.

Heather and Jason nod proudly.

'You can show that after the film,' Belle insists enthusiastically. 'Everyone sit down, let's get started.'

We all take our seats, but as Belle presses the play button Josh and Max emerge from behind a pile of beanbags.

'Forget this,' Josh strops as they head for the door. 'We thought you'd be watching something cool.'

'This is for losers,' Max adds with a nod, and with that they are gone.

As I feel my heart fill with pride I realise everyone is staring at me – obviously, this is my fault.

'Oh, just play the bloody film,' I insist.

Chapter 23

As I watch Jason and Heather perform their version of 'I've Had The Time Of My Life' that won them a couples' talent show, I have never felt happier to be single. I have also never been more sorry to have ears and eyes – though even without those two senses, I reckon I'd still be able to smell the cheese and feel my skin crawl.

'What, no jazz hands?' I ask, instead of joining in with the applause everyone else is giving them when they are finally finished.

My teasing isn't enough to faze the happy couple, who are beaming with pride at their routine. Belle and Nancy are in awe, but Mike looks just as disturbed as I am. The only difference is he's polite enough to clap.

'There is no moment a couple can share that is more intimate than singing together,' Heather muses breathlessly.

I go to raise my hand to suggest other things, but an amused Mike forces it back down.

'Well, that was awesome,' I lie, 'the film, the dancing – everything. Sadly I need to go and call work. It can't all be 24/7 fun, you know?'

My sister gives me a very brief dirty look, but no one else even acknowledges that I'm leaving the room, apart from Mike who gives me a salute.

As I begin climbing the stairs to my – sorry, Leo's bedroom, I can't help but think about just how unbearable things have become. Yes, things were awkward from the second I got off the train, but it only seems to be getting worse and worse. I know that Belle is my sister, but I can't help but think that it would be better for everyone if I hadn't bothered coming. I'm sure no one thinks all that much of me, especially after everything that has happened since I got here. They didn't think much of me before, but I'm sure I've made things worse. At least things are so bad that they can't get any worse, right?

As I reach the top of the stairs I spot my auntie, standing on the landing, her ear against Leo's bedroom door.

'Having fun?' I ask her.

'I was just, erm, just – I thought I heard a leak,' she tells me.

'Right, OK, and what's the verdict?' I ask.

'Well, you're here now, so you can go and check,' she tells me as she shuffled away sheepishly.

As I head for Leo's room I make a gun with my hand and hold it to my temple. 'Boom!' I say to myself as I 'pull the trigger'. I stand corrected, things can get worse, so *so* much worse. She's obviously trying to check up on me.

I grab my iPad, make myself comfortable on Leo's bed and take a deep breath before video calling the office. It's my assistant, Dalia, who answers, looking as miserable as ever.

'Hey Dalia,' I say brightly.

'How is England?' she asks. I don't think she actually cares, when she thinks of England she imagines a touristy London postcard with an added raincloud.

'Great, thank you,' I lie. 'It's nice to have a break, I might go and chill out on the beach after this.'

'No way, you guys have beaches?'

So stupid. So *so* stupid.

'Yes, we do. Anyway, how is work?'

Dalia gestures for me to lean closer to the camera, which I do.

'The boss is not happy,' she whispers.

'Tell me something I don't know,' I unnecessarily whisper back. My boss is never happy, in fact he always looks about one piece of bad news away from a heart attack.

'He's not happy with *you*,' she tells me. 'He, erm … he found out that you and Zack, you know.' Dalia widens her eyes for emphasis.

'How did he find that out?'

'They're totally BFFs now,' she informs me. 'He's talking about promoting Zack *already*.'

'But he's crap,' I reply – in bed *and* at his job.

'I know, right? He's also not happy about you taking vacation days.'

'He approved them!'

'Don't shoot the messenger, Mia.' Dalia searches around on the desk for something. 'I have a list here of the changes you need to make. I will email them over. Make sure you do them, or he'll have another reason to be mad at you.'

'OK, sure. I'll do it today.'

'I bet the beaches there are crappy there anyway, huh? Save the sunbathing for when you're back home.'

Our call comes to an end, and soon enough my to-do list flashes up on my screen. Boy, oh boy – this a lot of work considering I'm supposed to be on vacation.

'Hello,' Leo says as he enters the room. 'Ready to hang out?'

'Yes,' I reply with a big smile on my face. I'm sure work can wait.

Chapter 24

Leo and I have been strolling along the beach and chatting for a little while now. It's a lovely sunny day and the beach is packed with people sunbathing, walking their dogs and building sandcastles. Lots of people are splashing around in the sea, but the lifeguard on duty isn't one that I recognise, nor do I have any intention of sleeping with them – it's a woman.

Despite the lovely atmosphere, our conversation got pretty deep pretty quickly. One minute Leo was telling me about lunch with his mum, which soon turned into how close he is with her, and ended with him telling me that his dad isn't around anymore. He didn't go into the reasons why, and I didn't want to press him, so to change the subject I explained to him that even though both my parents are still around, I'm no better off for it. It only took a few stories about the way my family treat me before Leo had a smile back on his face. I'm just glad my misery can bring joy to some people.

'Do you want to grab a coffee?' he asks, nodding towards Shell's Café.

'I'd love to,' I reply, safe in the knowledge that Chris the lifeguard isn't working today.

It's pretty busy in the café today, but that doesn't stop Shell rushing over and giving me the kind of hug you usually reserve for an old friend. Leo receives the same treatment, despite this being the first time Shell has laid eyes on him.

'Hello, hello,' she says brightly. 'Who is this? Is this your boyfriend?' she asks, nodding towards Leo.

Leo seems a little taken aback by her forwardness, but he looks amused at the same time.

'Erm, no, he's the best man at Belle's wedding,' I tell her, hoping to quash any awkwardness.

An elderly couple is hovering around the counter so Shell signals that she'll soon be over to serve them.

'Let me take care of this couple and then I'll come and take your order. Get comfortable. Such a shame you're not a couple,' she mutters as she wanders off, 'you'd make such beautiful babies.'

Before either of us have a chance to say anything, we are interrupted by another voice.

'Ah, but we'd make blonde babies, they'd be way cuter,' Chris the lifeguard jokes in his unmistakable Australian accent.

I laugh politely.

'I can't believe I've been so wrong all these years,' Leo chimes in. 'I thought Hitler was Austrian, not Australian.'

Chris's face falls, and I'm not sure whether I should laugh at the joke, change the subject or run outside and throw myself in the sea.

For a moment Chris and Leo stare at each other, like a standoff from a Western, only with impressive arm guns for weapons instead of, you know, gun-guns. I rack my brain for a suitable subject change, but Chris saves me a job.

'So, are you all ready for the wedding?' he asks.

'Oh, I'm not sure things will ever be ready enough for Belle, but we're getting there.'

I take a seat at the nearest free table. Leo takes a seat on one side of me, and Chris on the other. They're facing each other, which I'm sure they're delighted about.

'I'm looking forward to it,' Chris enthuses. 'I've even picked up a new shirt. Well, I can't turn up in this, can I?'

As always, Chris is shirtless and wearing his lifeguard shorts.

'Oh good,' I tease. 'I was beginning to think you didn't own other clothes.'

'Well, it's always so warm on the beach,' Chris reasons, rubbing his hand across his muscular chest.

'Yeah, it is warm today, isn't it?' Leo agrees, pulling his own shirt over his head.

Their standoff resumes, only now it's a shirt-off standoff.

I glance at Leo, and then at Chris, and then back to Leo.

'I think I'll keep mine on,' I joke, still trying to diffuse the situation.

'That makes a change,' Chris jokes, and I know that he's referring to a few perfectly innocent occasions, but this doesn't go down well with Leo.

'So, how come he's going to be at the wedding?' Leo asks me, which only seems to wind Chris up even more.

'Haven't you heard? I saved Mia's life,' he tells him.

'Yeah, I heard about that,' Leo replies sharply.

'What can I say?' Chris leans back and puts his hands behind his head. 'If a beautiful lady needs help, I'm more than happy to give it to her.'

Chris gives me a cheeky wink, and all I can do is secretly wish that a tidal wave would come along and wipe us all out – this is *so* awkward. If I didn't know better, I'd think Leo was getting jealous, but being the ladies' man that he is, that's impossible after a one night stand. As for Chris, I think he's just enjoying winding Leo up.

'Hello, hello,' Shell beams as she comes over. She's got a jar of jam in her hands and she's struggling to open it as she talks to us. 'If you let me know what you want, I'll make a start on it after I've done this.' She stops suddenly as she realises both Chris and Leo are shirtless, and that they're both ripped with muscles.

'Why am I struggling with this when there's two strong men like you around who can do it for me?' she asks, placing the jar smack bang in the middle of the table. My eyes go straight to the jar. Oh Shell, what have you just done?

Everything seems to happen in super-slow motion, and I can hear the music from the finale of *The Good, The Bad and The Ugly* playing my head – it's a lid-off standoff.

Chris and Leo only stare at each other for a split second before both reaching for the jar at the same time. Their hands collide, which not only looks painful, but the jar gets pushed off the table and smashes all over the floor.

The busy café falls silent at this loud noise, and Shell frowns.

'Well, I could have done that myself.'

***

'Well, that was weird,' I eventually say. Leo and I are sat on the bench outside Shell's Café. He's holding a cider ice lolly on his hand.

Leo doesn't say anything, he just nods his head as he attempts to stretch his fingers out one at a time.

'Please tell me it's not broken. Belle will kill me if I've injured the best man.'

'It's fine,' he laughs, taking the lolly out from its wrapper and giving it a lick. 'It's just a bit sore, I'll be fine. I'm sure your friend will be, too.'

His voice changes when he talks about Chris.

'You didn't like him, did you?'

'Nope,' Leo replies confidently as he licks his ice lolly.

'Are you going to tell me why?' I ask. I know it's none of my business who Leo chooses to dislike, but that just seemed so unwarranted and out of character.

'Are you sure you want to know?' he asks, and now I definitely do, so I nod.

Leo pauses for a moment and it's almost as if he's figuring out how to tell me.

'This is going to sound really silly, but I was bullied by an Australian kid at school, and he just looked and acted exactly like a grown-up version of him so ... I know that's pathetic.'

I know exactly the type of kid he means because I had my fair share of dealings with those types of boys at school. The thing with the 'cool' boys is that you couldn't help but fancy them a bit, with their good looks, cheeky charm and charisma ... but it was a bittersweet crush, because boys like that are not nice to shy, chubby girls. If Chris had known me at school, there's no way he would've had anything to do with me and that's why I don't get too involved with the kind of guys I attract now. They may want me *now*, but they wouldn't have before, so I don't want them for much now.

'It's not pathetic,' I assure him, grabbing his uninjured hand and rubbing it. 'I was bullied at school, I know what it's like.'

'*You* were bullied at school?' he asks, and he couldn't sound more surprised if he tried.

'I could say the same to you. Why on earth would you get bullied?' I ask.

'I was an overweight kid,' Leo admits, sounding a little embarrassed, even though he looks perfect now.

I can't help but smile.

'Oi, don't laugh,' he warns me after seeing my smile.

'I'm not laughing at you,' I insist.

'Well you're not laughing with me,' he reminds me.

'I'm just smiling because that's exactly why I was bullied. I was bigger too.'

Leo widens his eyes. 'That's the last reason I would have guessed you were bullied for,' he tells me. I don't ask what the other reasons were.

'Yeah, well I don't tell anyone about it. Ever. I only told you because we were in the same boat.'

'Well you'll understand then – that guy just brought it all back for me. Imagine seeing your former bully now.'

I pull a face, unsure whether or not I should say what I'm about to say.

'What?' he asks.

I like to think that I'm a bigger person and that – to an extent – you should forgive and forget, but Nancy is still absolutely horrible to me, so why shouldn't I tell Leo?

'Nancy bullied me quite a lot when we were younger – Belle did too, although only after Nancy came onto the scene.'

'Really?' Leo asks, although he doesn't sound too surprised. 'No wonder you're trying to ruin the wedding.' I open my mouth to protest, but Leo doesn't let me speak. 'I'm joking, I'm joking,' he insists with a big smile. 'Well, I'm glad you told me.' Leo squeezes me hand.

I'm glad I told him too. I have never actually admitted that to anyone who I didn't know before my image transformation – because I always worried that would be enough for them to judge me. For a while after I lost weight, I felt like some kind of imposter, like I'd changed on the outside but I was still that shy, insecure dork on the inside, and it would only be a matter of time before people realised that. But with great abs, comes great confidence, so I soon got over it.

It's interesting that Leo used to be bigger too – that's probably why he's so nice now. You often find that people like Nancy, who was skinny *and* a bully at school, grow up and remain a bit of an arsehole for the rest of their lives, whereas people like Leo and I had to be nice to make friends. Now Leo is hot enough to be as horrible as he wants, but he isn't, and I really like that about him.

'Give me a lick of that lolly,' I insist, poking my tongue out in preparation.

'OK, but it's supposed to be for my hand, not you,' he jokes.

I playfully hit Leo on nose with the remainder of the lolly, but I must have done so harder than I realised because he jumps to his feet.

'Shit! My nose!' he cries out, his hands clapped over his face.

'Oh fuck! Don't tell me I've broken your nose, Belle will kill me if the photos are ruined,' I panic.

Leo stops and removes his hands from his perfectly fine nose as his face dissolves into a massive smile.

'Got you,' he teases.

'You bastard,' I shriek. 'Haven't you ever heard of *The Boy who Cried Wolf*? The third time you might not be so lucky.'

'It was worth it, just to see the look on your face,' he chuckles. 'You really are worried about this wedding, aren't you?'

'I just don't want another reason for everyone to be mad at me.'

'Come here,' Leo says, grabbing me and throwing me over his shoulder, fireman style. 'Let's get back to the house before they send out a search party.'

Chapter 25

This morning the family has gathered together for a 'formal breakfast' at Belle's request, because Dan is finally able to move and he's coming down to eat with us. This news has delighted Belle, because if Dan can make it downstairs for breakfast, then he'll probably be totally recovered by the day of the wedding. In fact, Belle is so delighted that she's even talking to me normally again – well, when I say normally, I mean normal for Belle.

As Dan enters the room slowly and takes a seat at the table, a few of us cheer his efforts.

'I thought I was going to have to stand in for you,' Mike jokes to his younger brother.

'Unlucky, bro,' Dan replies.

'Maybe on your wedding night?' Mike persists, and I can't help but laugh.

'Michael,' his mother snaps at him. She shoots me a filthy look too, for daring to chuckle.

With everyone sitting around the table, Belle goes off to the kitchen to start making breakfast and the conversation soon turns to the day ahead.

'So, where are we going for lunch?' my granddad asks.

My gran clicks her tongue. 'You haven't even had your breakfast yet, Jack.'

'I know, it's just I've been thinking about those delicious fish and chips we had the other day. We need to make the most of them while we're here.'

As my family all discuss the most incredible fish and chips they have ever tasted, I sit and twirl a piece of my hair with my fingers, bored out of my mind.

'They really are incredible, you know,' Nancy tells Leo, blatantly flirting with him.

'I'm not a big fan of fish and chips,' Leo replies.

'Well, you can have anything you want,' she reasons, leaning closer to him.

I'm sitting across the table from them so I can't help but watch, and for some reason it's really annoying me to see her flirting with him – probably because if she had known him at school, she would have made his life hell. I'm not sure if it's because of what I told him, but Leo isn't flirting back.

I'm only distracted from Nancy and Leo when my auntie mentions my name.

'Mia can look after the kids again,' she tells everyone.

'I *have* to work today,' I reply. 'The wedding is getting closer and I'm running out of time. Anyway, you sure got over the whole *Pulp Fiction* thing fast when you got hungry, didn't you?'

'Don't be rude to your auntie, Mia,' my mum reminds me, the same mum who preaches about treating others how you wish to be treated yourself – by that logic, my auntie is asking for it.

'Sincerest apologies,' I say sarcastically. 'But I really do have to work.'

'The damage has clearly already been done,' my auntie reasons, 'you couldn't do any more harm, could you?'

I could.

'We want to stay with you, Mia,' Josh chirps. Being one of the few people who genuinely likes me, I can't bring myself to say no to him.

'I'm sure I can manage a couple of hours,' I give in, unable to resist Josh and Max's cute little faces – although I'm not sure how I'll entertain them this time.

'Well, I could go and do some work now while you guys eat breakfast,' I suggest, standing up.

'You'll do no such thing,' Dan's mum snaps. 'This is Dan's special breakfast, and your sister has gone to a lot of effort. Sit back down.'

I look over at my own mum – is she really going to let someone else tell her child off? Surely only she can do that. I wouldn't mind, but I'm twenty-nine years old, no one should be able to tell me what I can and can't do.

The table has fallen silent during my ticking off. Leo, who is sitting opposite me, actually looks like he feels sorry for me, but I'm getting the same disapproving looks from almost everyone else.

'OK,' I say quietly as I sit back down.

Dan's mum starts serving drinks.

'Tea or orange juice?' she asks me.

'I might have coffee,' I tell her.

'I didn't say coffee. Tea or orange?' she repeats angrily.

'Neither. Thank you.' I reply through gritted teeth.

What I meant was that I would get my own drink, from the coffee machine they're all too scared to touch. I wasn't being smart with her. Am I being oversensitive or is she treating me worse than my mum, sister, auntie and gran combined? Still, no one else is speaking up, maybe it's just me.

'I'll stay and help Mia with the kids,' Leo says, breaking the silence.

'You don't need to do that,' Nancy insists, clearly annoyed that her prey is getting away from her.

'Mia knows how to look after us,' Josh says in my defence. 'She's really cool. She lets us watch good films and she teaches us new words.'

'Like what?' my auntie asks. That caught her interest. I rack my brains, trying to remember what words I could have taught them, and hope that it wasn't a bad one.

'Vulva,' Josh says proudly.

Oh shit. To be fair, I didn't even know I was saying that one in front of him, he was hiding in the room.

'Vulva?' my uncle echoes.

'Don't worry, I have a diagram,' Mike tells him quietly.

'Mia,' my auntie shrieks. 'What the hell is wrong with you?'

Dan's mum clicks her tongue and my own mum places her head in her hands.

'You see,' Leo chimes in, a big smile plastered across his face, 'she needs me.'

'I'm going to get a coffee,' I say as I head for the door, and this time no one insists I stay.

'Did I hear you upsetting Harriet?' my sister asks me the second I step into the kitchen.

'Who?'

'Dan's mum,' she reminds me angrily.

'Oh. Yes. Mum and Auntie June too.'

'Mia, please don't upset anyone, especially not Harriet.'

'Your mother-in-law hates me – I thought she was supposed to hate *you*.'

'You think life is a movie,' my sister laughs, and whether she's right or not, it's nice to see her looking relaxed, and if she's joking around with me then hopefully she's forgiven me for the little bedroom misunderstanding.

Hopefully things will get better now. Dan is mobile again, Belle seems to be OK with my existence, and if I can just get this work done then maybe I can actually enjoy myself at this wedding. Perhaps some of the oldies would still rather I wasn't here, but the kids like me, Mike is so much fun and Leo ... well, I'm just really glad he's here.

'I'm babysitting today,' I tell my sister as I make my coffee, 'so

I'm just going to nip upstairs and download some porn.'

My sister rolls her eyes at me as she fries bacon.

'I'm actually going to go and do some work, then Leo and I are going to entertain the kids while you guys go for lunch.'

'Ooh, Leo and I,' my sister teases. 'You two seem to be getting on well.'

'Yeah, he's cool,' I reply casually. 'A good friend.'

'I didn't realise you had friends, I thought you only had F buddies.'

'Very funny,' I reply, because I think she's joking. Not about the F word though; God forbid Belle would say such a naughty word.

***

Having a shower and washing my hair before I started my work seemed like a brilliant idea, that way I could make sure I was ready and then work right up until the second it was time to babysit. After swapping my shower for a nice relaxing bath, slipping on something sexy-ish (but hopefully still appropriate for babysitting) and curling my hair, I had only just sat down to work when Josh, Max and Leo came bounding into the room. Josh jumped up and down on the bed, cheering on Max who had Leo in a headlock. I couldn't help but smile as Leo jokingly begged and pleaded with a ten-year-old not to break his neck. He's got a way with kids, something I appear to be missing.

With no chance of getting any work done, Leo and I thought it best we take the kids out for the afternoon, although with neither of us knowing the area we don't exactly know where the child-friendly places are. I told Leo that finding somewhere to go is entirely his responsibility because, based on my track record, I can't guarantee I won't accidentally take them to a brothel, sign them up for the navy, or something else Auntie June probably wouldn't approve of. After a lovely stroll along the beach, we decide to pop into the café to see if Shell has any ideas.

'Hello my lovely,' she says, greeting me with a hug much warmer than any of my female family members have given me since I arrived. She greets Leo, and despite this only being the second time she has met him, he gets a lingering hug too – then again, Leo has one of those bodies that you just don't want to let go of.

'We're on babysitting duty today,' I tell her, nodding in the direction of Josh and Max, who are currently ripping open sachets of sugar and making neat little lines of white powder on the table. 'Leo, do you want to … erm …' my voice trails off. I don't need to tell him to intervene before the boys start snorting it, he's already on the case.

'They seem like a handful,' Shell laughs.

'They are,' I agree, failing to point out that they probably weren't so bad until they met me. 'I was wondering if you knew of anywhere we could take them today, somewhere that will keep them entertained.'

'What do they like?' Shell asks.

'Aside from doing lines and pretending to shoot each other? I have no idea,' I laugh.

Shell wanders over to the tourist display and grabs a leaflet before handing it to me.

'This will be perfect,' she says, smiling widely. 'And it will give you and that lush gentleman some time alone together. To talk,' she adds quickly.

As I look over the leaflet for Blazer, an indoor laser tag centre, I know that it will be perfect for the boys.

'Oh, they will love this,' I squeak. 'Thank you so much.'

'You're welcome,' Shell replies. 'I'll pack you up some cupcakes to go. I always find sugar much more enjoyable when eaten.'

Looking over at Josh, who is pretending to give Max an adrenalin injection to the heart, I think she might be right.

Chapter 26

As we arrive at Blazer, Josh and Max charge through the doors, closely followed by Leo and me.

Blazer is almost pitch black, even here in the lobby. There isn't a single light that isn't a bright neon colour, in fact the transition from the beautiful sunshine to these trippy lights is taking a little getting used to. Those, combined with the screams of joy from those already taking part, seem like the perfect conditions for creating one hell of a headache.

'Four is it?' the young lad behind the desk says.

'Very good,' I cackle. 'Just two, please.'

The young lad gives me a look and I realise he wasn't joking.

'It's not just for kids, you know,' he insists.

'Ah, but I'm sure it's just for those wearing flat shoes,' I reply.

I twist my foot slightly to show the persistent Blazer employee just how unfit for service I am.

'You can hire shoes,' the super-helpful employee informs me. 'We get lots of people coming here from the beach, I'm sure we'll have your size.'

'Hire shoes?' I squeak. The idea of handing over money for the privilege of flat, ugly shoes that have been worn by thousands of other people doesn't exactly have me reaching for my purse – but before I can say anything, Leo intervenes.

'Come on, Mia. It looks like fun and together we'll crush these little twerps.' Leo ruffles Josh's hair before giving his head a playful push.

I think for a moment.

'It will be good cardio,' Leo teases.

'Go on then,' I give in, and before I have the chance to change my mind I am being strapped into armour with brightly coloured flashing lights all over it, and being handed my gun. It's a big old thing, and not only is it flashing equally as brightly as I am, but there's a beam of light coming out of it which I shine on my cousin's chest like a sniper aiming at a target.

'You'll be sorry, turd,' I warn him. I'm actually quite excited now, even in my rental shoes.

Leo and I go through one door while the boys are ushered in through another. The aim of the game, I'm told, is to try and tag the other team with your laser, while avoiding their beams. It sounds simple enough, but as we are thrown into the dark maze with only the glow of the neon light and our armour to see where we're going, I realise we're going to have to play it clever.

'This way,' Leo says, ready to charge his way through the maze.

'Wait,' I whisper. 'We need to be tactical if we want to outsmart them.'

'They're kids,' Leo reasons. 'They'll be hiding. When was the last time you played hide and seek? I bet they play it all the time.'

'Yes, but they also think they're Jules and Vincent from *Pulp Fiction*, and they'd come at us guns blazing.'

Leo laughs and I'm not sure whether it's because I'm trying to be tactical or because of what I'm suggesting, but he looks so gorgeous when he smiles.

'OK,' he laughs. 'So, we hide?'

'Yes. Let them come to us. Then we waste them.'

***

'Can I get you a coffee from the machine?' Leo asks me.

'I'd rather eat something from one of the clinical waste bins,' I snap, regretting it instantly. 'Sorry. I've never been a big fan of hospitals.'

Leo takes me by the hands and looks into my eyes.

'Mia, it wasn't your fault.'

'The others won't see it that way,' I sigh.

'Kids hurt themselves all the time.'

'Kids hurt themselves, men hurt their backs, trousers get sent out in the wrong length ... it doesn't matter, it's always my fault as far as that lot are concerned.'

'Come on, Mia. All four of us were playing, any of us could have slipped and hurt our ankle. Anyway, at least we won,' he laughs.

I smile, but only for a moment, until I see the nurse heading in our direction.

'Josh will be fine,' she assures us. 'It's a nasty sprain, but he'll be better in no time. Ideally he needs to rest for a few days, but he mentioned that he's on holiday and that his cousin is getting married so we'll give him a pair of crutches. We're going to pop a support on his ankle, then I'll come back and go through the self-care techniques with you, OK?'

'OK, sure. Thank you so much,' I tell her. I exhale deeply – it feels like I've been holding my breath ever since I saw Josh hit the floor. It was no one's fault really, we were all running around, chasing each other and ducking behind the obstacles for cover – he just lost his footing and went down the wrong way on his ankle. Like Leo said, it could have happened to any of us. Maybe Leo is right, maybe people will understand that this one wasn't down to me.

***

I'm not saying it was the right thing to do, but I didn't call Auntie June and Uncle Steve from the hospital. At first it didn't occur to me, I just wanted to make sure Josh was OK. Then, when I found out that he was going to be fine, I decided it might be best to explain it to them in person. After all, dragging them out to the hospital would make things seem much worse than they were, it's much better to return him safe and almost sound, and then explain what happened.

As the four of us creep in through the front door, Josh on Leo's shoulders because Max wanted a turn on his crutches, we realise everyone is in the dining room having dinner.

'It will be fine,' Leo assures me with a smile before we head in.

'Oh God,' Dan's auntie squeaks immediately, spying her son hopping in on crutches.

'Mum, I'm fine,' he insists and she looks visibly relieved. 'They're Josh's.'

As Leo follows us in with Josh on his shoulders everyone drops their cutlery and starts asking questions. June and Steve rush over to see their son.

'What happened?' June asks him.

'I fell,' he tells her proudly. 'I had to go to hospital and everything, it was *so* cool.'

'It's just a sprain,' I interject. 'The nurse says a couple of weeks and he'll be back to normal.'

'*Just* a sprain,' my auntie echoes angrily. 'And you took the word of a nurse? He needs to see a doctor.'

'You know nurses are trained, right? They don't just dish out uniforms to anyone who asks for one,' I reply.

'How did you fall?' Steve asks Josh, carefully lifting him down from Leo's shoulders and sitting him at the table.

'Mia and Leo took us to play laser tag, it was *so* cool,' Josh chirps. Despite being hurt, he's had the time of his life.

'Seriously, Mia?' Belle chimes in. 'You thought laser tag was appropriate?'

'It wasn't Mia's idea,' Leo says. 'A local recommended it.'

'There's a homeless man who sits outside the amusement arcade who told me to kiss him on the whatsit, it doesn't mean I did it,' Dan's mum tells the room.

I let out a brief snort of laughter – I can't help it.

'This isn't funny, Mia,' my own mum warns me.

'That was a little,' Mike helpfully adds, but no one listens to him.

'I trust you with my child after you let me down once,' my auntie starts, 'and you let me down a second time. This time damaging his body instead of his mind.'

I sigh as I realise I don't have a single ounce of energy left to defend myself with. Ever since I arrived, all I have done is defend myself for the stupidest reasons, and I'm tired of it.

'It was a silly accident,' Leo insists in my defence.

'Don't blame yourself, Leo, you're a good man,' Dan's mum insists.

'But I was there too,' he insists, 'so that means we're equally to blame.'

'This is just what Mia does,' June tells him. 'She breaks things.'

'Wow,' Leo laughs to himself. 'How can you blame Mia and not me? We were both there, she didn't kick him or push him. *I* was the one chasing him at the time, so blame me, go on. Give Mia the night off.'

The entire room seems a little taken aback by Leo's angry rant, and for a moment no one knows what to say.

'Unbelievable,' he mutters to himself, storming out and slamming the door behind him.

'I'm really sorry,' Leo's mum insists to the room, her face red with embarrassment – or maybe it's anger. 'I don't know what's gotten into him at the moment.'

As Maria apologises on her son's behalf, I could swear she shoots me a dirty look. Clearly unwanted at the dinner table, I decide to go after Leo and thank him for standing up for me.

I eventually find Leo sitting on the beach behind the house.

'Leo De Luca, you're my hero,' I laugh as I approach him.

Leo smiles.

'I shouldn't have snapped like that, but you're right, they've got it in for you.'

'Mia Valentina.' I curtsey proudly in front of him. 'Public enemy number one.'

'Why are they like that with you, seriously?'

'I have no idea. When I was little, it was like I didn't exist – and since moving away, it's like I'm not a part of the family any more. Ah well.'

I lie down on the sand next to Leo and look up at the beautiful sky. It's only just starting to get dark, but the stars are out already. Leo lies back next to me.

'I suppose your only close friends are in LA now?'

'Yeah,' I lie. I mean, I have lots of friends, but I wouldn't say I had close friends. In all of the big movies I have written, the leading lady always has a best friend that she can count on. They always come in different shapes and sizes, but everyone has someone. That's not realistic though, and if there's one thing I've learned it's that the only person you should rely on is yourself.

'Thank you for sticking up for me,' I say, changing the subject.

'No problem,' Leo replies. 'I thought maybe you were being oversensitive or exaggerating, but something isn't right with that lot.'

'At least I've got you,' I tell him, edging closer and resting my head on his chest. Neither of us says a word, we just gaze up at the stars.

Chapter 27

Last night was fairly uneventful. I think people still hold me responsible for Josh's ankle, but after Leo's rant they are keeping pretty quiet on the subject. Leo is now public enemy number two by association. Even though everyone is treating him relatively well, he is being excluded from group activities. So am I, so we're spending pretty much every minute together, keeping each other entertained. No, not like that! I'm still on my sex ban, remember. I don't want to be blamed for anything else, so I'll see it through, get the wedding over with and then go home – and life can go back to normal. Belle is my only sister, so it's not like I'll be invited to any more weddings, and when she inevitably starts popping out babies I can't imagine I'll be invited to the christenings, lest I drown a baby or sleep with the priest.

It's been really nice getting to know Leo, actually. It's weird, we've developed this strong alliance or, dare I say it, friendship. It's been a long time since I've established any kind of relationship with a member of the opposite sex, and I have to admit, I'm enjoying having Leo on my side.

Yes, it's been nice being excluded from wedding-based activities for a few hours, but today is the day of the stag and hen parties, so I'll be dragged back in kicking and screaming.

Leo got up early to go and work out on the beach. Working out is something I have been neglecting slightly since I got here. I've never been that great at making my own exercise – I couldn't prance around on the beach like you see all the beautiful people in LA doing – I need a proper gym with machines that tell me how well I'm doing.

Alone in Leo's bed, I stretch out as fully as possible, occupying the entire bed in the shape of a starfish. It's strange, but sharing a bed with Leo at one end and me at the other is oddly restricting. If I roll over too far to the right, I find myself face to face with his feet, and knowing that I'm prone to wiggling in the night I keep my back to him, terrified I might kick him in the face or something. I don't get to relax for long, before Belle bursts through the door.

'Good morning,' she says cheerily, placing a cup of coffee down next to me. 'I brought you this.'

I rub my eyes to make sure I'm not dreaming.

'You … you managed to work the coffee machine?' I ask, because it seems more polite to be surprised about her getting the machine working than the truth, the fact that she is being nice to me.

'Oh no, no chance,' she laughs. 'It's instant.'

I am not usually a fan of instant coffee, but I am a fan of my sister treating me like a human being so I will drink every last drop.

'Thank you,' I tell her, sitting up and taking the mug in my hands.

'So …' I start, racking my brains for something to say. 'How are you?'

'I'm good. You?'

'Not bad,' I reply, sipping my coffee. It isn't nice at all, and she's loaded it with sugar, but I said I'd drink it so I will.

Belle nods towards Leo's pillow at the bottom of the bed.

'So, this is really what's going on, you two just sharing a bed, both sleeping at opposite ends?' she asks.

'Of course,' I tell her honestly. 'Is that why you're here? To try and catch us shagging?'

My sister shakes her head – not to say no, it's because she disapproves of my language.

'I told you I wouldn't and I haven't,' I tell her. 'Leo and I are just good friends. Really good friends,' I add.

'So, you keep saying,' my sister replies, 'but the two of you seem way closer than just really good friends.'

'And yet we sleep at opposite ends of the bed,' I remind her.

'Exactly, you're more like a married couple than Dan and me,' she laughs. A joke! My sister is being friendly with me all of a sudden. 'And if you sleep with the guys you don't care about, maybe this is what you do with the ones you do really care about.'

'Shut up,' I laugh. 'So, what's the plan for today?'

'You tell me,' she replies, smiling widely.

'What do you mean?' I ask.

'My hen party, duh! You're the chief bridesmaid, it's your job to arrange something. You have arranged something, haven't you?'

'Of course, I have,' I lie.

'What?'

'It's a surprise, silly.'

I'm not sure if my sister is buying it, but she'll go mad if she knows I have overlooked this small detail. It never even crossed my mind that she expected me to sort this. Not only because I live in another country, but because I would have thought her actual friends would want to do it.

'So what time should I be ready for?' she asks.

'Ten,' I reply, and my sister frowns. 'Sorry, I meant eight.'

'Coolio,' she replies. 'I can't wait to see what you've got planned.'

'Neither can I,' I say to myself as soon as my sister is out of earshot.

***

'Morning, gorgeous,' Leo says as he gets back from his workout. 'Just going to have a shower.'

'Can I borrow you for a minute,' I ask, beckoning him over to the bed.

'You sure you want me any closer? I stink and I'm covered in sand.'

'I'll risk it,' I laugh.

Leo does as he is told but he doesn't sit down on the bed, he just hovers next to me.

'What's up?'

'You can't tell anyone, but I didn't realise it was my job to organise Belle's hen party, so I haven't sorted anything. She thinks I have. Have you arranged Dan's stag do?'

'Of course,' he replies. 'But we're friends and he likes me.'

I laugh.

'I don't know what to do. She brought me a coffee and as far as I can tell it wasn't poisoned, but do keep an eye on me for the next few hours,' I joke. 'Honestly, Leo, she seemed so happy and excited. Despite the way things seem, I do want her wedding to go well, and I do want to make her happy.'

'I know you do.' Leo goes to hug me, before remembering that he's filthy. It was a nice thought though.

'Even if I do find somewhere to go, I don't have any of the usual tacky hen party junk you're supposed to have. I need inflatable men and L plates.'

'Look, don't panic. Let me grab a shower, and then I'll get my mum on board, she'll be happy to help. She can go buy your inflatables while you sort somewhere to go.'

'Are you sure she won't mind?' I ask.

'I'm certain. I'm her only son, she can't say no to me,' he laughs.

'Leo, thank you so much.'

'What are friends for?' he asks, pecking me on the forehead before heading off for a shower.

I'm not used to having a friend like Leo, but I'm glad that I do. If I can just find a venue, then we'll be sorted. Today was my last proper chance to get any work done before the wedding, but I guess it will have to wait. I've got a hen party to plan.

Chapter 28

The plan that Leo and I came up with should have been foolproof, but when a suspicious Nancy pressed me for the name of where we were going in front of Belle, I had to think fast. As luck would have it, when we were out with Josh and Max the other day we passed a pub called The Cock Inn, and for some reason the name just stuck with me.

'Oh, how funny,' Belle's friend Heather said at the time, thinking it was going to be some sort of smutty, hen-friendly joint, but now, as our party barge through the doors of The Cock, it's no laughing matter.

The place is quiet, and filled exclusively with men much older than us. The only real noise is coming from a particularly drunk older gentleman who is performing an excruciatingly bad rendition of Elvis Presley's 'Always on My Mind' with all the seriousness of an X Factor contestant.

'Mia, this is an old man pub,' Nancy moans.

'Don't be so quick to judge,' I snap. 'I'm told this is the place to be when it gets late.'

'And which opportunistic rapist told you that?' she scoffs.

'Anyway,' I ignore her comment. 'I'll get the drinks in,' I say, trying to inject some cheer into my voice. 'What's everyone having?'

At the hen party tonight it's just me, Belle and her friends Nancy, Heather and Beth. Thankfully the older female relatives decided that they would sit this one out and I daren't petition for my oldest cousin, Hannah, to tag along. There is not much in the way of eye candy here. This is clearly no place for tourists, it's a cliquey local pub for local people, and the old pint-drinking fellows don't look too pleased to have us here.

'Hello,' I say brightly to the man behind the bar. 'How are you?'

He snorts. The patrons propping up the bar share a laugh too.

'Anyway,' I continue, 'what kind of wine do you have?'

'Red or white,' the man laughs as he scratches his chin through his big, shaggy, grey beard.

I think for a moment. There's no way we can go anywhere else, not without Belle realising I never had anything planned in the first place. I don't know where else we could go, and I don't fancy my chances roaming the streets trying to find another venue when it could be just as bad as this place. I need to stay in Belle's good books and for now that means making the most of this place.

'I'll take a couple of bottles of each, please,' I reply, flashing him my biggest smile. The barman does as he is told – well he's not about to turn away money, is he? But I am no sooner sat at the table with the rest of a party when a beast of a man approaches us. He's the tallest man I have ever seen, or maybe he just seems it because he's very intimidating-looking and I am sitting down. He has messy, dark hair and a bushy beard, like so many of the other men here. He smells awful, like tobacco and soil, but I'm not about to tell him so.

'Hello,' I say as cheerily as I can.

'Hello,' he replies. 'What's five young ladies like you doing in a place like this?'

'It's my hen party,' Belle offers bravely.

'I guessed as much when I saw all the dicks,' he replies, causing Belle to wince at his choice of words.

When Leo had said his mum would go out shopping for hen

party supplies, I hadn't expected her to come back with so much penis-based stuff. I was thinking L plates and silly hats – and maybe a token, understated penis of some kind because my sister might be OK with just one, because it's practically tradition. What Maria came back from the shops with were penis-shaped straws, shot glasses on necklaces, headbands with dicks on and a variety of name badges that say inappropriate, and not even remotely clever things – my own says 'My name is Mia and I like big dicks'. My first instinct was to take everything outside and burn it before Belle saw, but she walked in on me bagging it up and she was delighted with it all. I suppose she's less of a prude when it's a wedding tradition.

'We've been talking, and we think you should leave,' the big man says. 'This is no place for little girls.'

'We're not as little as we look,' I joke. 'We'll be fine.'

'No, you'll be leaving now, and you can leave your drinks here.'

The girls begin to gather their things, but I'm not willing to be forced out of a public place so easily.

'You don't look like much of a wine drinker,' I reply.

'I'm not,' he laughs, 'but we're keeping it, and you're going.'

'When we're done,' I reply firmly, although as cool and calm as I may appear on the outside, I'm terrified on the inside. It seems like a great length to go to, just to stay in Belle's good books. I imagine she'll like me even less if her hen party turns into a bar fight.

'It's not worth it, let's go somewhere else,' Belle pleads with me.

'You want to listen to her, Mia,' the big guys says, clocking my name badge. 'You like big dicks, do you?'

Every bone in my body is telling me that the right thing to do is get out of here as fast as possible. But I don't.

'I don't know about that, I don't like you,' I reply. 'And I can see why they call this place the Cock Inn.' There are mixed reactions from the room. Some of the men look shocked, some laugh, the man singing karaoke has stopped to see how things play out and my own friends are just staring at me with their mouths wide open.

The big guy stares at me, cocking his head as he thinks things over.

'You think you're tough, don't you?'

'I'm tougher than you,' I reply, because there's no turning back now. 'Why don't you want us to stay? Is it because my girls and I could drink you and your beardy boys under the table?'

'You really believe that, don't you?' he laughs, and all his friends laugh with him.

'I do,' I reply confidently.

'Well let's make this more interesting,' he suggests. 'We'll have a competition. If you win, not only can you stay, but I'll pay for your drinks all evening.'

'And if we lose?' I ask.

'You'd better hope you win,' he warns.

I can hear Belle, Nancy, Heather and Beth all begging me to back down but if there's one thing I hate, it's men who think they are better than women.

'You're on,' I reply. 'But I'm picking the poison.'

'Whatever the lady wants,' the big bloke replies mockingly.

I grab my bag to head out to find an off licence, because if we're doing this, we're going to drink something I know we can handle, not the old man bourbon he's cradling in his hand.

'She won't be back,' the big guy laughs to his friends.

'I will,' I reply. 'You can keep these four as insurance, they shouldn't give you any trouble.'

Chapter 29

Now, I'm not stupid. I know that, despite Belle and her friends' best efforts on a Saturday night, they are not hardened drinkers, and that while I have a tolerance for alcohol that would be more suited to a rugby player, there is no denying that these men would probably be able to outdrink us based on body size alone … and yet I refuse to be beaten. In situations like these you need to think outside the box, so it got me thinking, it's not how much we drink that will help us beat these guys, it's what we drink.

The girls looked visibly relieved when I arrived back with my bags of booze, I think it may have crossed their minds that I might have left them here.

We are currently having a team talk – me and my girls at one side of the room and Jimmy and his guys at the other, over by the guy on the karaoke machine who is still singing Elvis tunes, only now he's on to 'In The Ghetto'. Jimmy, I found out, is the name of my massive opponent. I discovered this when he told me his team were called 'Jimmy and the Bastards'. Despite my best efforts to get my team motivated, I'm not having much luck. When I told them we needed a team name, Belle suggested 'Terrified' and 'Dead Meat' but neither seemed suitable.

'Listen,' I whisper to them, 'I have bought the most sickly-sweet drinks I could think of. It might be the kind of junk we knock back all weekend but there's no way these guys will have the stomach for it.'

'Do you think so?' Belle asks curiously.

'Look at them, they're all drinking beer or bourbon – do you really think they can chain drink Kapop Shotz like we can?'

Kapops is a popular brand of alcopops here in the UK, but Kapop Shotz are super-strong vodka-based shots in ridiculous flavours like candy floss and toffee apple. For girls who like to get smashed but don't particular enjoy the taste of alcohol, they're perfect. What I'm hoping is that big, tough guys like these won't be able to stand them.

'OK, I hate to admit it, but maybe she's right,' Nancy reasons.

'Of course, I am! Come on, Belle, what do you say? Don't you want a hen night to remember for the rest of your life? We can find a club, go dance around our handbags until we get bored or we can stay here, show these motherfuckers who's boss and let them pay for our drinks all night while we abuse their karaoke machine. What do you say?'

As I deliver the last line of my speech, the girls are all standing – excited and ready to kick some ass. I feel like a king addressing his army before a big battle.

Going up against us we have Jimmy and his four bastards. They have laid empty shot glasses out on the table, a row for each competitor.

'Go on then, what silly girly tipple have you got for us?' Jimmy asks, and when I produce the brightly coloured Kapop Shotz bottles from my bag, he bursts out laughing. 'That's what you've brought? Liquid sweeties? I almost feel sorry for you, we're going to crush the lot of you.'

I look at my teammates expecting to see terrified faces, but they look cool, calm and confident.

'F you,' Belle shouts. 'The sooner we start, the sooner we'll see who the winner is.'

'We will,' Jimmy laughs.

'And I look forward to you paying for our drinks all night,' Belle adds confidently, and it makes me smile to see her enjoying herself.

The barman pours the brightly coloured liquids into the lines of glasses in front of each of us.

'Here's the rules,' he starts. 'When I say go, you go. The winner is the first team to finish and if anyone throws up, their team loses.'

We all nod in agreement to the rules.

'OK, go!'

We all knock our first shot back in unison.

'Fuck me, that's sweet,' one of Jimmy's bastards gasps.

'Just get on with it, you big girl,' Jimmy yells back.

As we all carry on knocking back drinks I can't help but notice that the boys seem to be going through them faster than we are, but Jimmy looks like he is struggling.

'Are you OK there, Jimmy? You don't look so good,' I tease.

'Shut up and drink,' he snaps.

'Gladly,' I reply between drinks. 'Mmm, they're so yummy and sweet. Is this one the toffee apple?' I ask no one in particular. 'You can really taste the toffee.'

'I think so,' Belle replies. 'It's like pure sugar, it's so yummy.'

Jimmy has just one glass left in front of him, but as he downs his second to last shot he brings his hand up to his mouth and his eyes widen.

'You feeling OK, Jim?' I ask insincerely. 'You're looking a little green. You know, like when you're on a boat and you're bobbing up and down and up and down.' As I say this I sway from side to side in front of him, and just when I think Jimmy is about to reach for his final glass his mouth erupts with brightly coloured vomit. He raises his hands to his face but all this does is force the sick to splatter his teammates either side of him. It is a truly revolting sight, but battles are never pretty.

Even though Jimmy's team had far less left to drink, we are the winners because he couldn't keep his down.

I pick up one of the remaining shots and sip at it leisurely.

'Take your time, ladies, we'll be here all night.'

You would think that a big man like Jimmy might be ashamed about losing to a bunch of girls, but he roars with laughter as he wipes his mouth.

'You're OK by me, ladies, you can stay. Dave,' he calls to the barman, 'start a tab for my new friends.'

As my teammates all cheer and hug each other, I can tell that my sister is genuinely delighted, and having the time of her life.

'So, we're staying here?' I ask her.

'We're staying here,' she replies.

Chapter 30

As I watch my sister drunkenly performing 'Jailhouse Rock' on the karaoke machine, I sit on one of the cushioned pub chairs with my feet up and sip at my glass of DIY rosé wine, which Jimmy created for me by mixing red and white, because that's what his daughter drinks. Jimmy and his bastards are actually pretty nice guys, and despite my sister's terrible singing voice, they're all cheering her on.

The karaoke machine, it turns out, is only programmed with Elvis Presley songs. Thankfully, even though we're not hardcore fans of the King, we all seem to know quite a few of his tracks. Singing along with the guy who was occupying the mic when we arrived soon turned into us all agreeing we would do one track each. I don't think any of us are particularly gifted in the singing department, but we're all feeling very brave since our drink-off, and we've had quite a bit since.

As Belle finishes her song she cheers herself just as loudly as her audience is cheering for her. She grabs herself a glass of wine from the bar and plonks herself down next to me.

'You didn't plan this hen party at all, did you?' she asks.

'No,' I admit. 'I didn't know I was supposed to. I'm really sorry,' I slur.

'That's OK, I am having *so* much fun!' Belle cheers and points at Jimmy who is performing an actually beautiful rendition of 'The Wonder of You'. Heather and Beth are watching him and screaming with delight, like he's Michael Bublé.

'Really?' I ask.

'Really,' she replies. 'None of the other girls would have brought me somewhere like this, and we wouldn't have had this much fun anywhere else. You're my favourite sister.'

'I'm your *only* sister,' I remind her.

'You're my favourite only sister though.'

I laugh and thank her. That might be the nicest thing she has ever said to me.

'My name is Belle,' my sister reads her name badge out loud. 'And I like to be on top.' She giggles quietly. 'I do like to be on top.'

I down the last of my drink.

'I'm pretty sure I imagined that,' I say to myself.

Over in the corner of the room, two men are having a disagreement and it's getting pretty heated. One punches the other in the face so the barman grabs him by his shirt and throws him out of the front door.

'Oh, it's all kicking off, isn't it?' Nancy says excitedly as she sits down with us.

'I'm having so much fun,' Belle says again.

I have lost count of the number of times my sister has expressed how much she is enjoying herself tonight, but it is music to my ears. I have finally done something right and I'll drink to that. I pour the three of us a bright green shot.

'To my sister's last night of freedom,' I toast, and we drink.

'You can have your room back now that Dan is better,' my sister says generously. He's been better for a few days, but this is the first I've heard about being allowed my own bed again – she must be really pleased with my efforts tonight. 'That way you won't have to sleep with Leo anymore.'

'I thought you wanted separate rooms for the night before the big day?' I remind her.

'Yeah, but Dan can sleep on the sofa or kick Mike out of his bed or something,' she babbles.

I shrug my shoulders casually.

'Is something going on between you and Leo?' Nancy asks.

'Nope,' I reply firmly.

'But you seem so close, you're always together—'

'And they sleep in the same bed,' Belle interrupts.

'And you sleep in the same bed,' Nancy echoes. 'And Belle offered you your own bed back and you clearly don't want it. Do you have feelings for him?'

'Nope,' I reply, although I'm slightly less confident with the delivery of that one.

'You like him,' Belle assures me. 'You sleep with the people you don't like, so by that logic, you don't sleep with the ones you really do like.'

'You're the one stopping me sleeping with him. Anyway, that makes no sense, drunk woman,' I laugh.

'I think you like him too,' Nancy insists. 'I've been watching you together and I can just tell.'

I bat away the suggestion with a wave of my hand, just as Jimmy finishes his song.

'Up next we have Mia, give her a round of applause,' he shouts down the microphone.

'But I haven't even picked my song,' I insist.

'I picked it for you,' Belle informs me. 'It's super-appropriate.'

I make my way to the makeshift stage and take the microphone from Jimmy. As I start singing the words as they appear on the screen, it doesn't take me long to realise what I'm singing – 'Can't Help Falling in Love'. Oh, very funny, my sister is suddenly a comedian it seems. As the words leave my lips, I really think about what Belle and Nancy were saying. It's ridiculous, isn't it? I mean, Leo and I are just friends. If we were shagging instead of sleeping at opposite ends of a bed, and kissing instead of watching movies and messing around on the beach all day, then maybe I could understand why they're thinking what they're thinking. What am I talking about? I'm drunk, I have no idea what *I'm* thinking.

I finish my song to a massive round of applause, but I can't help but feel annoyed. I'm not sure why, but that conversation about Leo has just rubbed me up the wrong way and suddenly I'm not in the mood for partying any more.

Chapter 31

As I stroll along the quiet street towards the beach house, I swig from the bottle of blueberry Kapop Shotz that I grabbed before leaving the pub. I scrunch up my face and make funny noises after each sip because it really is so sweet, and I've had way too much.

I'm struggling to stay on my feet. This either has something to do with my very high heels or the fact that I have had far too much alcohol, even by my standards. My legs are like jelly and it feels like I'm walking on a waterbed, not a pavement.

The other girls are far drunker than I am. So drunk that, when I told them I was going home because I was tired, they didn't even question it. Weirdly, they seemed gutted that I was leaving – we've actually had a really fun night, but with my mood taking a turn for the worse, all I wanted to do was leave. I'll slip off my dress, climb into bed and try and get to sleep. The boys will almost certainly still be partying, so I'll make the most of having the bed to myself and not being squashed on my own side.

The beach house is in sight, but walking just feels so difficult. Deciding that my shoes are just holding me back, I kick them off in the street, picking them up in my free hand. As I walk the final few feet towards the stairs to the front door, I alternate between swigging my drink and quietly singing 'Can't Help Falling in Love' to myself, dancing my way along, pretending my life is a musical.

I let out a little yelp as I make out a figure sitting on the bottom step. I was expecting everyone to either still be out or be fast asleep by now – it must be after midnight.

'Hello you,' Leo says cheerily, sounding like he's had his own fair share of alcohol tonight. He's looking really good in a pair of black trousers and a white shirt. He's drinking a bottle of beer and as he lifts it to his lips to take a drink, the sleeve of his shirt looks like it might burst open courtesy of his bulging bicep. I remind myself not to look at him like *that*, we're just friends, we're just friends.

'Leonardo,' I greet him, clumsily plonking myself down on the step next to him. 'What are you doing home so early?'

'I could ask you the same thing,' he replies, smiling that dreamy smile of his that shows off the cute dimples in his cheeks … stop it, Mia!

'I don't know,' I reply. 'I'm just drunk.'

'Me too,' he laughs. 'Cheers.'

Leo holds up his bottle and I clink it with my own. We both drink.

'Beer, though,' I start. 'That's not a man's drink. *This* is a man's drink.'

I wiggle my bottle of blueberry, sugary vodka at him.

'Men don't drink that,' he tells me.

'Real men can't drink this,' I tell him. 'They can't handle it.'

Leo laughs and takes the bottle from me. He takes a confident swig, but scrunches up his face as soon as he swallows.

'My God, that's sweet,' he gasps. 'I'll stick to my beer.'

'No, you won't,' I inform him, pouring the remaining contents of his bottle into the nearest plant before pushing the neck of the bottle into the soil. 'You can't let me drink this on my own.'

'If I drink that I'll end up with a blue tongue like you,' he insists.

'My tongue isn't blue,' I mumble, opening my mouth as little as possible when I speak.

'Prove it,' he demands, but I keep my mouth tightly closed like a little kid refusing to eat her peas.

Leo, who isn't willing to take my word for it, gently opens my mouth with his hand and pinches my tongue between his fingers.

'There you go, it's blue.'

'Eww,' I squeak. 'I know where those hands have been. There's only one thing for it, I'll have to drink more blue alcohol to try and clean my mouth.'

I take a big swig from the bottle and jokingly swish the liquid around inside my mouth.

'You look like you went down on a Smurf,' he laughs. His joke catches me by surprise, causing me to erupt with laughter, spraying blue drink all over his lovely white shirt.

'Shit, I am so sorry,' I cackle. 'Take it off, I *will* fix it.'

'You *will* fix it?'

'I will. I'll just pour some of the candy floss flavoured one on it, it'll bring the blue right out.'

Leo laughs and shakes his head.

'Give me that bottle,' he demands as he takes off his shirt. I do as he asks, and watch as he takes a drink. It never ceases to amaze me just how perfect his body is – he's like a statue. He has splashes of blue all over his chest so I brush them off with my hands. Maybe it's because I'm drunk, but I just can't seem to remove my hands from his rock-hard chest, it's like a magnet is holding them in place. Leo reaches out and places the bottle on the side before gently grabbing me by the wrists and pulling me close for a kiss. No one has ever kissed me like this before, it's slow and it feels like it lasts a lifetime. It isn't like the sexy, passion-fuelled kiss we shared on the day we met, but it isn't a friendly kiss either.

As Leo releases me I lose my balance a little, falling into him.

'Let's go upstairs,' he says as he picks me up, throwing me over his shoulder.

I giggle with delight – well, isn't this every girl's fantasy? To be carried to bed by a fireman.

Chapter 32

My head hurts. Not just my head, but my hair too, every last strand of it is causing me physical pain every time I dare to move my head on the pillow. I feel like I've been hit in the face – by a wrecking ball, a really big one with a butt-naked Miley Cyrus warbling away on top of it.

My eyes are closed, but my eyelids are glowing red from the bright sunlight. I would bring my hands to my face to cover them but I just can't find the strength. As my stomach grumbles and bubbles like a pan of boiling water, it occurs to me that when I do find the energy to move my arms, I should probably cover my mouth. It's not a case of *if* I'm going to be sick, it's a case of *when*.

What the hell happened last night? I remember arriving at The Cock, our drinking game with the locals and my sister treating me like a human being (although that last part sounds like something drunk-me might have wishfully made up). I left early, didn't I? I made my own way home and then …

My body remains perfectly still, but my eyes open suddenly. I allow myself to stare into space for a second so my eyes can adjust before allowing myself to glance down at my body. It turns out that it isn't a lack of energy or some kind of alcohol-induced paralysis that is stopping me from moving, it's a man's arm wrapped around my body.

'Shit shit shit,' I shout, jumping out of bed at such a speed I go lightheaded.

'What's wrong?' Leo asks, his voice is croaky and he's rubbing his eyes.

At least it's Leo. For a second I thought that I might have got into bed with Dan again.

'Sorry. Waking up with a naked man kind of freaks a girl out,' I explain.

'I'm not naked.' Leo yawns. 'Neither are you.'

Leo pulls back the covers, showing me that he's still wearing his trousers. I turn around to look in the mirror behind me and sure enough, I'm still wearing my outfit from last night.

'So we didn't …'

'We didn't,' he laughs. 'We chatted for ages and then we fell asleep. How drunk were you?'

I attempt to run a hand through my knotted hair as I think, but my fingers get caught and it's unbearable – but not as unbearable as what I have just realised.

'Oh my God,' I start slowly. 'We snuggled!'

'So?' he laughs.

'We chatted and then we cuddled each other to sleep – who does that?'

'We do.'

'*I* don't,' I start as I pace around the room. 'Sleeping cuddled up to a guy, fully clothed! I don't do that.'

'Mia, relax,' Leo insists. 'You're talking like we spent the night engaging in really weird sex acts. We cuddled and you're acting like we had a one night stand.'

'No, because we already had a one night stand, and I was fine with that. This I'm *not* fine with.'

'Look, just calm down,' Leo says as he approaches me. 'You don't look so good.'

'You don't look that great your—'

I don't get to finish what I am saying. I run to the bathroom, making it to the toilet just in time to be sick.

'Was cuddling me really that disgusting?' he jokes cautiously as he rubs my back. It was kind of him to follow me, but I'm not crazy about throwing up in front of an audience.

'My vomit is blue,' I tell him, although he can probably (and unfortunately) see that.

'It's that blue crap you were drinking last night,' he tells me. 'It's upset your stomach.'

'My stomach isn't upset,' I reply. 'It's furious.'

***

Leo ran me a bath before heading down for breakfast. That's the difference between most men and women: men can simply eat their hangover away.

After holding back my hair as I threw up the bright blue, blueberry flavoured contents of my stomach, Leo and I didn't say much to one another. I didn't mean to act so oddly, I just freaked out when I realised what we'd done. It's all coming back to me now: I came home last night because Belle and Nancy were teasing me about having feelings for Leo and how did I prove them wrong? By having a nice chat and then falling asleep in his arms – and all done with pants on.

As I wonder why I reacted so badly, and why I care so much about people thinking I have feelings for Leo, I realise it's because I do like him a lot. I didn't know much about him when I slept with him, but when Belle put a stop to that, we had no choice but to become just good friends. The thing is, without the sex, the cuddling feels too intimate. Mates don't cuddle. If you have sex with a friend he's a fuck buddy, but there's no name for a friend that you share platonic intimate moments with because there's no such thing. That, right there, is a boyfriend, and not only have I not had a boyfriend for a very long time, but Leo isn't boyfriend material. I mean, he's handsome, kind, funny and all the other things you'd want a boyfriend to be, but he's made it very clear that he's a good-time boy with no interest in settling down. He's the male equivalent of me, and that's why we get on so well.

I kind of wish I hadn't turned down Belle's offer of getting my bed back, but if I ask her now she'll know something is up. The best thing to do is just pretend last night didn't happen, get back to normal, get the wedding out of the way and then fly back to LA where I need never think of my trip here again.

I squeeze a blob of shampoo into my hands and begin massaging it through my long hair ever so gently. My headache is still booming, so today will most definitely be a straight hair day; no way could I endure curling it.

There's a knock at the bathroom door.

'Hello,' I call out.

'Hey, it's me, can I come in?' Belle calls back. She's actually asking for permission to invade my privacy, rather than just doing it. That *is* progress.

'Sure,' I call back.

'Oh, sis, you look as rough as I feel,' she says, sitting down on the edge of the bath.

'This might be the worst hangover I've ever had,' I tell her honestly.

'And you went home early,' she reminds me. 'We kept going until four a.m.'

'Did you go to a club?'

'No, we stayed there all night. You were right, the Cock Inn really is the place to be when it gets late.'

Well, who would've called that one?

'I thought I'd better check on you when we got back, make sure you were in your bed and not swept away by a wave or something.'

Oh God.

'It wasn't what it looked like,' I insist, causing my sister to laugh. She's smiling widely at me, like she knows something I don't, and it's making me want to hold her head under the water.

'It looked like you and Leo were spooning. With your clothes on,' she adds.

'Oh God, don't, it sounds so bad when you say it out loud,' I whine, covering my face with my hands.

My sister splashes water at me.

'Mia, what's wrong with you? Just be happy. You like him, he likes you.'

'Yeah, but not like *that*,' I insist, but Belle is clearly sick of hearing it.

'OK, we get it, you're just friends. What I actually came for was to tell you that we're having our hair done today.'

It's not like the wedding is today or even tomorrow, so having our hair done today makes no sense at all. Surely whatever ridiculous style my sister has chosen will be messed up by then …

'Well, we're getting the colours done today,' she informs me, seeing my puzzled look. 'There was a little leftover money in the wedding fund, so Mum's taking all the girls to have their hair coloured, to treat us, that way we just need styling on the day.'

I protectively place my hands over my honey blonde hair. There is one person I trust to colour my hair and she is over five thousand miles away, so no way am I going to let some random have a go at it.

'I've just had mine done,' I insist, but Belle is having none of it.

'Mia, it's free,' she reminds me as she leaves the room. 'Hurry up and get ready.'

I love that my sister is being nice to me and treating me like a friend for once, but no one is touching my hair. I'll just have to tell her straight and face the consequences.

Chapter 33

I nibble my thumbnail anxiously as we make the journey to the hair salon. Everyone was in such a rush when we were leaving, I didn't get time to speak to Belle. I was going to try and talk to her while we were driving, but we're travelling in separate cars and, unlucky for me, I'm travelling with my mum and my gran.

'Mum,' I start, hoping I'll find the right words as I need them. 'I've actually just had my hair coloured, so while I appreciate the offer, I can probably sit this one out.'

'Nonsense,' my gran replies. 'Just have it brightened up a little. We're not doing this for you, it's for Belle and for us all to spend some time together.'

My mum nods in agreement.

'I get that, and I'll happily sit with you all and watch. It's just that I've had the same colourist for years, and she won't be happy with me if someone else messes with her work.'

'Colourist, she says,' my gran snorts.

'Just join in Mia, it will be fun,' my mum insists, and then the subject is closed.

The thing is, this is my hair. Everything else on this trip may be short-term, but when I go home my hair goes with me. The subject is not closed.

'It's just that I'm not exactly comfortable letting a stranger put chemicals on my hair,' I persist. 'I won't know what kind they're using, and it might not be right for me and—'

'For God's sake, Mia,' my mum yells. 'I don't understand how my little girl can have changed so much, simply by crossing the Atlantic.'

'Being a snob doesn't suit you,' my gran insists.

'It's not just that,' my mum continues. 'You used to be so sweet and caring – you'd do anything for anyone. Belle told me all about last night, how you made sure she enjoyed herself, and she's been banging on about you all morning. I thought we had the old Mia back, but you're still being selfish. Belle will be heartbroken if you snub this gesture, she thinks the two of you are working things out. Just endure it. What's the worst that can happen?'

***

As I twirl aimlessly in my chair I look at my reflection in the mirror. It doesn't matter how much makeup I put on this morning, my eyes are so dark I look like I've been punched in the face. There's something horribly honest about the mirrors you find in hair salons. You're sat so close to them, for extended periods of time with nothing to do but take a long hard look at yourself.

Without the safety blanket of my hair (because it's wrapped up in foil, like leftovers) I have no choice but to take a long hard look in the mirror, and I don't like what I'm seeing. No one wants to be a bad person really (although the jury is still out on Auntie June), do they? I don't want people thinking that I'm stuck up or selfish. I don't look down on my family; they raised me and at the end of the day I'm still one of them, so why do they think I'm looking down on them?

If that isn't a snob looking back at me, then what's the alternative? A pathetic little girl who allowed her mum to guilt her into getting her hair done. I'm really happy that Belle and I are working things out, so when she said that Belle was happy too, I knew what I had to do.

So much for this being a social thing though. My mum and gran have gone for a cup of tea because they don't believe in colouring their hair now that they're grey, they think a woman should grow old gracefully – further proof that I was accidentally swapped at birth because I plan to grow old as disgracefully as possible. Give me Botox or give me death.

The rest of the group are all sat chatting at the other side of the room. Not only am I sitting apart from them but, with several noisy hairdryers on the go, I can't hear a thing.

I am sitting over here alone because of my 'overly fussy request' as my mum put it before she left. I love my warm, honey-blonde colour. It like it more than that bright, Barbie-blonde you see most naturally brunette girls rocking. One thing I made very clear to the girl doing my hair today is that I didn't want to end up with bleach blonde hair.

A girl called Amber is doing my hair today. When she was assigned to me I instantly regretted giving in to my mother, because Amber's own hair is awful. It's a sort of burgundy colour and is scraped up in a bun on top of her head. As she admired my long hair she told me how her own was quite short because she had damaged it over the years by repeatedly colouring, straightening and curling it. Still, I didn't want to make a scene, and if she's still working here at Dyevine she's clearly good at her job. Dyevine, what a stupid name for a hair salon. I understand the love we have in the UK for giving salons names with terrible puns, but I don't think this one quite works.

'Let's check you,' Amber says, peeling back a piece of foil. 'Just a little while longer,' she concludes, leaving me sitting under the heat lamp.

'I don't usually need heat when I'm having my hair coloured,' I tell her, but it falls on deaf ears. I really hope I'm not going to leave here today looking like a Playboy Bunny, with hair so blonde you'll need sunglasses to look at it.

After sitting a while longer, I notice everyone else is finished. As Belle walks over to see how I'm getting on, I notice that her shoulder-length, chocolate brown hair isn't much different than it was before we arrived, so that's encouraging.

'Will she be much longer?' Belle asks.

'Nope,' Amber chirps. 'We just need to rinse and dry. Follow me,' she instructs me, walking towards the sink.

I lie back, my head resting on the uncomfortable sink, as Amber washes my hair. I always find something very relaxing about having someone else washing my hair, but Amber obviously hasn't been taught the art of the head massage. She's sloppy, splashing water in my eyes – water that is far too cold. My headache was bad enough this morning, and that's before my hair was pulled into foil and rinsed like a dog getting a bath. As soon as we're done here I'll go pick up some painkillers, then I'll maybe take a nap and pray that I feel better. Tonight I might actually be able to get some work done!

'Right, back over here,' Amber instructs, leading the way.

I sit down in front of the mirror, but as Amber removes the towel from my hair I can't help but notice it looks a little different than usual. I mean, I know my hair is still wet, and it's pretty dark here in Dyevine, but something isn't right.

'There you go, that isn't too blonde, is it?' Amber says victoriously, in an I-told-you-so kind of way.

I shake my head silently as she begins drying my hair. At first she has me lean forwards so she can dry the underneath, but as I sit upright again the true horror of what she has done to my hair hits me. My hair is orange.

At first I can't speak. Well, what do I say? It's orange. Maybe I should say that? But Amber doesn't seem to think anything is wrong with it – she's happily blowing away.

'There,' she says when she's done. 'One sec, I'll grab the mirror.'

Amber positions a small mirror behind my head so that I can

see the back, which is also orange.

'It's a bit ... orange,' I say, my manners getting the better of me. What I want to do is hit her over the head with that mirror she's holding and yell: 'You stupid bitch, you've given me clown hair!'

'Oh, that's just the lighting in here, it's quite dark. Once you get out in that lovely sunshine you'll realise it's not much different to when you came in. Just better,' she adds.

I stare hard at the mirror. It is dark in here, but it looks orange to me. Still, I give her the benefit of the doubt and leave with the rest of the gang, but the second I step outside I take my compact from my handbag and check it out. I gasp dramatically because out here in the light it only looks even more orange.

'Holy shit, I look like Hayley Williams from Paramore,' I announce before turning on my heels and heading back in.

I march up to the front desk where Amber is stood chatting to another employee.

'So, I went outside,' I start, trying to keep my cool, 'and it looks an even brighter shade of orange.'

'You said you wanted it warm,' Amber starts.

'Yes, Amber, warm. Not on fire,' I reply through gritted teeth. 'Honey-blonde is what I asked for.'

'Well honey is orange in colour,' the other girl interjects.

'Oh, come on, everyone knows what honey-blonde looks like. It was the colour I came in with, which Amber knew.'

Amber shrugs her shoulders.

'Look, I'm Pearl, the manager here,' the other girl replies. 'And it looks to me like Amber has done what you asked for.'

'I asked for Cara Delevingne, not Coco the Clown,' I insist. 'You can't expect me to go out in public like this.'

'Well we're fully booked for the rest of the day,' she insists, although the place is currently empty.

'So, what?' I ask.

'We don't give refunds,' Pearl informs me.

'Screw the refund. Do you think I care about that? I care about walking around with disgusting-coloured hair.'

'That's offensive to gingers,' Amber tells me off.

I roll my eyes. So, I'm some sort of ginger-basher because I'm not happy with my orange hair – that's the distinction here: orange. Ginger hair is beautiful, some of the sexiest women in the world are redheads, but my hair isn't ginger, it's a very unnatural shade of orange.

'If you come back tomorrow, maybe we can run a toner through it or something,' Pearl offers reluctantly.

'Thanks, but no thanks,' I reply, storming outside where the others are waiting for me.

I'm no expert, but I'm not sure a toner is going to do much to dampen the orange fire that burning brightly on the top of my head. And even if it would, there's no way I'm letting Dyevine's two precious stones, Amber and Pearl, anywhere near my hair ever again.

Chapter 34

We drove most of the way home in silence. When my mum first clapped eyes on my hair she tactfully told me it was a 'nice change', but I gave her such a filthy look she hasn't spoken to me since. This is all her fault, really. I told her I didn't want my hair doing – several times – and she guilted me into it by making out like I'm a selfish snob. She made me feel like my relationship with my sister depended on it.

Sitting alone on the bed I share with Leo, I sigh. There's no use blaming my mum, I should have stood my ground and gone with my instincts. I should be strong enough not to give in to guilt trips, and to know that you should never trust a hairdresser with bad hair.

I grab my iPad and open up the file I need to work on. It's hard to get on with work when I'm feeling sorry for myself. The truth is that I'm devastated, but I haven't cried about my appearance since I was younger and I don't plan to start now. The last time I burst into tears was before I moved to the States. I was in the town centre when a complete stranger – who I imagine was the 'top dog' of a gang of lads – called me a minger in front of all his mates. I went home and I burst into tears, in private, like I always used to do when people called me names. When it was Belle and Nancy that were teasing me when I was younger, it wasn't so easy, finding a private place to cry. When Belle and Nancy saw my hair I think they both actually felt sorry for me, which was better than them making fun of me, but having people feeling sorry for me doesn't feel very nice either.

I abandon my work by brushing my hand across the screen and open up Google, but as I search for ways to quickly fix my hair it seems that, unless I manage to find (and trust) another local hairdresser, my only option is to buy a darker colour and go over it myself. I love my hair, and it will break my heart to dye it brown again. Maybe it's just the way I'm feeling, but going back to brown feels like I'm regressing, going back to being teenage me – perhaps I can move back in with my parents and go back to the miserable life I had before. I put my lack of confidence in the past down to not feeling good about myself. It sounds silly, but the hair just feels like the first step towards being that person again.

'Whoa,' Mike says as he peeps through the door. 'Everyone's talking about your 'do downstairs. I had to see for myself.'

'Hello Mike,' I say unenthusiastically.

'Hello Ginger Spice,' he replies, sitting down on the bed next to me. 'What are you up to?'

'I'm just wondering if Belle would be mad at me for punching her fiancé's brother in the face. What do you reckon?'

Mike laughs.

'What a fiery temper you have,' he teases as he heads for the door. 'I'll give you some space.'

Mike has no sooner closed my door behind him when I hear a knock. It will be him again so I storm over to open it, to tell him to piss off.

'If you call me any more names I'll shove this iPad up your arse,' I snap as I rip open the bedroom door, except it isn't Mike standing there, it's Leo and his mum. The three of us stand in silence for a second before I find the right words to explain myself.

'Sorry, I thought it was Mike. He's been teasing me. You don't have to knock your own door,' I tell him.

'I know, I thought you might be upset though. Are you up for visitors?'

I nod my head and let them in. I suspect the real reason he knocked is because his mum is with him, and he probably expected me to be half-naked.

'Oh, love, your hair,' Leo's mum fusses around me, despite my little violent outburst in front of her just then.

I give her a half-smile, but why are they here? Am I some sort of freak show? I'll probably have everyone up here before the night is done.

'My mum is a hairdresser,' Leo tells me. 'A really good one. She says she'll fix your hair.'

'Really?'

'We'll wait until tomorrow,' she says. 'I'll go out and get the things we need in the morning and we'll have you back to normal in no time.'

I grab Maria and I hug her, only releasing her to hug Leo too. I know that I don't know Maria very well, but I trust Leo, and if he tells me she's up to the job then I'm all for that. Anyway, if it doesn't work out, I can always head to the shops and pick up a brown dye as a last resort.

'Thank you so much,' I say to them both, my arms still around Leo's neck.

'Well, I'll head back down,' Maria says, although it seems like she's making an excuse to leave. 'Be up bright and early tomorrow,' she tells me, closing the door behind her.

I place my hands on Leo's face.

'I suppose I have you to thank for this,' I say, and he nods. I get up on my tiptoes and kiss him on the cheek. 'What would I do without you?'

Leo's cheeks flush a little.

'It's nothing,' he insists. 'So, do you think you can make it until morning?'

'I'm sure I can put up with it for one night,' I smile. 'I can't promise I won't kill anyone though.'

***

'So, do you have any plans to release another Simply Red album?' Mike asks me across the dinner table. Until now, everyone had remained tactfully silent about my outrageous orange locks, but I should have known Mike would have plenty of material to work with. I notice Leo look over at him, shooting him an angry look through narrowed eyes, but he's getting a few laughs from select others and that's enough to encourage him.

'Very funny,' I reply as I pick at my dinner. For once we're having something healthy, chicken and vegetables, and typically I have no appetite tonight.

'What's the Hamburglar like in real life?' he asks, an obvious nod to my Ronald McDonald hair.

'That one's a little dated,' I say. 'But OK.'

'Sorry, Lindsay Lohan,' he replies, and while I can't help but giggle at his unrelenting ginger jokes, his mum gets angry.

'Michael, enough,' she snaps. 'We're trying to enjoy dinner. Leave her alone.'

Mike looks down at his plate like a scolded child. With Mike no longer playing jester to the group, people start making conversation with those closest to them.

'You actually make that colour look good,' Leo says to me quietly.

'Really?' I squeak in amazement. I'm not sure anyone could make *this* colour look good.

'Yeah. You could have any hair colour, you'd still be beautiful,' he replies.

I smile at him. That's exactly what I needed to hear right now.

'Well, we'll have you back to normal soon enough,' Maria interrupts us. She's sitting across the table from us and I didn't realise she was listening. There's a strange bluntness to her reply, like she's putting an end to whatever moment I'm having with her son.

'I can't wait,' I tell her sincerely. It's strange, but it's knocking my confidence, having bad hair.

'I can't wait to meet my cake,' Belle interrupts me, addressing the whole table.

'What's the deal with this cake?' Mike asks through a mouthful of food. 'All I keep hearing about is this bloody cake.'

'Michael,' his mum warns him. He flashes me a cheeky grin before shovelling in another mouthful. I feel sort of sorry for Mike, he's the 'Mia' of his family. He's the older sibling, unmarried, and his parents seem to disapprove of his lifestyle choices and cheeky sense of humour – that certainly sounds like me to me.

'There's this bakery in Paris,' Belle explains, 'called Le Papillon, and they made this TV show about it because people travel for miles to get cakes from there. Dan knows that I love it, so he insisted we'd get our wedding cake there, didn't you, Dan?'

Dan just smiles and nods. He clearly loves Belle and and he knows how to make her happy.

The other guys might not get it, but this cake means the world to Belle. It's sweet that Dan has gone out of his way to get it for her – no one has ever done anything like that for me, unless you count the croissant a certain world-famous actor picked me up on the way back to his trailer. We were filming on location in New York and the director was a nightmare; everything had to be perfect and the Pink Inc. team had to be on hand to make changes to the script. This guy was playing the lead in the movie, and I spent most of my time on set in his trailer. One day he brought me this croissant, and although I had no intention of eating it, I appreciated the gesture because he couldn't even remember his assistant's name. He was one of the most selfish people I have ever met, so the fact he did anything at all for me felt like a big deal. Still, it doesn't compare to flying in an expensive cake from Paris. This is the life I have chosen though, and I don't keep anyone around long enough to buy me cake, so the occasional pastry from the on-set buffet table is the best I can hope for.

'I'll be sure to take lots of photos of it for you,' my mum assures my sister.

'I don't see why we're not having a proper photographer. We can afford it,' my dad reminds them, even if it is coming from my half of the wedding fund.

'Ted, we've told you a thousand times, Belle wants fun and informal snaps – selfies and what not.'

Did my mum just say 'selfies'? Today it's selfies, tomorrow it will be YOLO and twerking, just watch.

'So, is it ginger cake?' Mike asks, hardly able to contain his laughter as he does so.

'Very good,' I sigh.

'Thanks,' he replies. 'We started talking about cake, I saw my chance, I ran with it.'

I push my chair out from under the table and excuse myself.

'I don't have much of an appetite. I think I'll go get some work done.'

'Can you get me a drink first?' Mike calls after me.

'Orange juice?' I hazard a guess.

Mike's smile drops.

'It's no fun if you guess them.'

I shake my head as I leave the room. I only have to endure these jokes for a few more hours and then everything will be back to normal. I'll be counting down the minutes.

Chapter 35

'Can you make me one of those please?' my uncle asks as I fire up the coffee machine.

'Sure, what would you like?'

'A cappuccino, please.'

'Coming right up,' I tell him. I'm making a drink for Maria and myself anyway. She's about to fix my hair, so a latte is the least I can do.

Uncle Steve reads the paper at the table while I make the drinks. Being the only person who can work the machine, the last thing I need is a queue of people lining up for one.

'There you go.' I place the drink down in front of him and he thanks me.

'Mmm, that's good,' he says after taking his first sip. 'Dope hat, by the way.'

'Thanks,' I laugh. He's referring to the bright yellow SpongeBob SquarePants cap I borrowed from his son. 'I thought the yellow would offset my orange hair nicely.'

'I don't see what's wrong with your hair, it looks lovely,' he insists.

'Lovely and orange,' I remind him.

I search around the cupboards for biscuits, eventually finding a packet of chocolate digestives. I'll take these for Maria too.

'I'll never understand why women are so worried about how they look,' he says. 'Hannah spends forever in the bathroom. Then she comes out looking like a clown.'

I have noticed that my cousin is a little slap-happy, but we all go through that phase as a teen. She'll figure out what's right for her eventually.

'That's women for you,' I tell him, grabbing the latte glasses and heading for the door.

'Does Hannah seem OK to you?' he asks, and there's something about his voice, he sounds genuinely concerned. I hang back for a second.

'Yeah, I think so. She's a cool kid,' I tell him, but then I remember that conversation we had, when she mentioned a secret she didn't think she could talk to her mum about.

I take a seat next to my uncle. I should probably tell him, shouldn't I? He might be a bit of a butt-kisser, but he's not a bad person.

I open my mouth to speak, but we're interrupted.

'Why is it that whenever I can't find my husband, I eventually find him with you?'

'Talking in the kitchen.' I gasp in faux horror. 'I was just making some drinks.'

'And you made Steve one.'

'I did,' I reply confidently. 'I'll make you one if you like.'

My auntie frowns at me.

'We were just talking,' my uncle tells her.

'Yeah, I was just—'

'You two always have excuses,' she interrupts.

I have no idea why my auntie doesn't like my uncle talking to me. Yes, sometimes I misbehave, and sometimes I land myself in some strange situations, but this is just ridiculous. And I was only trying to be helpful by talking to them about Hannah. Well, fuck them. They can sort out their own problems.

Chapter 36

'Sorry I took so long,' I tell Maria as I finally arrive with our drinks, more than ready to have my hair fixed. 'I was chatting with my auntie and uncle.'

I decide not to mention what we were talking about.

'That's OK. Shall we start?'

'Oh, yes please,' I reply, taking a seat at the dressing table. We're in Leo's bedroom. He's gone for a run, giving us some privacy.

This is the first time I've had a proper conversation with Maria and she seems nice. She's quiet and much warmer than the female members of my family. She speaks softly and there's something very reassuring about the tone of her voice. Having such a lovely mum is probably why Leo turned out so well – if that's true then I never stood a chance, did I?

We chat while Maria works on my hair. It's the usual hairdresser small talk – work, holidays and the impending wedding of the summer.

'Your sister is a lovely girl,' Maria tells me.

'Yeah,' I reply. I don't mean to sound unconvincing, but Maria notices something in my voice.

'You're not too close with your family, are you?'

'Not really,' I admit. 'Even before I moved away – before I

started work, it was like no one really noticed me. I was very plain and quiet, I just blended in.'

I sigh as I think back. I remember when I bagged my first writing job. I never thought they'd want me – no one else did – so when they told me I'd got the job, I was over the moon. You might find this hard to believe, but my family were over the moon too. Suddenly unremarkable little Mia was doing something remarkable, and suddenly I existed. My dad invited the family over for a celebratory dinner, popped open a bottle of champagne – the works. For a short while I got a glimpse of a family who wanted me around. At family parties, people actually introduced me to guests I didn't know, my parents took an interest in what I was working on and, for a brief moment, I overtook Belle as far as attention goes. It didn't last though. People were impressed I had bagged the job, but when they found out I was good at it, it was like they resented me for it. I was attending big industry events and spending more and more time in London, and I don't know if people were jealous or just bored of it, but suddenly no one wanted to hear about it anymore. No one wanted much to do with me and I felt like an outsider again. That's why I moved away as soon as possible, determined to change things to try and make myself a little less unremarkable.

'Well, they notice you now,' Maria replies.

'They do – for all the wrong reasons,' I laugh.

What is it about hairdressers that compel you to tell them your deepest, darkest secrets? There's something so warm and friendly about them, you feel like you can tell them anything and everything.

'Leo notices you,' she starts, and I feel like she's going somewhere with this.

'He's such a lovely man,' I tell her. 'You should be proud.'

'I am.' Maria smiles, but her face soon falls. 'He's a lot like his dad.'

During all our lengthy conversations, Leo has always danced

around the issue of his dad. All I know is that he isn't around anymore.

'Is he?'

'Oh yes, not just in his looks, but his personality too – we even named Leo after him, we must have known.'

'What happened to him?' I ask, curiosity getting the better of me.

'Leonardo was a firefighter, that's why little Leo followed in his footsteps. One day the three of us went to the park. It was a lovely summer's day; we had the most perfect time, eating ice cream and kicking a football around. We were walking home afterwards, but as we approached the convenience shop at the end of the street you could just tell that something wasn't right. I visited the shop most days, picking up bits for tea and what have you, but that day a crowd had gathered outside. Then we smelt the smoke.'

For a moment Maria stops everything. She stops talking, stops doing my hair and I could swear she has stopped breathing.

'Of course, Leonardo wasn't officially on duty, but there was one thing he used to say to me again and again: that firemen were firemen, always on duty. So, while everyone else was running out of the building, he was running inside. There was this one woman, I'll never forget the look on her face. She lived in one of the flats upstairs and had popped downstairs to pick up something from the shop. Her little boy was still up there though and she was absolutely beside herself, she could hardly speak. Leonardo gave me a nod and in that moment I knew what he was going to do. He didn't say a word, he just disappeared inside and soon enough the little boy emerged from the smoke. I waited for Leonardo to follow him, but he didn't. Each second felt like an eternity, but I held little Leo in my arms and I waited and waited. Eventually the fire engines arrived, but it was too late.'

Maria chokes back the tears and you can tell that the wounds are still as fresh as the day this happened.

'We later found out from the little boy that Leonardo had died saving his life. Part of the building collapsed and he pushed the boy out of the way, but he ...'

Maria doesn't finish her sentence – she doesn't need to. As she reaches for another piece of my hair, I catch her hand and hold it for a second.

'He was a real hero,' I tell her.

'Leo used to say his dad was a hero, but his dad would just say that he was doing his job. Leo was eight when he lost his dad; he was robbed of so much. He clung to me after that, that's why we're so close. As he grew up, he started taking on the roles of the man of the house. He joined the fire service when he was old enough, and he still takes care of me.'

I smile. It's great that he's close with his mum, and that he takes care of her. His dad would be proud of him, and it does sound like he's inherited all his best qualities.

'I don't want you to hurt him,' Maria says assertively, wiping away the one tear that has escaped her eye.

'What?' I'm taken aback by her comment.

'We all see how the two of you are together, and I see what's coming.'

'You can see the future, can you?' I snap. I don't mean to, and I instantly regret it, but I don't like where this is going.

'I have eyes,' she snaps back. 'I see the two of you getting closer and closer – he doesn't do that lightly.'

'Look, I know he might not have the best track record with the ladies when it comes to sticking to the same one, but he's treating me like a friend, nothing more.'

'Is that what he told you?' she laughs. 'Mia, Leo isn't like that. He's terrified of getting too close to anyone so he keeps them at arm's length. I hardly ever see him with a girl at all; he doesn't want them to go through what I went through with his dad. I am his mother, I know him better than anyone, so trust me when I tell you that he is falling for you. So, what are you going to do about it?'

For a moment I just sit there, stunned. I hold eye contact with Maria in the mirror. She's just looking out for her son, but I had no idea Leo felt that way about me. He's a ridiculously handsome man, why wouldn't I believe he's some big player who loves and leaves every girl he meets? Don't get me wrong, I really like Leo, more than I've liked anyone for a long time, but the idea of being anything more than friends never entered my mind. Not just because I'm not a relationship kind of girl, but because in a matter of days I'll be going back to my life in LA and I doubt I'll ever see him again. I do care about him a lot though, and I don't want to hurt him.

'OK, point taken,' I tell her. Maria pleads at me with her eyes – she must be after a more reassuring answer. 'I'll make sure he knows the score; I'll put a bit of distance between us.'

'You'll let him down gently?' she asks.

'I will,' I reply. Well, what else can I say? I feel like I've been ambushed by sweet, little Maria. She's in the middle of doing my hair, so there's no escaping her.

We both remain silent until my hair is finished – Maria doesn't even ask me to head into the bathroom to rinse my hair, she simply nods and expects me to follow her, which I do. I just want everything to be normal again.

She finishes blow-drying my hair just as Leo gets back, and she has certainly done a good job – it looks exactly as it did before.

'How are my two favourite girls?' he asks cheerily, but in light of recent conversations, I can't even muster up a smile.

'Look at that, good as new,' he says before grabbing his mum and kissing her cheek. 'Thanks, Mum. Mia, I told you my mum would set you straight.'

'She certainly has,' I reply, exchanging a knowing glance with the woman who just warned me off her son. Now the only issue is how to tell him.

***

Maria didn't stick around for long after she tidied up. Leo hopped straight in the shower, so before his mum left she reminded me one last time to stay away from her son.

I'm sat on the bed, hugging my legs, waiting for Leo to finish up in the bathroom.

On the one hand, I don't see why I should have to stay away from him. We both know the score, we both know this is just a silly holiday thing – we're just keeping each other sane. Although his mum seems to think he has more on his mind than that. Still, if it is just a silly holiday thing then it won't be difficult to cut it off, will it? So why am I feeling so hesitant? We *have* grown close – maybe too close. Sharing secrets, spending all our time together, sleeping snuggled up and fully clothed … shit, I can see why people think we're more than friends. We're not though, are we? These feelings I'm having, it's just a friendship thing. I try to consider how I feel about my friends back in the States, but I don't have that many close friends. Well, I don't really get on with girls, and as for the guys … any time I have built up a close bond with someone, sex has got in the way and I've panicked and put a bit of distance between us. I can't explain it, but relationships are just not for me. Even if they were, I can't afford to get close to Leo.

I think about what to say. We're not a couple, so it's not like I can break up with him. What does his mum expect me to do? Tell him I don't want to play with him anymore? Tell him that his mum forbids it? We're not kids, we're adults.

'Hello blondie,' Leo says cheerily, walking out of the bathroom with nothing but a towel around his waist. This would probably be a lot easier if he had a top on.

'Hello. Can we have a quick chat?'

'This doesn't sound good,' he laughs as he sits down next to me, but as he notices the serious look on my face, his smile vanishes. 'What's up?'

'Belle says I can have my room back, so I just thought I'd let you know you're getting your bed back.'

'You don't have to, you know. I've kind of gotten used to having you around; the bed will seem empty without you.'

What might have seemed like a cheeky, flirty remark yesterday, seems very sweet today. As I think about the way Leo is with me, something hits me: he *is* falling for me. The way he defends me, helps me out, strokes my cheek when we look into each other's eyes and the way he plays with my hair as we chat … no one has ever treated me that way before.

'You'll get over it,' I joke. 'After the next few days are over, you'll probably never see me again.'

'And you're OK with that?' he asks seriously.

I have to be OK with it.

'Course.' I smile, grabbing the bag I filled with my things while he was in the shower. 'See you around.'

And with that, I disappear. As I walk towards my bedroom, my heart feels kind of heavy. I'm doing the right thing though. I don't want a boyfriend and if that's where he thinks this is going, then it's only right I nip it in the bud. It's called being cruel to be kind, isn't it? So why don't I feel at all kind right now?

Chapter 37

After a fairly uneventful evening and a night in my own bed – alone – I woke up feeling restless at six a.m. I laid there for an hour, just thinking about things – mostly how I can't wait to go home – before getting up and dressed. I'm going to pop downstairs, grab a coffee and then sit in my room and work all day. I promised my boss that I would work while I was away and so far I haven't written one word, things just keep getting in my way. It's the rehearsal dinner tonight, and I imagine tomorrow will be busy, so today is my last chance to get something done.

As I reach the bottom of the stairs, I notice my cousin Hannah heading out the front door.

'Hey cuz, where are you headed?' I ask.

'I'm just popping to the shops for some stuff,' she tells me, but there's something shifty about her. I know I said that I was going to leave that lot to sort out their own shit, but I just can't.

'I'll come with you,' I tell her. 'I fancy some exercise.'

'It's not even that far to the shops,' she tells me, but I won't be put off.

'I need to pick up some stuff too,' I insist. 'I'll grab my bag.'

My cousin is unable to hide her annoyance.

'So,' I start as we walk down the street, 'how are you?'

'I'm cool. You?'

'Yeah, I'm good,' I tell her, suspecting that neither of us is telling the truth. 'Fancy grabbing a coffee after this?'

'That would be cool,' she replies with a smile. Her phone beeps for the billionth time, which isn't unusual for a fifteen-year-old girl, but she looks worried as she reads it. I'm going to have to find some way of getting her to open up – I'd get her drunk but my auntie would probably have something to say about my interrogation techniques.

We stroll around a few shops, neither of us picking anything up, before I spy a nice-looking coffee bar across the street.

'Shall we go there?' I ask.

'Sure, I just need to pop in here.' My cousin nods towards the pharmacy behind us. I don't say anything, prompting her to continue. 'Time of the month,' she tells me.

'Oh, not while you're on holiday,' I sympathise. 'Shall I come in with you?'

'It's cool, you go order the drinks.'

'Sure. Latte?'

'Please,' she replies, disappearing into the shop behind us.

Poor girl, she must not like talking about it. My mum has never wanted to talk about things like that with me. It's a good job they gave us 'the talk' at school or I probably would've been terrified when it finally kicked in. My auntie must be that way too, which doesn't surprise me. My money would be on that or the extreme opposite, having a chart up in the kitchen for the girls to track their cycles with little star stickers.

I do as instructed. It isn't long before Hannah joins me.

'So, do you have a boyfriend?' I ask. Full-on prying is the only way I'm going to get anywhere, but my cousin looks hesitant. 'Don't worry, I won't tell your mum.'

'Sort of,' she replies.

'Sort of,' I repeat. 'I hear that.'

'Is Leo your sort of boyfriend?' she asks. 'He is well fit. I would.'

'Would you really?' I laugh. I like Hannah, she's a Mia in the making. Perhaps when I go home and she gets a bit older she can take over my role as the family's least favourite.

She nods her head.

'So why do you only "sort of" have a boyfriend?' I ask.

'Well, I'm not sure if he really likes me or if he just wants me for …'

'Ah, got it. Well, guys can be like that.' Girls can be too. 'You've just got to see what happens, you'll soon find out if he's genuine.'

'So, if I sleep with him and he sticks around then he's cool, but if not he only wanted one thing,' she thinks out loud.

'You don't have to sleep with anyone,' I tell her. 'Listen to me, only do what *you* want to do. If you want to wait then tell him that, and if he's cool he'll stick around. If he isn't up for waiting, then you can do better.'

'That makes more sense,' she giggles. 'Thanks, Mia. You're pretty cool.'

'You're part of a very small and exclusive group that believe that,' I tell her, and she laughs.

'Did you really sleep with Leo?' she asks me. I'm not sure if she maybe has a bit of a crush on him, but who could blame her?

'Yes,' I tell her quietly, probably because I'm not sure I should be telling her at all.

'But you guys don't want to be together?'

'Well, we can't be together, it's too difficult,' I tell her. 'We live so far apart.'

'But if you love each other, you make it work,' she says casually. 'Like in your movies, the couple always end up together.'

It hasn't escaped my notice that my life is starting to resemble one of my movies, although unlike my leading ladies, I'm not about to learn some valuable, life-changing lesson towards the end. In my movies the couples always end up together because we make them end up together, because women wouldn't pay to see film after film about heartbreak and dying alone. No matter what the circumstances in the movies I write, there's always a way to give the couples a happy ever after. It doesn't matter how farfetched or unrealistic it may seem, the people who watch these flicks are willing to suspend their disbelief if it means a happy ending. Life isn't a romcom though, and even I can't think of a happy ending for this story.

Chapter 38

The rehearsal dinner is finally upon us. I'm in Belle's room, helping her get ready along with my mum, my auntie and Nancy. Belle is sitting in a chair while we all fuss around her, doing whatever she asks. She looks like a pampered queen sitting on her throne while her subjects run around after her.

'I haven't seen you and Leo spending as much time together today,' Belle observes. 'You two OK?'

'We're fine,' I reply, aware that everyone is listening.

I am saved from going into further detail when Heather burst into the room.

'Disaster. Does anyone have a tampon or a pad? I've been caught by surprise.'

It just goes to show that, even though Heather is much older than Hannah, we never quite get the hang of these things.

No one in the room offers to help her out, so I make a helpful suggestion.

'Maybe try Hannah.'

'You'll have no luck there,' my auntie insists. 'She's not due on for a couple of weeks yet.'

What did I tell you, she'd be one of the two extremes. Hannah must have forgotten to mark the family chart last month, tut-tut.

'I'll have to pop to the shops,' Heather sighs, dashing out of the room as fast as she came in.

'My doctor gave me something so that my period didn't ruin my wedding day,' my sister informs us all.

'Really?' I reply, not actually wanting to know.

'Yeah, it's like when they send those planes up to clear the sky of clouds before a festival.'

There's an obvious joke to be made, but my mother pre-empts my dirty mind and shoots me a warning glance not to make it. I wasn't even going to, I'm just happy to be on better terms with my sister. If one good thing has come from this holiday, it's that.

'So, you and Leo,' my sister persists.

'What? I don't have to spend every minute with him, do I?'

'It's preferable to you spending all that time with my husband,' my auntie interrupts. 'Those little talks you're always having, shutting up when I walk into the room.'

'Mia, what *do* you talk to Steve about?' my mum asks curiously.

'You mean my uncle?' I remind them. 'Nothing – we hardly talk. He asks about my job and LA and stuff. He keeps telling me things are dope. Am I not allowed to talk to my uncle now?'

'Mia, go and ask your dad what time he needs us downstairs, will you,' my mum asks, diffusing the situation.

'Are you sure you can trust me to talk to your husband?' I ask sarcastically as I head for the door.

'Don't be vulgar, Mia,' my mum scolds me.

Downstairs the house is buzzing with people getting things ready for the rehearsal dinner.

I run my hand along the beautifully set table as I pass it, reading the name cards to see who is sitting where. A second after I see my name, I notice Leo's and he's going to be sitting right next to me. My heart jumps into my mouth. Would anyone notice if I changed the seating plan a little? I mean, it's only the rehearsal dinner, and I doubt anyone would even notice. I wait until no one is looking and quickly swap Leo's card with another.

'Mia,' my dad says in his usual blunt manner.

'Father,' I reply, echoing his enthusiasm. 'Mother would like to know what time we're kicking off.'

'I'll go and have a word,' he tells me. He gives me a nod before heading upstairs. A nod is my dad's take on a hug and he doesn't give them out lightly.

Not wanting to get in the way, I head into the living room and plonk myself down on the sofa. I'm wearing a very short red dress that doesn't seem to want to protect my modesty, no matter how much I try and tug it down, and a very high pair of heels. I'm careful to dangle my feet over the side of the sofa so that the spikes don't damage the leather.

'Wow,' I hear my uncle say. 'Dope dress. Like something you'd wear to a movie preimer, I'll bet?'

Again with the word dope.

'Erm, thanks,' I say awkwardly, sitting up straight and crossing my legs.

'I'm sorry June is giving you a hard time,' he tells me. 'She's just threatened by you, I think. She's a bit funny about all women – we think it's *the change*.'

I mean, she doesn't seem like she's changed to me, this feels pretty on-brand for her.

'Ah, it's fine,' I reply. 'I think, as her husband, you're supposed to dislike me too. Out of loyalty.'

'She doesn't dislike you,' he tells me. 'She's just … struggling.'

'Speaking of struggling, I wanted to talk to you. It's about Hannah,' I start, but once again I don't get to finish.

'You two, *again*,' my auntie moans.

'Oh here we go,' I say under my breath.

'Well,' she prompts, expecting some sort of explanation.

'Well, what?' I reply.

'Less of your attitude, Mia. I'm getting very tired of it,' my auntie says through gritted teeth.

'You're not the only one,' I reply, standing up as ladylike as possible, although it's hard when you're having to keep yanking your dress down. In hindsight, maybe it is a little too short.

I remind myself that the wedding is imminent. I can go home the day after and then who cares what this lot think of me? I can go back to the lovely sunny weather, writing movies and spending my time with handsome actors who don't want to learn my name, let alone snuggle me all night.

Chapter 39

If the big event goes anything like the rehearsal, then things are going to be just fine. Everyone is well, mobile, present and correct. The dinner isn't going too badly either. It turns out I swapped Leo's name card with Mike's, so we've been joking around and having loads of fun. Leo is sitting with Nancy, and despite our new sort-of friendship she's in full-on flirting mode which isn't easy to watch – not that I'm letting on.

'You know, the ginger jokes really made me realise just how funny I can be,' Mike jokes to me.

'Well, I'm back to blonde now,' I reply.

'It also made me realise that I know far more blonde jokes than I do ginger jokes, so let the laughs continue, Barbie.'

'Oh good,' I reply sarcastically, but I can't help but laugh. Say what you want about Mike, but he's kept me amused from day one.

'What does a blonde say if you blow in her ear?' he asks.

'I don't know, what?'

'Thanks for the refill,' he replies, laughing at his own joke.

Mike leans closer to me and takes a break from chuckling to blow in my ear. I laugh it off and give him a playful shove, but it's only as he moves away from me that I notice Leo giving us the filthiest look. Seeing that look on his face causes my heart to jump into my mouth. I pick up my wine to take a sip, although I'll probably need more than a sip to block out the pesky rush of emotions suddenly bubbling in my chest.

'I doubt Mia will ever marry,' I overhear my mum say, taking my mind off Leo and dragging me into her conversation.

'You don't?' I ask. I don't either, but I'd be interested to hear whatever fantastically offensive reasoning she has for saying so.

'It's not that I don't think you could find a husband,' my mum assures me.

'No, they do always seem willing,' my auntie adds.

'It's just that you're more of a …' my mum pauses to think of the appropriate term. '… a good-time girl.'

I laugh. Spectacularly offensive, but she might be right.

'Well, it's like Michael,' Dan's mum joins in, happy to participate in a subject that seems rather inappropriate to chat about during a wedding rehearsal. 'He's thirty,' she mouths his age, rather than say it out loud, like the big three-oh is a dirty word.

'Thanks, Mum,' Mike laughs, he's taking it in good humour like me – even if that's not the way it is intended.

'All I'm saying is that you're getting older, you refuse to get married and you work in a computer game shop,' she continues. This comment finally gets to Mike and his face falls. 'At least Mia has a well-paid job, even if she doesn't have a man.'

The table falls awkwardly silent as everyone stares at Mike, the unmarried freak with no prospects in life. I feel terrible for him because he's not a bad person. He's got a great sense of humour and he's so much fun, and while I may not be into his scruffy style, he's quite a good-looking guy – any girl would be lucky to have him.

'Remember the time I let the kids watch *Pulp Fiction*,' I blurt out.

'Yes, it was a matter of days ago and I think people are still pretty upset about it,' my sister fumes. 'Why would you bring that up?'

'She's an attention seeker,' June reasons.

The attention shifts from Mike back to me. No one thinks much of it – it's like pantomime, they love to hiss and boo me – but Mike realises I've taken a bullet for him and he reaches under the table and squeezes my hand. I smile at him, happy to have done it. In a couple of days, I'll be back home and he'll be stuck with this lot. I'm happy to take the heat.

I glance over at Leo almost on autopilot – I've been doing it all night – and notice that he's watching us, and boy does he look unimpressed. I quickly let go of Mike's hand, banging my own on the table in the process and catching the attention of the others.

'What are you two doing under the table?' my sister asks, like we're a couple of naughty kids, although I suspect she secretly thinks the hand job queen is striking again.

'We were shaking hands,' Mike tells her. 'If we're not married by the time we're forty, we'll marry each other.'

His mum nearly chokes on her glass of wine.

'Over my dead body,' she scoffs, and if she keeps saying things like that, it could almost certainly be arranged.

***

Another awkward dinner done and dusted, now almost everyone is heading to the pub for celebratory drinks and more bonding.

'You coming in the taxi with us?' Leo asks me as he heads for the door. Obviously, because there are so many of us, it's going to take several taxis to get us all to the pub. The thing is, tonight really is my last opportunity to get any work done, so I have to take it. If I go back to LA without having done any work at all my boss will go mad, and I'm already in his bad books. The grandparents aren't going and the kids are staying here too. It's getting late so everyone will be in bed and it will be nice and quiet, I'll be able to get loads done.

'I think I'll stay and do some work,' I tell him. 'Have fun though.'

I hadn't meant to sound so casual and cold, but I did, and

Leo doesn't look happy. He nods across the room, instructing me to follow him.

'What's going on?' he asks after taking me to one side.

'What do you mean?' I ask.

'I mean, you're avoiding me. What's wrong?'

'Nothing. I'm not avoiding you, I need to work.'

'You've needed to work this entire time,' he reminds me, 'but you haven't, you've been hanging out with me, and now you've stopped.'

'I have work to do,' I tell him again, sounding no more convincing than the first time I said it. I *do* have work to do, but that's not why I've been avoiding him.

'You've found time for Mike,' he says, a slightly accusatory tone to his voice.

'You're jealous?' I ask.

'I just don't understand what's going on here.' He takes me by the hands. 'Mia, I like you and I know that you like me, so why are you pushing me away?'

I exhale deeply. Had his mum not warned me this would happen, a comment like that would have totally floored me. The fact that I knew this was coming doesn't mean I feel any less anxious about what I have to do next though.

'Suddenly we're liking each other – how old are you?' I ask cruelly. 'We both knew the score when we met, so why are you getting all clingy?' Cruel to be kind, cruel to be kind. 'Maybe I'm just bored of you now.'

Leo lets go of my hands, laughs and shakes his head.

'You tell yourself that if you want to, Mia, but I think you like me just as much as I like you. You just don't want to admit it. Stay here and do your work, you know where I am when you're ready to accept it.'

And with that, he leaves. Everyone leaves or goes to bed, leaving me all alone.

I am so angry, I want to scream and swear and smash things.

How infuriating is that man? Thinking I'm in love with him and just kidding myself. What an egotistical arsehole. He'll sit down in the pub with his pint and laugh and joke with his friends and family, thinking I'm just being stubborn and that I'll go running back to him, begging him to be with me. I shake my head. Not tonight, mister. Not tonight, not tomorrow, not ever. I'm going to take a stroll and see if I can find sexy Chris the lifeguard. I think I need a little mouth to mouth resuscitation.

Chapter 40

My sort-of holiday sort-of romance is like the one I always wanted but never had as a teenager. Sneaking around behind the family's back and most of our romantic moments playing out on the beach – well, Chris removing my knickers in the sea while he did impressions from *Pirates of the Caribbean* wasn't that romantic, but you know what I mean. Like a technology-free holiday romance from years back, Chris and I never swapped numbers. He knows where I'm staying but I don't know exactly where he lives, so I'm not sure how I'm going to locate him. I know he doesn't live too far from Shell's Café, but I headed down that way without seeing a soul. What did I think was going to happen, that he'd be strolling around on the beach just waiting for me to pounce on him?

It's late, and with Shell's Café being closed up for the night, things are eerily quiet down this end of the beach. I should probably head back to the house.

As I walk along the beach, I have nothing but my thoughts and the waves splashing at my feet to keep me company.

Leo thinks he's got me all figured out. He thinks I'm deeply in love with him – as deep as this sea – and that I'm just kidding myself. Why is it so hard for people to believe that I don't want a boyfriend of *any* description? Much less one who lives thousands of miles from me.

I wonder why it is that I'm so angry. Why don't I just leave him to think what he wants? He'll soon realise he's wrong when I'm over five thousand miles away and he isn't getting so much as a like on Instagram from me. For a split second, I consider just how much I feel for Leo. Could it be possible that I like him like he likes me? Am I even capable of feeling that way about a man? I am distracted by my thoughts when I realise I'm not alone out here.

As I approach the house I see a shadowy figure sitting on the steps leading up the back door. As I get closer I realise it's Mike. He's drinking vodka and looking very sorry for himself.

'Not enjoying the company at the pub?' I ask.

'I'd much rather be here with my friend, vodka,' he tells me, raising a silent toast before taking a swig.

Uh-oh, something must be wrong.

'Can I have some?' I ask, sitting down on the step next to him.

'Any friend of vodka is a friend of mine,' he tells me, handing me the bottle. I take a swig before passing it back to him.

'So, what's up?' I ask.

'Were you not at dinner?' he asks me. 'When my mum told everyone what a loser I am?'

I notice a towel on the wall, probably left by one of the group earlier – I don't care either way. I grab it, dry my feet and slip my heels back on.

'Wait, let me get my shoes back on, I want to look my best for your pity party,' I tease.

'Very funny,' he replies. 'That was so fucking embarrassing, you've got to admit.'

'My mum, gran, auntie – entire family – tell people what a loser I am at every opportunity. They just don't get that we want to live different lives to them.'

'My mum thinks I should be married, making babies and working some boring job.'

'As does mine,' I remind him.

'So, we're both losers,' he concludes, taking another drink.

'I don't know, I have a pretty cool job, I don't work in a computer game shop,' I joke, doing my best impression of his mum. Mike finally smiles.

'Ah, there we go, I got a smile out of you. I'll drink to that.'

I grab the bottle and take another hit. It's powerful stuff; I'm feeling a little lightheaded already. I don't think it's mixing well with the wine I had with dinner.

'Thanks for earlier, for getting them off my back,' he says.

'Ah, it was nothing. I didn't need to try too hard, no one likes me.'

'I like you,' he tells me, looking deep into my eyes.

For a moment, we just stare at each other. Apart from the sound of the waves, it's very quiet out here. The house is pretty much in darkness but the moon is so bright. You know, Mike really is quite handsome.

It's almost as though he is reading my mind. Mike takes one big swig of vodka before discarding the bottle, grabbing my face and kissing me passionately. His approach may be a little sloppy, but I kiss him back. He's a good-looking guy, we're both single (oh-so single, as we are constantly reminded) and I actually want to do it. By kissing Mike, I am proving to myself that I don't have any feelings for Leo, and the reassurance feels good – the kissing feels good too, Mike is pretty good at this. Frantically passionate to the point of being a little on the rough side, but I'm not complaining.

Mike pushes me back against the hard steps before pressing down on top of me. As he fumbles with my clothes, I realise what a terrible mistake we're making.

'Wait,' I say, my words sounding muffled because he won't stop kissing me, not even for a second. 'We can't do this, not here. We should go inside.'

'Good thinking,' he replies, releasing me from his grip and

chasing me up the steps. Well, the last thing we need is for some poor dog walker to see us, call the police and land me in all sorts of trouble less than forty-eight hours before the wedding. Imagine that.

We sneak in through the back door, into the almost pitch-black kitchen.

'Right here,' Mike insists. 'I can't wait long enough to take you upstairs.'

I shush him and listen carefully. The house is not only in darkness, it's in complete silence. The oldies and the kids will surely be asleep and I imagine everyone else will be at the pub for quite a while yet.

For a moment, we stand and stare at each other. It's too dark to see much, but I can hear Mike breathing heavily, I can feel his body pressing against mine – and then our lips meet again.

We stand there kissing for a while before I feel Mike's lips travel to my neck and then down my body. Kneeling in front of me, he runs his hands up my legs, takes hold of my knickers, pulls them down and then removes them.

'Do you know why blondes wear knickers?' he asks in a whisper.

'Why?' I reply.

'To keep their ankles warm,' he tells me, coming back up to eye-level and stuffing them down my cleavage.

'They won't keep my ankles warm there,' I tell him.

'Well, we'll just have to find another way to keep you warm,' he replies.

Mike's brief yet effective moment of slow-paced seduction is over. He grabs me by the hips and pushes me back towards the kitchen counter, lifting me up and sitting me down on top of it.

As he unbuttons his trousers and moves in close I wrap my legs around his waist, but I can't get comfortable.

'What have you sat me on,' I ask, practically talking into his mouth as we kiss. 'It feels really wet.'

'You're just really into it,' he jokes. He clearly couldn't give a damn, but whatever it is, I hope it doesn't ruin my dress.

He may not be as strong or as hot as Leo, but Mike certainly knows what he's doing – why am I even thinking about Leo? He's not important right now, all that matters is that I was right. I feel nothing for him, right? No, this doesn't feel right, this feels wrong and I need to stop this before this kiss goes too far ... but I don't get the chance.

I notice the kitchen light turn on a split second before I hear Dan's voice.

'Surprise,' I hear him call out, followed by a number of shocked gasps.

We both freeze, neither of us daring to look.

'What the hell is going on?' Belle shouts.

I finally look towards the kitchen doorway and see that Belle, Dan, my mum, my auntie and Mike's mum are all standing there.

'It's not what it looks like,' Mike blurts out, still pressed up against me, my legs still locked around his waist.

'Really?' Belle asks. 'Because it kind of looks like you're bumping uglies with my sister in the kitchen.'

'It's like a sexy version of Cluedo,' I whisper into Mike's ear and he chuckles briefly. I know that this is a fairly awkward situation, but it's just sex – well, nearly sex. To be honest I'm glad someone else stopped things, because I'm not sure how I would've let Mike down gently after coming to my senses.

'Do you think this is funny?' Harriet asks. I know she's a bit of a prude, but her son is thirty and unmarried, you'd think she'd be pleased to see him interact with a member of the opposite sex.

'You should be ashamed of yourself,' she tells him before pointing at me. 'And you're a harlot.'

'How could you, Mia?' I hear my own mum ask.

'Oh, come on, we're all adults, and we were only kissing. No harm done,' I insist. Despite Mike's trousers being undone, they're still up around his waist and no one knows I'm missing my knickers – again. These guys really need to lighten up.

'Do you think Mike's girlfriend will think there's no harm done when she finds out?' Harriet asks angrily.

Wait, Mike's single, isn't he? I look at him and wait for him to put his mum right, but he doesn't.

'Mike, you don't have a girlfriend, do you?' I ask.

'Sort of,' he replies.

'And he "sort of" has for the past four years,' his mum adds.

'You told me you were single,' I say quietly through gritted teeth.

'No, I told you I wasn't married. My mum goes on at me to pop the question, but I don't want that, I—' he begins to explain, but now isn't the time.

'I tell you what, you can explain this little misunderstanding to me later, when we're not practicallly joined at the crotch, surrounded by our families,' I reply. 'In fact, now might be the time to let go,' I suggest helpfully.

'I can't, can I? Everyone will see.'

I shake my head in disbelief. He's still standing so close to me because he's worried he'll flash when he fastens his trousers. Surely that's the least of his worries.

'You think we have any modesty left?' I ask him, shaking my head before burying my face in his chest. I want the ground to swallow me up.

'Leo,' I hear Belle squeak.

I look up and follow her gaze across the room to where Leo is sitting.

'How long have you been there?' I ask in astonishment.

'Longer than you've been sitting there,' he tells me. With all the arguing going on, none of us even noticed he was in the room.

'I came looking for you,' he tells me. 'When I couldn't find you I thought I'd sit up and wait for you to get back. When you guys came in you didn't even notice I was here.'

'So, you were just sitting in the dark?' I ask angrily. 'Why didn't you say something?'

'You were having too much fun,' he replies. 'And you have no right to angrily quiz me.'

'Wait, was this my surprise?' Belle asks Dan. 'Because this isn't funny at all.'

'No, no,' Dan babbles. 'I brought you all to see the cake.'

'Well, where is it?' Belle asks.

Dan, who isn't the sharpest knife in the drawer, scratches his head as he tries to remember where he put this cake, and he remembers where he left it around the time I realise that the soft, wet sticky something I am sitting on is my sister's wedding cake. The custom made, one-of-a-kind, ordered months ago and flown in from Paris cake that Dan spent a ridiculous amount of money on to make Belle's day perfect.

We exchange concerned glances. I can't be sitting on top of the cake, can I?

Up until now, things were weirdly calm. People were angry, but in that reserved way English people have perfected – not mad, disappointed – but as Belle slowly approaches me, she learns the fate of her cake.

Mike is still pressed against me, so with nowhere to run my sister is able to fully express her rage, blindly slapping us both using both hands.

'Get them off it, get them off it,' she cries as Dan and my mum try to restrain her.

'It's too late now,' my mum tells her softly.

You're damn right it is. I have icing so far up my butt I can taste it. This cake is a write-off, I've inadvertently helped Mike cheat on his long-term girlfriend and Leo looks both distraught and furious having watched me getting off with his best friend's brother. Everyone is looking at me like I'm the most disgusting person in the world, my sister is crying her eyes out and if Mike doesn't get his cake-covered crotch away from me right now, I will rip *it* off with my bare hands.

Leo storms out of the back door, slamming it behind him.

Everyone else filters out of the kitchen and it takes several minutes before I can no longer hear my sister's crying. It's just the two of us now.

'I don't suppose you want to finish?' Mike jokes as he swipes a little frosting up with his finger and tastes it. At least I hope he's joking.

'Get off me before I shove the rest of this cake up *your* arse,' I warn him.

Mike does as he is told, finally releasing me before pulling his pants up and running upstairs.

Finally alone, I hop down off the counter and examine the cake. You can't even call it a cake any more, it's just the remains of something delicious-smelling with my butt-print right in the middle of it. Thank God there wasn't a little plastic bride and groom on top.

In my defence, the room was very dark and it's quite a small cake. It didn't stand a chance, but letting Dan carry my heavy case, showing the kids *Pulp Fiction*, jinxing the wedding, hitting my sister in the face with a rounders ball – none of that compares to this. This really takes the cake.

Chapter 41

There is cake everywhere. It's all over the counter, the floor – me! I have cake in places I didn't think possible. It can't have been a very big cake, which only makes me feel worse. As expensive, TV show worthy cakes go, this one was in their budget and I've literally fucked it. I suppose that's why it was so easy for Mike to plonk me down on top of it, the fact it wasn't that big. I'd guess there were two tiers. Maybe. The only reason I know it was a cake is because it smells like buttercream and because my sister repeatedly cried out 'my cake, my cake' as they carried her upstairs.

Completely unsalvageable, I scoop the cake into a plastic bag and wipe myself down as best I can. Now I have a choice to make: I can run upstairs and apologise to my sister or I can go out and search the beach for Leo. One thing I know for sure, is that it did not feel good doing that to Leo. It wasn't my intention for him to watch me kissing someone else, but I was doing it to prove that I feel nothing for him. So why do I feel so bad? A pattern has occurred to me: when I'm around my family, they give me such a hard time I end up doing stupid stuff like this … which only seems to give them more reason to be mad at me. It's a never-ending cycle.

I decide to go and speak to Belle – she's my sister. Leo can wait.

I practically tiptoe up the stairs, ever so cautiously just in case my sister thought to booby-trap the place in case something like this were to happen. I don't have to hover on the landing wondering which room she is in for long, because I can hear her sobbing loud and clear. I have upset her so many times in the short time I have been here, but this time I take full responsibility. I didn't do it on purpose, but I did do it, and I have to apologise.

I knock on the door and wait to be called in. No one shouts, but my mum shuffles out to talk to me.

'She doesn't want to see you, Mia. Just go to bed,' she tells me sternly. 'Your own, if you don't mind.'

'I suppose I deserved that,' I start, 'but I just want the chance to apologise.'

My mum opens the bedroom door a small amount, just loud enough for me to see my sister crying.

'Do you think apologising will do anything to mend that?' she asks me and I shake my head.

'Let her in,' Belle calls out.

My mum does as she asks and reluctantly leaves the two of us alone to talk.

Belle is sitting up in bed, surrounded by used tissues. Her eyes are full with tears that turn black as they escape her eyes, leaving her with a face of messed up makeup that Alice Cooper would be proud to rock.

I sit at the end of her bed, as far from her as physically possible. She scared me a little when she started hitting me – she just went wild. All sense and reason went out of the window, her emotions and her anger got the better of her and I don't know what she would have done if people weren't around to stop her.

'I'm sorry,' I start, knowing that my mum is right, that sorry won't be good enough, but it's all I've got right now.

'Well, as long as you're sorry,' she sobs sarcastically. 'Is that for destroying my cake, cheating with Mike or breaking Leo's heart?'

All of the above.

'The thing is,' I start, and my sister rolls her eyes. 'The cake thing was a complete accident, you know I wouldn't do that on purpose. Mike didn't tell me he had a girlfriend, and no one else has mentioned her to me, so how could I have known that? And as for Leo …'

My sentence trails off as I struggle to find the right words to come next. My sister stares at me expectantly.

'After talking to his mum, I realised Leo might be thinking something was happening that wasn't, so I needed to nip that in the bud.'

'And you had to do that by having sex on my cake in front of him?' she snaps.

'No, look, we didn't have sex, we just kissed. I didn't know Leo was there. And that wasn't for his benefit, it was for mine.'

'Nice.'

'Not like that,' I insist. 'Look, I don't do feelings or relationships, this is hard for me. I needed to prove to myself that I didn't have any of those kinds of feelings for Leo.'

'By having sex on my cake?'

I sigh.

'And did you prove that to yourself?' she asks.

'Yes,' I lie. The truth is, I thought I was proving it to myself but even if we hadn't been interrupted, I knew there was no way I'd have been able to go through with it. And as soon as I realised Leo was there to see it, all kinds of feelings kicked in that I'm not used to feeling. I feel embarrassed, not because I was caught kissing, but because of who I was kissing and who we were caught by. I feel guilty for hurting so many people; my heart feels like it has dropped right down in the deepest part of my body. And then there's the way I feel about Leo … I *do* feel strongly about him, stronger than I have ever felt about anyone, but is it worth acting on when we live so far apart? Is it love? How are you supposed to know? No one tells you what love feels like. I mean, I write about it often enough in my movies – it's like walking on air, butterflies in your stomach, the best feeling in the world with your heart full of joy, etc. – but that's fiction, it's rubbish I write to sell movies to hopeless romantics. I certainly don't feel any of those things. I don't feel like I'm walking on air, I feel like I'm trying to balance on a tightrope with no safety harness. I don't feel like I have butterflies in my stomach, I feel like I've been trapped on a malfunctioning rollercoaster for twelve hours. And as for the so-called best feeling in the world, my heart doesn't feel like it's full of joy, it feels like it's made of really thin, fragile glass that could shatter at the slightest touch.

'Oh, well, at least you're sorted,' my sister says sarcastically, a terrifying false smile plastered across her face to help get her point across.

'I'm far from sorted,' I reply.

'My God, it's all about me me *Mia*!' she shouts, jumping out of bed. 'You come here, you ruin my wedding, you sleep with *everyone*! And then you're all "poor me, I need to sleep with more people just in case I'm in love".'

As my sister approaches me angrily, my mum rushes back into the room and gets between us.

'Just leave,' she insists, and I think it's for my own safety as well as because I am upsetting Belle. I have never seen my sister so hurt and angry in my entire life.

Well, there's my failed attempt to smooth things over with Belle. Now I can go and find Leo, I'm sure he'll be equally as pleased to see me.

Chapter 42

I woke up thinking last night must have been a terrible nightmare, that there's no way it could have happened, but as I spied my cake-stained dress on the floor, I knew that it absolutely did.

After having no luck with Belle last night, I went out looking for Leo. I didn't find him, but that's probably for the best. I didn't know what I was going to say to him anyway. Babbling 'sorry I got off with another guy in front of you, it's just I know you like me and I was scared I liked you so I had to prove a point to myself' probably won't cut it.

It's only two days until the wedding, and as much as I want to hide away, I only have to tough it out for a little longer and then I can go home and write this off as a holiday from hell. But, as I walk into the kitchen where lots of people are gathered, I realise that it's not going to be that easy. As I headed downstairs I could hear the kitchen buzzing with people, I could hear chatting, cutlery on plates, the clinking of mugs … now that I'm here, everyone is silent, which means everyone knows. There isn't even the slightest trace of the cake. I had cleaned up as best I could, including the base it was sitting on, which I left on the table. That's gone too.

'Hi,' I say, but no one replies. Not Belle, my mum, Maria,

Nancy, my gran or Dan's mum Harriet so much as give me an acknowledging nod. It's all women in here, and I wonder if the men would judge me as harshly – women can be so judgmental of other women. Then I remember it's not the act that's making them mad, it's the who, the where and the why.

'Is there anything I can do today?' I ask.

'Yes, pop over to Paris and pick me up a replacement cake,' Belle snaps.

I suppose I deserved that, but I do want to help.

'What *are* you doing about a cake?' Harriet asks her future daughter-in-law.

'I don't even want one now,' she replies. 'I'm just not going to bother. It's just one more thing for Mia to ruin.'

I open my mouth to protest, about how it was an accident and how I would never do anything like that on purpose, but a furious looking Auntie June bursts into the room and I don't get a chance to speak.

'Something you want to tell us?' my auntie yells, and I realise she's talking to me.

'Me? No.' I don't know what else to say.

She nods down towards my outfit. I'm wearing a pair of denim shorts and a bikini top because the plan was to go for a long walk on the beach, to give everyone some space. I self-consciously run my hands down my body. I didn't think I was dressed too inappropriately, certainly not for the beach, and definitely no worse than the way I've been dressing this entire time.

'About this,' she says as she thrusts something white and plastic towards me, holding it just inches from my face. I have to take a step back just to focus on it, it was that close to me. That's when I realise it's a pregnancy test – I've never seen one in real life before, I've never had reason to – and that she wasn't nodding towards my outfit, she was nodding towards my womb, and unless some cake found its way up there, it's definitely empty.

'Eww, get that out of my face,' I tell her with an awkward laugh.

No one has ever waved a pregnancy test in my face before, I'm not sure what I'm supposed to say.

'Where did you get that?' my mum asks her.

'In the downstairs bathroom, in the bin. It's positive.'

Under normal circumstances I'd ask why she was rooting around in the bathroom bin, but she seems quite angry, I'd best not antagonise her.

'It's not mine,' I squeak in amazement. 'Why would you think it was mine?'

'You used the bathroom yesterday,' she replies.

'Everyone used the bathroom yesterday,' I reason, although my auntie has another reason up her sleeve.

'You're the only one who is … promiscuous.'

I feel almost grateful she paused to find an appropriate word, but I don't like what she's suggesting. And why would she assume I wasn't careful? As if I'd risk getting pregnant, I can hardly take care of myself. A baby would ruin my life right now, so of course I use protection. Not that it's any of her business.

'You have been sleeping with everyone,' my sister interjects, and everyone stares at me.

My jaw drops in shock, does everyone think it's mine? I know that I didn't take that test, so who did? No one in the room is speaking up or looking guilty: most of the other female relatives are probably too old, Heather was frantically looking for tampons last night so it's not hers … that's when it hits me. I know who took that test and I know who is pregnant. It's Hannah. I thought she was being odd, sneaking off to the pharmacy, and her mum knew her period wasn't now – that must be what's wrong with her at the moment, and the thing she told me she was too scared to tell her mum. As Auntie June stares at me angrily, the test still held up accusingly in front of my eyes, I'm not surprised Hannah is too scared to talk to her. With my auntie branding me as careless and promiscuous in front of everyone, I would love nothing more than to wipe that look off her face by telling her it's her fifteen-year-old daughter who is knocked up, but I would never do that to my cousin. She needs support, not to be shouted at in front of everyone. I'll make my excuses and go find her. People already hate me, let them think it's me if they want, but all I want to do is find Hannah and tell her that she's not alone.

Before I have a chance to speak, my auntie ups the dramatics. If my jaw hit the floor before, then hers has dropped straight through to somewhere just off the coast of New Zealand. She drops the pregnancy test and slaps her hand across her mouth, the same hand that was holding the test that someone has definitely peed on. My auntie goes a ghostly shade of white. Has it crossed her mind that Hannah might be pregnant? If so, I hope she doesn't blurt it out in front of all these people.

'Tell me it the dad isn't someone in this house,' my auntie says with real panic in her voice.

'How could it be?' I reply.

'You've been putting it about a bit – and that's just the people we know about,' she replies.

I mean, forgetting the fact that I've actually only slept with one person while I've been here, she must know that no one gets pregnant that quickly. She's seriously overreacting.

'Do you need me to explain to you how babies are made?' I ask her.

'Don't get smart with me, young lady, we've all seen your antics – men on the beach, Leo, even poor Mike.'

I hear a gasp from my gran, who, it turns out, hadn't heard about Mike's part in destorying the cake until now.

I massage my temples for a moment. I've put up with so much already, there's no point losing my temper now.

'You're all so judgemental,' I tell them. 'And so critical of me. I've had enough.'

I turn on my heel to head back upstairs.

'We're not done with you,' June calls after me, but I ignore her and head upstairs.

Would you believe it, the first person I clap eyes on is Uncle Steve, who is about to head down.

'Good morning, bestie,' he says brightly.

'Where's Hannah?' I ask, cutting to the chase. 'I need to talk to her.'

'I think she went for a walk on the beach, is everything OK?'

'It will be,' I tell him. 'I promise you it will be.'

My uncle looks confused but smiles as he heads downstairs.

'You might want to avoid your wife,' I call after him, stopping him in his tracks about halfway down.

'Why?' he asks nervously.

'Just trust me.'

Chapter 43

As I sit on the sand and look out to sea, I think about how I can't wait to get away from here. If these people are normal and I'm unconventional, then I'm happy to be different. I can't imagine being like Belle, obsessing over this one day like her entire life depends on it, because if her wedding doesn't go well, her marriage will be doomed. What's so great about marriage anyway? Look at the couples in my family. My dad hardly speaks to my mum, my auntie thinks my uncle is cheating on her and even people who were happy, like Leo's mum and dad – well, he died. There's no such thing as a happy ending.

I had a quick look around for Hannah, but it's a big beach and I don't know which way she went. I'll just sit here until I figure out what to do.

'Mia,' I hear Leo's voice from behind me. As he approaches me I consider how I'd do anything to avoid this conversation. In fact, I would jump in the sea and swim home were it not for the fact I'd probably be headed for Spain/die trying.

'Hello,' I chirp. 'Go on, let me have it. I have no fucks left to give.'

'My mum told me about what happened this morning,' he says seriously. I thought he was going to yell at me about last night.

'Crazy, isn't it?'

Leo sits down on the sand next to me and takes my hand.

'Someone said you thought it might be mine,' he says softly.

My eyes widen with horror as I snatch my hand back from him.

'Not you as well,' I babble, jumping to my feet. 'I expect this crap from everyone else, but not you.'

'I just mean … I know it's not, but I'd support you …' he calls after me as I'm walking away.

'I don't have time for this shit,' I call back. I just need to find Hannah.

***

After sneaking back into the house and creeping upstairs unnoticed, I eventually find Hannah in the room she is sharing with Meg, her younger sister.

'My mum says you're pregnant,' Meg says to me in wonderment, like it's the coolest thing she's ever heard. 'That's awesome!'

'Sorry to disappoint you, but she's wrong,' I tell her gently. 'Can you give your sister and me a minute, please? And don't mention to anyone that I'm up here.'

Meg, disappointed, grabs her phone and leaves the room.

'Nope, I'm not pregnant,' I say again, now that it's just Hannah and me, 'but, someone is, and I think that someone is you.'

Hannah doesn't need to say anything, the terrified look on her face confirms everything.

'Shit, Han, you should have told me sooner.' I sit down on the bed next to her and put my arm around her. 'How long have you known?'

'I only found out for sure yesterday,' she admits. 'I guess I already knew. We did it, but we didn't use anything – Lee said I couldn't get pregnant the first time.'

'Well Lee is a fucking idiot,' I tell her. 'Did he put pressure on you?'

Hannah nods.

'He said there were plenty of other girls who wanted to do it with him, but I was his girlfriend. I wish I hadn't now.'

'I meant what I said before, never ever sleep with someone you don't absolutely want to do it with. Wait for someone you trust.'

Hannah raises her eyebrows at me – she's obviously heard at least something about last night.

'Look, I'm not going to tell you that you should only ever sleep with one person, and that it should be when you're madly in love and getting married, but you should only sleep with someone you want to, who you trust, when you are absolutely one hundred per cent ready – and with protection,' I add. 'Always use protection.'

'It's a bit late for that now,' she laughs. Bless her for smiling in what must feel like such an awful situation.

'You're not going to want to hear it, but you need to talk to your mum,' I tell her.

'She'll go mad,' she squeaks. 'Look at how she reacted when she thought it was you.'

'Yeah, but that's just because she hates me,' I joke. 'Look, don't worry, I'll talk to her with you, OK? She'll be cooler than you think.'

'Will you tell her for me?' she asks.

'Tell you what, I've got some stuff to do today, your mum needs to calm down and you need to prepare yourself for telling her. Think things over and then later tonight take your mum to one side, come and find me and we'll see what happens. You should try to tell her but if you really can't, I've got your back, OK?'

Hannah nods her head and smiles. She still looks terrified, but there's a hint of relief there now too. She knows she's not alone and that's all I care about.

It would be awful to say that I'm happy to be tackling Hannah's problems instead of facing my own, but I am pleased to be helping her instead of making things worse for myself. Like I said before, I'll be back home soon enough, but this lot are stuck with this life, and I don't envy any of them one bit.

Chapter 44

Helping Hannah gave me a real rush of something, because it turns out I *can* make a difference if I want to. That's why I have decided I will do everything I can to find my sister a replacement cake of some description. I'm not having much luck though, and as I sit alone at the kitchen table after hours of making calls and searching the net, I decide it's probably best to call it a night. It's nine p.m. after all, and there's always tomorrow. I'm just not sure where else to try.

I sip my coffee, but it's gone cold. It's the third one I've made that has gone cold, which either has something to do with the fact I've been trying so hard to find a cake or the frosty atmosphere in this house. Everyone is so mad at me, for so many things, that no one wants to talk to me. Throwing myself into finding a cake isn't just about making things right with my sister, it's also a very welcome distraction from being public enemy number one.

I am startled by someone falling in through the outside door. As he climbs to his feet I realise it's Leo, and he's drunk.

'Mia Valentina,' he greets me. 'What are you up to?'

'I'm trying to find a cake,' I tell him, but he's not really listening. 'Jesus, you're absolutely wasted.'

'Enough about me,' he babbles. 'I am here for my refund.'

'What?'

'My refund, from you. I went to see your film. *For Better, For Worse*,' he informs me. 'It was shit and I want my money back.'

'Well you're not exactly my target audience,' I tell him, only a little wounded by his unconstructive criticism.

'It was all a lie,' he practically shouts. 'All that love stuff, you don't even know what love is.'

'The other two write the love stuff, I do the sex scenes,' I joke, trying to diffuse the situation. 'Let's get you a coffee.'

'Money back first,' he demands.

Oh, for God's sake, I have absolutely no time for emotional drunk men right now.

'You do realise the cinema don't just pop the money in an envelope and post it to me, right?'

For Better, For Worse is my latest movie, currently showing in cinemas here. It's your typical wedding rom-com, although I'm especially proud of this one because for once I got to make our leading lady a bit of a bad girl, not your usual naive ditz. She's called Lulu and days after getting engaged to her long-term boyfriend she meets this other guy. Her boyfriend is safe, sweet and dependable, but this other guy is a bit of a bad boy, he's exciting and he makes her feel alive. Like bad boys do, he tries to convince her to ditch her boyfriend and run away with him, and while I certainly know what I'd do in that situation, this is a romcom, so by the end of the movie she realises that she loves her boyfriend far too much to leave him, even if he isn't the most exciting option.

'There's this bit towards the end,' Leo slurs, 'when the girl decides she isn't going to leave her bloke, and she says that she knew she was in love with him the second she set eyes on him. Do you believe in love at first sight?'

'Does it really matter?' I ask, pulling a face as I force him to sit down at the table. I fire up the coffee machine. I suppose the one good thing about Leo being so drunk is that we don't have to have any serious conversations – I doubt he'll even remember this in the morning.

'And another bit,' he continues to ramble, 'where she says falling in love is like walking on air, but you don't even know what love feels like, so it's all a lie.'

'Once again, I didn't write that part,' I explain, but I'm on the verge of losing my temper with him. 'Falling in love isn't like walking on air, it's like jumping off a fucking building. You jump and then sooner or later you're going to hit the ground and it will leave you crushed.'

'So, you're just going to stay up on top of your building, admiring the view and never getting too close to anyone?'

'It's one hell of a view,' I tell him, placing a strong coffee down in front of him. 'Drink.'

'You're wrong,' he tells me, his breath stinking so strongly of alcohol that I can smell it from across the table.

'Oh, am I? Because you're such an expert when it comes to love. Drink,' I prompt him again. The sooner he starts to sober up, the sooner I can send him off to bed.

'OK, falling in love *is* like jumping off a building, because it's scary and it takes your breath away but being in love … that's different. Real love is the person on the ground with their arms open, just waiting to catch you.'

'That's awfully profound for a drunk person,' I tell him. 'And it's that kind of shit that makes women swoon over my movies – you could get a job with me if you come out with more shit like that.'

I like how I talk about women, as though I'm not one of them.

Leo finally takes a sip of his coffee.

'Are you going to keep the baby?' he asks, still slurring but in a far less confrontational manner.

'Leo, there's no baby,' I tell him. 'It's all a big misunderstanding.'

'Everyone saw the test,' he continues.

'Well, they've got it all wrong,' I reply firmly.

'It's like the film,' Leo reasons. 'You can have me and I will support you both or you can have Mike, but he's a cheat and a liar. You have to make the right choice,' he babbles, but I've had about as much as I can take.

'For fuck's sake,' I snap, because I can't take a second more of this. 'I am not fucking pregnant. Hannah is.'

There's a look of shock and horror on Leo's face.

'What?' I hear my auntie say angrily. I turn around to see her and Hannah standing in the doorway. When Hannah asked me to tell her mum, I don't think this is what she had in mind.

Chapter 45

I've made a lot of mistakes in my twenty-nine years on this earth – most of them recently. From inter-office relationships to destroying wedding cakes to accidentally announcing my cousin's pregnancy to her mum, I just seem to be fucking everything up. I'm down, but I'm not out. I'm just hoping people will judge me on how I fix my mistakes, rather than the mistakes themselves.

My first job today – the day before the wedding – is to try to help Hannah. After what happened last night she ran away and her mum ran after her. The coffee didn't help to sober Leo up, it just made him sick, so I made myself scarce while he was in the bathroom. I haven't spoken to Hannah or Auntie June yet, instead I popped into town while everyone was still in bed, printed out some information on pregnancy – especially the stuff with advice for teens – and slipped copies under their bedroom doors. I also slipped an apology note under Hannah's, not that it will change anything. I seem to be throwing apologies all over the place at the moment but they don't do much good, that's why I'm hoping my actions will speak louder than my words.

So, the other two problems that need tackling. Well, as far as work goes, I know that if I knuckle down and do some work today that I will begin to find my way back into my boss's good books, but my efforts to find a cake aren't going so well. That's why, instead of doing my own work, I have decided that I will bake. Yes, you heard me right, I'm going to get my hands dirty (instead of my dress) and try and make a wedding cake – wedding cupcakes to be precise. Well, I wouldn't know where to begin making a proper wedding cake with tiers and stuff, but when Belle and I were younger, making cupcakes was our thing. Hopefully that, plus the fact I am making a real effort, will mean something to her, or at least save the day.

Before I left the house I poked my head into the dining room where most of the household were eating lunch. The room fell silent when my face appeared – something I'm getting used to. I noticed that Belle and Dan weren't there, but I didn't stop to take stock. I said that I was going to Shell's Café to make cupcakes as a surprise for Belle, and casually mentioned that if anyone fancied helping, it would be greatly appreciated. Of course, no one stepped up, no one even answered me. So far Shell is the only one willing to help me by letting me use the kitchen at her café, along with most of the supplies I'm likely to need. I told her that I was responsible for the demise of the wedding cake, but I thought it probably best not to mention the details.

As I climb the few steps to Shell's Café, I somehow manage to drop my bag and a bunch of stuff falls out. I quickly retrieve it all, hoping no one saw me. I only had to buy a few things, just specific colours and decorations. I went shopping to find food colouring to match the dresses and the ties, as well as finding edible flowers that match the last-minute wedding flowers we organised. I really am trying here.

Pushing my way through the door with the shopping in my arms, Shell can't help but laugh at me.

'Oh, love, let me help you,' she says, taking a few things from me.

We head for the kitchen where I finally set everything down. I can see that Shell has got everything ready for me, but she can't help me bake because it's business as usual in the café. I'm just so happy she's letting me use this place. I promised to find a way to set a scene of a movie in her café in exchange – she didn't need any extra incentive to help me, but it's the least I can do, and I know it will make her happy. I'm not exactly sure how I'm going to swing that, but I'll do my best.

'Right, you know where I am if you need me,' Shell assures me. 'I'll be popping in and out anyway.'

'Thank you,' I call after her.

OK, I can do this. We were kids when Belle and I used to make these, how hard can it be?

I open up my recipe of choice on my iPad – one of the simplest I could find – and begin measuring things out. I have no sooner started when Mike pops his head through the door.

'Hello gorgeous,' he says.

'Have you come to help me?' I ask, skipping the pleasantries. 'I can't even work the scales.'

'Oh, no, that's women's work,' he replies. He'd better be joking.

'Well, if you're not here to help you can fuck off,' I say with a laugh. 'This isn't going to be pretty.'

'I just wanted to talk to you,' Mike says, approaching me slowly. As he gets close to me he stands behind me and wraps his arms around my waist. 'About the other night.'

'I really can't talk about that right now,' I begin to tell him, just as Shell pops in to grab something. I smile at her but remain frozen in Mike's grasp until she's gone.

'Look, get off me.' I wiggle free, knocking a box of eggs to the floor. Every last one of them falls out of the box and smashes on the floor. 'Shit.'

'I'll go,' he assures me, 'I just need to know where I stand.'

'You stand with your girlfriend, you moron. I can't believe you let me think you were single.'

'You didn't ask.'

'Oh, come on, you made out like you were. And anyway, it's

your business. You want to be a cheater, be a cheater. I'm not getting involved.'

'Another visitor,' I hear Shell call from the other room, shortly before we're joined by Leo. Brilliant, another member of my angry male fan club, just what I need.

'I found these chocolate flowers on the step,' he tells me. I must have missed those when I was picking up my dropped shopping.

'Fancy that,' Mike replies. 'I came across a cake the other night.'

Leo doesn't look impressed at this joke at all. I shoot Mike an angry glance.

'If you're not here to help, you can get out,' I snap at them both.

'Fine. To be continued,' Mike chuckles. As he passes Leo on his way to the door he gives him a pat on the back. 'See you, bud.'

I exhale deeply and wipe my forehead with the back of my floury hand.

'Not going well?' Leo asks me when we're finally alone.

'It was never going to, was it? I don't know what made me think I could do this.'

I get down on my knees and start scooping the gooey egg mess into the box they came in. As hard as I try, it just slips through my fingers – story of my life.

Leo gets down on the floor with me.

'You can't make an omelette without breaking a few eggs,' he tells me encouragingly.

'At this rate I *will* be making her an omelette, at least I'm capable of that.'

Leo laughs, flashing me his gorgeous smile, and however guilty I felt before, I feel a billion times that now.

'Mike not helping you then?' he asks, and I finally feel like I should explain, I just don't know how.

'No. Nothing really happened with him, you know. I mean, we kissed, but it wasn't ever going to be more than that.'

'It looked like it was from where I was sitting.'

'Honestly,' I reply, and hopefully he can tell that I'm being sincere. 'I couldn't have done it.'

Leo nods his head thoughtfully.

'I feel like you should be angrier at me than you are,' I tell him. 'Not that I want you to be, just …'

'I'm here to help you. The fact that you're doing this is admirable.'

I feel my heart jump into my mouth. The fact he's helping me is what's admirable, he should hate my guts.

'Grab me some salt,' he insists. I do, handing it to him before joining him back on the floor. I watch as he sprinkles salt over the broken eggs.

'We wait for it to dry, then it will be much easier to clean up.'

I stare at him in amazement.

'You're like a little old lady trapped in the body of a smoking hot man,' I laugh. 'Where did you learn to do that?'

'From my mum. One of the many benefits of still living with your mum in your late twenties,' he insists. 'She teaches me all the vital survival skills, she doesn't want me getting hurt.'

And don't I know it.

'Well, if you do want to help, that would be incredible. Thank you so much.'

'It's nothing,' he tells me.

We do most of the cleaning up and preparations in silence, occasionally looking at each other and exchanging smiles. It means a lot to me that, after everything, he's still willing to help me. And thankfully Shell has more eggs.

'Belle will appreciate this, you know,' Leo tells me once we're well on our way, mixing the batter.

'I wouldn't be so sure about that, she's pretty angry. She'll probably accuse me of doing this on purpose to ruin her wedding, and then trying to fix things to make myself look good.'

'Why would you do that though?' he asks. It might not make sense, but it's nothing new to me.

'She thinks I'm jealous. Everyone does actually. Little sister having her dream wedding, tying the knot with the man of her dreams and then there's me, accumulating dust on the shelf. Something like that.'

'*Are* you jealous?' he asks.

'No.' I laugh. 'Sounds like my idea of hell.'

'Why?'

I shoot Leo a look.

'I didn't realise I was going to be interrogated.'

'Humour me,' he insists with an irresistible smile.

'Look, I'm annoyed that I have been summoned here to spend time with a family who hate me, and I'm even a little pissed off that my parents have decided Belle should have my half of the wedding fund – not because I want the money, but because they've just written me off.'

'But marriage sounds like your idea of hell,' Leo reminds me. 'So, what does it matter?'

'I don't care about the fact that it's gone, I care about why.'

'But why does it matter if you're not getting married?'

'Look, you're never going to get it. Your mum worships you, you couldn't possibly understand.'

'Do you know what I think,' Leo starts, raising his voice as I switch on the noisy electric mixer. 'I think you're lonely.'

'You think *I'm* lonely?' I repeat, equally as loudly. 'Do I seem short of attention to you?'

'Well, what have you got in LA? You don't have a boyfriend—'

'Oh my God, I don't have a boyfriend, the be all and end all,' I interrupt him, my voice still raised even though I've turned the mixer off.

'Well, you don't sound like you have many friends either.'

'So, what, you're going to move to LA with me? Be my BF, my BFF and a total pain in my ASS?'

As Leo beings preparing the frosting, I angrily dollop blobs of batter into bun cases. I imagine I'll be marked down for presentation because with each one I grow angrier and angrier, slopping batter all over. If he's not careful, I might say something I'll regret.

'OK then, why not?' Leo starts enthusiastically. 'I'll move to LA, we'll see what happens.'

'What about your job?' I ask.

'You have fires in LA, right?' he says with a smile. I really love that smile of his. When he isn't giving any emotion away, his dark eyes and chiselled features make him look quite moody and intense, but when he smiles his face just comes to life. He lights up. Would it be the worst thing in the world to see that smile every day? No, but it's not realistic and we both know it. He knows how I feel about relationships and commitment, and suddenly he's suggesting moving thousands of miles to be with me.

'And it's that simple,' I say with a laugh, but it's not an amused laugh, it's an angry laugh, the one that seems to serve as a warning shot when I feel like I'm being cornered. There's only one thing to do when you're being cornered and that's attack.

'It is,' he tells me. 'We're meant for each other, Mia. You can keep doing your job, I'll find work as a firefighter.'

'What, so you can just die in a fire and leave me heartbroken?' I snap.

And there it is. The thing that I say before instantly regretting it. I almost can't believe I said it, so I instantly turn my back to him and bend down to put the cakes in the oven. I jump up as I hear a loud noise, only to see the bowl Leo was using on the floor and Leo standing over it. He's holding his hand like he's hurt it, he must have hit something in a temper.

'Why are you so afraid of people loving you?' he yells before storming out.

I place a hand over my mouth, the mouth that just said such a cruel thing. Leo has been nothing but incredible to me since the day we met – he has stuck up for me, he was disturbingly calm when he found me with Mike ... but he's finally snapped. Well, of course he has, because I stupidly brought up the way he lost his dad as a reason for us not to be together. His dad died in a fire saving a child's life, that's a huge sacrifice and I feel like such a fucking bitch for bringing it up.

As I clean up the mess Leo has made, I notice Shell standing over me.

'These are not thick walls,' she informs me, without her usual warmth.

'Oh God, I'm sorry, did people hear?'

'I heard,' she tells me. 'I heard everything – what happened, the things you said to Leo. He loves you, what's so wrong with that?'

'Well, maybe I don't love him back, or does that not matter?' I ask defensively.

'If you believe that, you're an even bigger fool than I thought.'

'You don't know the first thing about me,' I tell her.

'And you don't know the first thing about love, Mia. It's hard, but we still do it.'

I place the bowl in the sink and grab another to make some frosting that hasn't spent any time on the floor.

'Maybe some of us weren't designed to love,' I say quietly.

Shell exhales deeply.

'I don't want your sister's day ruined any more than it already has been. Finish the cakes – quietly – and then get out. You're not who I thought you were. You can store them here overnight, but after you collect them I never want to see you again. And don't worry about setting a scene from your next movie here, I've had enough of your scripted rubbish.'

For a moment, I am speechless. Shell has gone from worshipping me to wishing I was dead and it took less than an hour. She was warm and bubbly and now she's angry and shouting ... and it's all my fault.

***

It took me a long time but eventually I made enough cupcakes and I decorated them all with pink frosting and chocolate and orange flowers. I'd never get a job at Le Papillon but I've done a pretty good job, even if I did lose my sous chef halfway through.

Shell's is empty now, apart from Shell herself, who had no interest in saying goodbye to me.

It's getting cold out, and as I walk home along the beach I realise there isn't another soul around.

I freeze on the spot as I feel my breathing stop. I can't breathe, why can't I breathe? As I drop to my knees I bang my hand on the sand, willing myself to take a breath. It works and I gasp as I manage to suck in and push out air, but it doesn't feel natural, it's like I am having to consciously think about each breath. In ... out ... in ... out. A panic attack – it's been so long since I had one, but that's what this is. And it's not just a panic attack. As I feel my heart pounding in my chest I feel my throat close, my eyes burn and then the tears come flooding out. Crying is something else I haven't done since I was younger, I forgot how consuming it was. I sob as I watch my tears dampen the sand on the ground in front of me. I concentrate on my breathing, in ... out ... in ... out ...

I think it's finally hit me that everyone hates me. Everyone. And everyone can't be wrong, can they? They're all right about me. I'm a selfish monster and I am broken. I don't know what's wrong with me, or where it all went wrong, but I've really done it this time.

As I kneel here, wailing away, I realise that not only is no one around to notice, but no one would actually care if I disappeared.

As my breathing eventually calms, I stand up, compose myself, wipe my eyes and carry on walking back towards the house. I don't ever want to feel like this again.

Chapter 46

If there's one thing I can take back to LA with me, it's a better understanding of the act of crying. Until today I had probably written more crying scenes than I had shed tears of my own as an adult, but I had forgotten just how ugly it could be. In my movies it's always the slight quivering of the voice, a few beautiful tears rolling down the cheek that leave a pretty little glistening trail behind them – it's all shit. Crying isn't beautiful, it's horrible. As I sobbed, I couldn't have spoken if I wanted to, even breathing was difficult. When you're truly upset, it isn't a few pretty little teardrops from each eye, it's just constantly flowing, making your eyes burn until you feel like you can't keep them open for a minute longer. It's not even just tears you have to deal with – I didn't know it was possible to produce so much snot, I felt like it was choking me. Even now, after drying my eyes and washing my face back at the house, my head feels absolutely full. Full of thoughts and full of snot. The skin on my nose feels tight, my ears feel blocked and my eyes feel like they are being sucked into my skull. Crying looks and feels ugly, and 'letting it all out' certainly hasn't made me feel any less ugly inside.

Just when I think I am about to make it to my bedroom without seeing a soul, I hear someone call my name.

'Mia.'

It's my granddad. I recognise his voice, but I don't turn to face him.

'You OK, Kid?'

'I'm fine, just tired,' I tell him as I feel that tight lump returning to my throat. I'm pretty sure he knows exactly what has gone on and it breaks my heart, because he's the only person to ever stick up for me, and even he's going to struggle to do that now.

'Are you crying?' he asks, sounding almost shocked to see me displaying such an emotion.

I shush him, grabbing his arm and pulling him into my bedroom, probably a little rougher than I should considering his age, but I don't want anyone else to see that I'm bothered.

'You should let them see you cry,' he tells me once the door is closed.

'Crying shows weakness,' I reply.

'No, it shows honesty,' he corrects me. 'Words come so easily. It's only a matter of seconds between them being thought and uttered. Parrots can apologise – it doesn't make it sincere, it's a habit that they've learned, they're just repeating the same thing. You need to realise that saying these words after each mistake means less and less each time. You don't say you're sorry, Kid, you show people.'

I don't think I have ever known my granddad to be wrong. He always tells me that between them, he and his dad knew absolutely everything. I would ask him difficult, sometimes impossible to answer questions, and if he didn't know the answer he would simply tell me: 'my dad knew that one'. Jokes aside, he has never steered me wrong before, and it means so much that he is still looking out for me.

'How do I do that?' I ask as the tears start flowing again.

'I heard you've been baking, that's a good start. After what happened to the cake …'

OK, he definitely knows. I cover my face with my hands.

'Come on, Kid, we've all made a mess in the kitchen at some point in our lives,' he laughs. I look at him and my eyes widen, because I can't imagine my gran ever being down for anything like that.

'Just show them this side of you. Don't put up a front, just tell everyone how you really feel – even that lad,' he adds.

'Leo?'

My granddad nods.

'I don't think he'll ever speak to me again. I said some pretty unforgivable things.'

'You'd be surprised what people will forgive when they're in love – just like when people say and do stupid things because they're in love. Think about it, Kid. I'll give you a bit of privacy.'

As my granddad heads for the door I go after him and throw my arms around him. As he hugs me back – and I mean really hugs me back, not like the occasional empty hug most of the other family members throw around – the idea of going back to LA makes me feel sick. The thought that one day my wonderful granddad won't be around anymore makes me want to never let go of him.

'Steady on, Kid,' he laughs. 'I can hardly breathe.'

As always, he's given me great advice, but being honest about my feelings is not something I am keen on doing – I am scared of being honest with myself, let alone the others.

***

After washing my face again and blowing my nose for the billionth time, I finally feel emotionally balanced enough to re-apply my makeup. I know I told my granddad I'd be honest, but the idea of crying my eyes out and begging everyone for forgiveness is not one that I am crazy about. My sister, my mum, my auntie, my gran … these people hardly know me now, there's no way they'd be able to recognise whether I was being genuine or not, and I doubt they'd even care. Maybe given time they will listen to my apology, but not in time for the wedding.

I am snapped from my thoughts by my phone ringing. It's work.

'Dalia, hello! Boy, am I glad to hear from you,' I answer, breathing a sigh of relief as I await a familiar voice that will remind me of my new life and how I will soon be back to it.

'Hey, you might change your mind when you hear why I'm calling,' she starts, and I feel my face fall. 'Mia, you haven't sent any work, we are seriously behind with the project, Savannah and Molly are on the verge of a fucking breakdown, the boss is majorly pissed. We need you back here.'

'Well, I'll be back in a few days, so don't worry.'

'Mia, the boss wants you back *now*, or else.'

'He realises it's quite far?' I ask sarcastically.

'He does. He wants you to catch a flight ASAP and be in the office tomorrow.'

'The wedding is tomorrow,' I tell her, but she already knew that. 'Level with me, Dalia. How serious is he?'

'Super serious,' she tells me. 'He says you have to show him you're willing to commit to this one hundred per cent. He's worried you're becoming a bit of a liability.'

Bloody hell, you turn up late now and then, sleep with the occasional co-worker, take owed vacation days to go home for your sister's wedding and suddenly you're a liability. When I took the job, I knew that it was going to be demanding, and at the time it wasn't a problem – but it's this damn wedding, it's ruining my life.

'OK, I'll sort it. I'll find a flight and I'll be back tomorrow. You can promise the boss,' I assure her. Well, what else can I do? My job is on the line and it's all I've got left. I've burned whatever bridges I had left with the family – and those flimsy old, petrol-soaked rope bridges disintegrated to nothing pretty quickly – Leo hates me, and he was right, my job is the most important thing in my life. I can't afford to lose it, it's not just what I do, it's who I am.

Let's be honest, no one even wants me at this wedding now. I've trashed my sister's wedding plans, broken Leo's heart, and caused unnecessary chaos for my auntie and my cousin ... I know I would half-joke that everyone hated me before, but now I think they truly do. There's nothing to stay here for – so the sooner I leave, the better.

Chapter 47

I woke up with a start – and in a cold sweat, as the sweet dream I'd been having turned into a screaming nightmare. I was dreaming about the wedding and it was weird, because *the* cake was there, only it was after I sat on it, so it was totally destroyed but no one acted any differently. Then, suddenly, I was with Leo. We were holding hands and smiling, walking down the street as the sun shone and the birds sang, it was beautiful. Then we happened upon a burning building and I screamed after him as he ran inside – I don't even think there was anyone in there, I think he was trying to get away from me. That's when I woke up and realised it was three a.m., and that I was still here.

I'm not only warm, I'm really thirsty. I hid in my room for most of last night, I just couldn't face anyone. The good news is that I managed to book myself a flight for the morning, but I'm yet to break the news to anyone. Still, they'll probably be relieved when I do tell them.

I grab one of my beach dresses and slip it on over my underwear so that I can go downstairs and grab a drink while everyone else is sleeping. The moon is bright tonight, illuminating the house just enough so that I don't have to turn the lights on, which is fortunate, because I'm terrified of waking anyone. I tiptoe through the kitchen and open the fridge, which lights the room a little better, just as I hear a voice behind me.

'Hello,' my sister says from the kitchen table.

I jump out of my skin.

'What is it with people sitting in this room in the dark?' I can't help but ask.

'I know, if only people would turn lights on ...' she replies.

I know what she's getting at, I'm surprised she's even speaking to me though.

'Sometimes it's better to be in the dark,' I sigh, closing the fridge door behind me and then heading for the hallway.

'Wait,' my sister calls after me.

I flick the light on and look at her, just to make sure I didn't just imagine her encouraging me to stay in the same room.

'Sit down,' she insists.

I cautiously do as she asks, not entirely convinced she isn't hiding a weapon under the table.

'I hear you baked,' she says softly, looking at her hands as she speaks to me.

'I did.'

'Can I see?'

'I left them in the fridge at Shell's. I have a photo though.'

I have my phone with me – I never like to be too far from it, especially in hostile territory – so I show my sister a photo, careful not to get too close in case this is some kind of trap.

'You made those?' she asks, her eyes widening as she looks at them. My cupcakes are by no means amazing, but even I was impressed by how well they turned out. I didn't know I had it in me.

I nod my head.

'They match the colour scheme and the flowers,' she tells me.

'Yeah, well I thought that would be the best way to go,' I explain. 'I just wanted to fix the mistake. It really was a mistake, Belle.'

She exhales deeply.

'I know. It's just ... it was a *big* mistake.'

My sister lets out a little laugh but I'm still too terrified to join in.

'Planning a wedding is stressful,' she tells me. 'It's not like it is in your movies.'

'Nothing in real life is how it is in my movies,' I tell her – the same thing I keep telling everyone when they meet me and expect a slushy romantic. They expect love to be my life, for me to have been planning my own wedding since I was a child – they probably suspect I have a scrapbook that I carry around with me with clippings and collages. What no one expects, and what they actually get, is someone who couldn't be less romantic if she tried.

'I'm sorry,' I tell her again. 'I'm really *really* sorry. I'm going to be honest, when I first arrived I thought you were being a bridezilla – the superstitions, demanding attention, falling to pieces over the slightest thing—'

'OK, I get it,' Belle interrupts.

'Sorry. Again. But, yeah, I take full responsibility for recent events. I am fucking it up from all angles, but I'm doing my best to put things right.'

I should tell Belle that I'm going back to the States, she will probably feel relieved that I'm not going to be here to mess up her big day.

'Mia, I haven't really said so yet, but thank you,' she starts before I get the chance to tell her anything. 'I am grateful for everything you've done. Babysitting, helping me sort the flower crisis, making endless coffees because no one else can use the machine.' She laughs, and as she does she smiles warmly. 'You have caused a few problems,' she continues. 'You forgot to plan my hen party, but you gave me an amazing one! And you ruined my cake, but you put it right.'

With every word Belle says, this incredible feeling washes over me. To be putting things right and to be forgiven feels amazing.

'Anyway, Dan probably shouldn't have left the cake just sitting there, on the worktop, uncovered, on a warm night, in the pitch black. He can be so dumb sometimes,' she chuckles.

I laugh, but only a little. Dan can be a little on the dim side, but he can't be blamed for this.

'Dan is a lovely guy, and he loves you so much,' I tell her, but of course she already knew that.

'I know,' she smiles, 'and I love him too. That's the thing, when you love someone you can look past the little things, like them being a bit dumb.'

I smile and nod my head.

'Or like them wanting to be with you so much, but going about it all wrong because they don't know how you'll react if they tell you.'

I nod, even though that one seemed a lot more specific, then I realise she's talking about Leo and me.

'Wait, what?'

'Leo loves you *so* much,' she tells me. 'I think he has since the second he laid eyes on you. And ...' she pauses, '... I think you love him too.'

With everything such a mess and with nothing left to lose, I pause to consider my feelings for Leo. I knew there was something between us the moment we met, but I thought that was just sexual chemistry because I heard the word 'fireman'. When I heard that Nancy was into him, I was jealous. When I've needed him, he's been there for me. When Belle put an end to our sexcapades it forced me to do something I hadn't in a long time, to build a proper relationship with someone, and when I was so drunk that my defences were completely down, I fell asleep in his arms. Normally people get drunk and have meaningless sex; when I get drunk I let my meaningful feelings get the better of me. That's why I feel so bad about everything I've done, because I love the people I am hurting and that includes Leo.

'Oh fuck,' I say, hiding my face with my hands. 'Why did this have to happen to me?'

My sister laughs.

'I think you're the last person to realise you're in love,' she tells me, highly amused. 'And stop freaking out and treating it like it's something awful that has happened to you – just feel lucky that it did.'

I don't feel lucky though, I feel a billion times worse. Leo and I live very different lives, very far apart. I have written one movie about a long-distance relationship, and as we penned our usual happy ending, this one felt particularly bullshit to me because everyone knows that no relationship can survive distance, especially when there's no goal to work towards.

'So, this is love,' I laugh. 'I thought if I ever experienced it, it might feel better than this. And I needed it to happen with someone who lives in the same country as me, then I might have gone through with it.'

'You don't get to choose who you love,' my sister reminds me. 'Like you, you're my sister and I'm stuck with you. You're every bit as dramatic as the movies you write, you might not have had sex on my cake but I'm pretty sure you had sex *with* the cake – my *wedding cake* ... but I love you.'

'I love you too,' I tell her, grabbing her from her chair and hugging her tightly.

'And I love you both,' I hear my mum say. I release my sister to turn around and look at my mum who is standing in the doorway in her dressing gown, her hair up as perfectly as it appears during the day.

'Wait.' I grab my phone. 'Can you say that again, I need to film it.'

My mum laughs, but I'd be lying if I said I was kidding.

'You're good girls,' she tells us. 'Both of you.'

She takes a bottle of water from the fridge before heading back upstairs.

From my usually frosty mother, that means the world.

'The next time she's driving me crazy, will you remind me that happened, please?' I laugh to my sister.

'I will,' she giggles. 'Mia, I'm so glad you're here. It wouldn't be right without you.'

As my sister holds my hands and swings them gently, I remember the promise I made to my boss, and how I had already decided I would skip the wedding to go home. Well, when I said that, I thought no one wanted me around.

'Why did you pick on me when we were teens?' I ask my sister. I've always wondered.

'I suppose I was jealous,' she admits.

'You were jealous of me?' I ask. 'You're remembering that the wrong way around. I was jealous of you.'

'Nope. You were smart and funny – I've never been either of those things. School was so hard for me and you sailed through.'

'I didn't sail through, I was bullied for being different. And things like PE were a living hell for me – and you were awesome at that. You were friends with the cool kids,' I remind her.

'Yeah, but you had proper friends who liked you for you, not just because you were cool,' she replies.

'So, we were jealous of each other,' I laugh. 'I wish we'd had this conversation sooner, we could've been friends.'

'We *are* friends,' she replies, hugging me again, and for a moment we stay like that.

'We should get to bed,' my sister sings, finally releasing me. 'I'm getting married tomorrow!'

'Yey,' I squeak, but it's hard to muster up the same enthusiasm when I know I'm supposed to be working. If I don't go back, I'm in big trouble, but how can I leave when things are finally getting better with my family?

Chapter 48

It might be late here, but it's still evening back at home. That's why I'm going to call Dalia and try to sort this out sooner rather than later. The longer I leave it, the more trouble I will be in for not going back when I said I would.

'Hey Mia, yikes, it must be really late there,' she squeaks as she answers the phone.

'It is,' I laugh nervously.

'Is everything cool with your flight?'

'About that,' I start, searching my brain for the right words. It turns out I don't need to, because Dalia speaks first.

'Mia, listen, Mr Skinner told me that if you called me with any excuses, I had to let him know straight away. Is it an excuse?'

I can tell from Dalia's voice that she isn't entirely happy about having to do this, but Mr Skinner is the boss, I don't suppose she has much choice.

'It is,' I sigh.

'Hang tight and I'll get him to buzz you now, cool?'

'Cool,' I reply, although it absolutely isn't cool, I'm going to get one hell of a telling off.

I sit and twirl a piece of my hair between my fingers as I wait for my phone to ring. It's hard to know how to play this because, somehow, I don't think explaining to my boss that I'm not coming back because I am finally patching things up with my family will work for him.

My phone rings, and Mr Skinner's name flashes up. It's his home number, and I know how much he hates having to deal with work when he is home. I wouldn't have called now if I'd known this was going to happen.

'Hello,' I say, as brightly as I can considering it's the middle of the night here, I'm terrified, I'm going to have to tell him the opposite of what he wants to hear and I've just found out I have this terrible disease called 'love'. 'How are you?'

'I was fine until someone disturbed me as I was about to have sex with my wife – do you know how rare that is?' he replies grumpily.

'Wow, over-share, OK. Sorry about that, I had no idea Dalia was going to call you,' I explain.

'Well, I asked her to call me if we were going to have a problem getting you back here to do your job – do we have a problem?'

'Well, the thing is, my sister's wedding is tomorrow, and that's why I took this time off. But if I can just get the wedding out of the way, I'll hop on a plane the next day – maybe even the same evening. So, I'll definitely be at work on time – no, early – the next day.'

'Yeah, OK, sure.'

'Really?' I squeak, amazed at his generosity.

'In fact, why don't you take an extra week?' he continues.

'Really?' I ask, although I'm suspicious now. That's too much.

'Yeah, and I'll have my wage for this month sent directly to you. In fact, when you come back, you can have my office.'

Ah, he's being sarcastic.

'Look, I know I promised I'd be there tomorrow but come on, it's my sister's wedding.'

'Mia, what this tells me is that you have no respect for your job,' Skinner starts. 'You promise you will be here, and you go back on it. You have inappropriate inter-office relationships. You show up late for work almost every day. You are great at your job, but you are not irreplaceable, do you understand?'

'I do.'

'So, will you forget the silly wedding business and come back to do your job? We both know the happy families shit isn't you, you make movies!'

He bellows that last part, like everything is supposed to fall into place for me when I hear it, and it does, but not in the way he's expecting. He thinks that instead of living my life, I should be writing about people who are, to make him far more money than I will get for doing much more work.

'No.'

'No, you won't be returning to work on time?'

'No.'

'What do you think is going to happen now?' he asks, unable to hide the amazement in his voice.

'I suspect you'll fire me,' I reply casually. I always thought that if my dream job was ever on the line, I would do whatever it took to save it, but if whatever it takes is ruining my sister's big day then I suppose that's that.

'Correctamundo,' he replies, and even though he is confirming it, his little accidental nod to *Pulp Fiction* only reminds me of the fun times I've had with my family – even if they were few and far between.

'Well, you get back to having sex with your wife,' I tell him.

'You get back to your wedding,' he replies.

And with that, the call is over. I am officially unemployed.

***

I always thought I was a free spirit. One who is not restrained, as by convention or obligation; a nonconformist. Freedom is a wonderful thing. You can do what you want, when you want to.

Take the internet, for example. You can watch absolutely anyone doing anything YouTube, you can Facebook stalk your old school boyfriend and sob at how handsome he is/dance with joy because he's going bald (delete where applicable), and you can even see exactly what two girls can do with just one cup (but let's not and say we did).

It's a cliché, I know, but until I lost my job I took pride in the fact that I was a free spirit. I could do what I wanted, wear what I wanted, sleep with whomever I wanted. I didn't have to answer to a boyfriend, I didn't have kids to look after; the world was my oyster.

I thought I was free. I thought I was spreading my wings, looking down on everyone – flying onwards and upwards. But now I realise I was just disconnected, I just kept doing the same old empty routine of work and gym whilst everyone else moved on with their lives. I thought I was flying onwards and upwards; turns out I'm the one who's been left behind.

I know it may seem like I think life is one big movie reference, but I think Norman Bates was onto something in *Psycho*. I know I probably shouldn't read too much into the ramblings of a serial killer with a split personality, but he thought that we were all caught in private traps, unable to ever get out. Of course, Norman was bothered about this, but he said that he wasn't. Well I am bothered, but unlike Norman, I'm not about to give in to it by throwing on a wig and getting stabby in the shower. My job was a huge part of my personal private trap. I thought it was the only thing that mattered – and I was surrounded by people who encouraged that mindset. So it's surprising really that, after losing my job, instead of losing my mind too, I feel weirdly liberated.

It's the morning of the wedding, and as I stand on my balcony and look out over the beach, I take in a deep breath of sea air and it feels amazing. This is what free feels like. I mean, I will have to find another job, because even with my savings, I won't last long in LA, but we won't worry about that today.

I am snapped from my thoughts by a knock on my door.

'Come in,' I call out.

'Good God, you're naked,' my auntie comments as she spots me standing undressed on the balcony.

I look down at the pretty vest and pants I slept in, which cover far more skin than the bikini she has seen me in previously.

'Hello, Auntie June,' I say brightly. Nothing can quash this good mood.

'I need to talk to you,' she starts. 'Well, actually, I need you to talk to Hannah. She won't speak to me.'

'Oh,' is the only reply I can manage.

'I mean, you must have had a trip or two to a clinic in your time,' she starts, but then she softens a little. 'I know you and I have never seen eye to eye, but she looks up to you. And I know you're a sensible girl, and I know that you've been looking out for her.'

'Auntie, I will happily speak to her. She's a tough little thing, try not to worry, OK?'

My auntie nods, and for a brief moment she gives me a sincere smile.

'Look, I'm trying this new thing where I sort my shit out with everyone,' I start, although probably not as eloquently as I could. 'So, what's your problem with me?'

'I don't have a problem with you,' my auntie replies coolly. I give her a look and she sighs.

'Look, I see the way Steve idolises you. He seems to gravitate towards younger people. I notice him looking sometimes. I'm not getting any younger, I wouldn't be surprised if he left me for a younger model at some point.'

I am shocked by her moment of honesty. I don't point out to my auntie that there's no way a younger model would want boring old Uncle Steve, instead I try a different approach.

'Auntie, listen, Uncle Steve just likes me because I'm he thinks I'm cool, because he thinks I'll get him a part in a movie or something. And as for younger models. I've spent a lot of time on the beach these past few days, and men just stare at women, it's what they do. And the women don't stare back, they don't even notice. It's just men being men. Steve loves you.'

My auntie nods her head. That's probably the best I can hope for.

'So, Hannah,' I remind her.

'Well, she's alone in her room if you want to try now. I'll wait outside.'

'OK.'

I head for the door.

'Mia,' my auntie calls after me.

I stop and turn around, preparing myself for a heartfelt thank you.

'Put some clothes on first, will you?'

I laugh to myself as I grab something to throw on. Perhaps that was too much to hope for.

'Hey, Teen Mom,' I say as I walk into Hannah's room. I hear the click of my auntie's tongue as I close the door behind me.

Hannah, who is sitting on her bed, hugging her knees, gives me a half-hearted laugh.

'First up, I am so sorry for the way your mum found out about this, that was not my intention. It's just Leo was going on and on about it—'

'It's OK,' she interrupts. 'I'm fifteen and pregnant and your life is messier than mine.'

'Thanks for that,' I reply, when I realise she's serious.

'I was too scared to tell my mum anyway, so you sort of did me a favour, but now she's being a total freak about it.'

'I don't think she knows what to say or do,' I tell her honestly. 'The important thing to remember is that you have so many options. No matter what you decide, your life isn't over. Do you know how many familiar faces returned to sit their GCSEs with baby bumps in my year? Three. And if you don't think you're ready to be a mum, then there are so many options for that too.'

Hannah nods, listening attentively.

'The important thing is to make an appointment with your doctor when you get back home, get it confirmed and then she'll let you know what's next.'

'How do you know so much about so much?' Hannah asks.

'I watch a lot of movies,' I laugh. 'Shall I call your mum back in here? If she's being a freak, I'll tell her to chill. She *does* want to be there for you.'

'OK, yeah.'

'Oh, Grandma June,' I call out, shortly before my unimpressed auntie walks in.

'I think she thinks she's funny,' June tells her daughter with a slight snigger as she sits down next to her.

'I'm sorry for not telling you sooner,' Hannah tells her mum.

'And I'm sorry for reacting the way I did,' she replies. 'Let's just enjoy the wedding, go home and then we'll discuss what to do.'

Hannah nods before hugging her mum.

'Aww, that's nice,' I say as I back towards to the door. 'I think the wedding is going to be a blast. No alcohol for you,' I remind Hannah.

'Mia, she's fifteen!' my auntie snaps.

I roll my eyes. Underage drinking is unthinkable, but underage sex is fine.

Just as I am about to leave, my auntie mouths the words 'thank you' to me.

I wave my hand at her, to tell her it's nothing. I'm just glad I could help them. It feels weird to admit it to myself, but I'm going to miss this lot when I go home.

Chapter 49

I didn't stay on top of the world for very long – a matter of hours – before I came crashing back down to earth.

The wedding ceremony took place on the beach earlier today, and as I walked down the aisle ahead of my sister, I came face to face with Leo, who I had successfully avoided up until then. Seeing his face – his sad dark eyes – and how gorgeous he looked in his suit, only served as a reminder of just how much I like him. He gave me a brief smile as I approached him, but that was that. No further interaction.

Now we're all in the beach house, in the middle of dinner. I have noticed Leo and Nancy getting on well, talking lots and laughing together. This is absolutely unbearable for me now, so I'm sitting on the stairs alone, drinking champagne. Were it not for the alcohol in my hand, I'd look like a stroppy child, refusing to go on stage for her ballet recital. It's the grumpy face, the tutu and the tiara that's doing it.

'You OK, Kid?' my granddad asks as he passes me.

'I'm good, just going over my speech,' I reply.

'You're giving a speech?'

'Belle asked me to.'

My granddad laughs mischievously.

'Oh, she'll approve of it, don't worry. Mushy junk that would be at home in one of my movies.'

'I'll leave you to it,' my granddad tells me, patting me on the shoulder as he heads back to the dining room.

I pull out my speech from the depths of my cleavage and give it the once over. Thankfully I wrote this before my own encounter with love, so it's just false instead of bitter. Not that anyone will be able to tell, not if I've done my job properly.

I wander back into the room where Leo and Nancy are still laughing together. It's the first thing I notice and trying to block it out is burning my eyes.

'Your dress suits you,' my mum tells me as I pass her. She's standing around with a drink in her hand, and I would guess it's maybe her twelfth of the day judging by how fresh and friendly she looks. And I think that might have been a compliment she just paid me.

'Thanks, I think,' I reply. 'You're looking pretty foxy yourself.'

My mum laughs and rolls her eyes before taking me by the arm and pulling me close.

'I'm proud of you,' she tells me. 'Everyone is amazed you're doing so well in America.'

Now is definitely not the time to tell her I lost my job last night, because I don't think she's ever told me that she is proud of me.

'Shame I'm such a mess in other areas,' I half-laugh.

'No, you're a smart girl. Belle has always needed that bit of extra attention, but not my Mia. You're smart and independent. You don't need anyone's approval, you're happy with who you are. I know I can be hard on you sometimes – I think sometimes I do it to make Belle feel better, she feels so plain and stupid compared to her successful sister. Don't tell her I said that.'

Perhaps quizzing my mum while she's drunk isn't my most ethical move, but ethics have never been my strong suit.

'If you're so proud of me, why don't you act like it?'

'Because it might go to your head,' she explains, gesticulating wildly and sloshing a little of her drink onto the carpet. 'When you got that first job, we hardly saw you. It was like you didn't have time for us anymore.'

'Mum, it's a demanding job, I was working—'

'I know,' she interrupts me. 'Then you moved away. I suppose we thought maybe you'd got above yourself.'

'And now?'

'You're still my little girl. You may be more grown up – and your clothes may be much smaller these days,' she adds as she nods towards my short dress. Well, it wouldn't be my mum if she didn't get a dig in. 'But I love you.'

My jaw drops, but I don't get the chance to say anything before Belle appears.

'Am I up first with my speech?' I ask her. She is every inch the blushing bride. She is positively glowing as she floats around the room in her white dress, thanking everyone and smiling for photos.

'I'm first,' Leo interrupts. I hadn't realised he had crept up on us.

'Oh, OK.'

Everyone takes their seats and Leo gently taps his glass with his fork.

'Ladies and gentlemen, if I could have your attention,' he starts, instantly commanding the attention of the room. 'Thank you. So, I had this funny speech all planned out. I've known Dan and his family for as long as I can remember. Growing up, it was just my mum and me, and the Ryan family made us feel like we were one of them. So, instead of teasing Dan, I just want to wish him and Annabelle all the best. It's not that true love is rare these days, I think it is just as common as it ever was, but people don't always respect it. People fall in love, and they let other people fall in love with them, and then they just walk out of their lives like it means nothing, like they can just find that magic with someone else,' he rants.

Oh God, this is so blatantly for my benefit.

'Anyway,' he continues. 'I'm going to keep this short. To Dan and Annabelle, and to respecting love.'

Leo raises his glass and everyone drinks to his toast.

As everyone chats about Leo's speech, I pull myself to my feet, careful not to let my tutu knock everything off the table in front of me.

'Excuse me,' I start, but no one can hear me. No one that is except Leo, who is just staring at me, and looking amused because no one is listening to me.

'Hello,' I try again, still with no luck, so I grab a knife and tap it on the side of an empty glass on the table, only for it to smash into a thousand pieces. Everyone falls silent and stares at me.

'What? It worked,' I tell my audience. 'Right, my turn to give a speech.'

I pull the piece of paper from my bra and stare at it. I want to tell everyone the wonderful things I wrote about love, and about how my sister and Dan are perfect for each other, but who does Leo think he is? Blatantly talking about me in front of everyone like that. I just need to keep my cool, deliver my speech and then get so drunk the rest of the day goes as quickly as possible.

'Anyone with eyes can see that Belle and Dan are perfect for each other. Belle told me that she knew she loved Dan from the second she laid eyes on him, and love isn't always easy to get to grips with.'

'You got to grips with Mike pretty easily, didn't you?' Leo calls out, causing Belle to shoot him a filthy look.

Is he heckling me? Seriously? I look down at my speech again before promptly screwing it up. There's no turning back now.

'Love is a funny thing. People seem to think if you have strong feelings for someone, that's all that matters. If you're in the right place at the right time, you can get a fairy tale ending, but if you don't have those perfect conditions, then you're going to have to ruin your life to make it work. And is it really worth it?'

My audience stare at me, clearly confused by both the dark

route my speech has taken and how off-topic it is.

'But, yeah, erm, Belle and Dan are happy together and perfect for each other and they just work. Neither of them has to try really hard or force anything; it's just natural and I hope they have a long and happy life together.'

I raise my glass, safe in the knowledge I fucked that up. As everyone raises their glasses and drinks to that – if only to shut me up – Leo taps on his glass again and stands up.

'Actually, sorry, if I could just have your attention again. I just wanted to say that, I think if you truly love someone, it isn't difficult at all. It's the easiest thing in the world to just love someone and have them love you back, and you're really lucky if you find that. You would have to be crazy to throw away something so amazing for a bunch of stuff that doesn't matter.' He raises his glass again. 'Anyway, to Belle and Dan.'

No one has time to raise a glass for the third time before I'm on my feet again.

'But,' I start, 'at what point does love become more important than a career or your friends or your home? People are too quick to think they're in love. Belle and Dan might know it was love at first sight now that they're married, but you can't be certain at the time. You build on it and it becomes love; you don't throw your life away because you *think* you're in love.'

'Oh, so that's why you kissed me within five minutes of meeting me?' Leo interrupts me, and if it wasn't before, now it's clear to everyone that these are not our speeches.

'Are you fourteen years old?' I snap. 'People meet in clubs and kiss in less time, it's called lust.'

'So, what, you used me for sex?'

'Enough!' Dan bellows, bringing our little argument to an end in the loudest and scariest tone of voice I have ever heard – or maybe it just seems that way because it's quiet little Dan.

I probably should have risen above that, but Leo just makes me so angry.

'I want both of you to get out,' Dan insists. 'I will not have you ruining Belle's day. Out.'

He points towards the patio doors that lead out onto the beach.

'Out!' he shouts, because neither of us makes a move.

Like a couple of kids being removed from the classroom for disruptive behaviour, we both make our way outside.

Chapter 50

After my little performance with Leo, I feel about as ridiculous as I probably look in this tutu. Safe in the knowledge I will never wear this dress again, I plonk myself down on the sand and look out to sea. Leo sits down next to me and stares out in the same direction, neither of us saying a word.

He seemed so cool and calm before I started causing drama for him. I never would have had him down as the kind to go rogue during the speeches. In a strange way, I'm impressed.

'What do you want from me, Mia?' he asks, finally breaking the silence.

'I don't want anything from you,' I reply forcefully, but as I catch the sad look on his face I soften a little. 'I don't know what I want from you.'

'I *do* love you,' he tells me. 'I know that's not what you want to hear, but I can't help it.'

'I have strong feelings for you – stronger than I've ever had for anyone – but I don't know how to process them,' I admit. He deserves a little honesty. I was terrified of saying that out loud, but Leo instantly makes me feel at ease.

'You do a very convincing job of acting like you understand love in your movies,' he tells me with a smile.

I shrug my shoulders.

'Walt Disney wrote a very convincing talking mouse,' I reply – that one always serves me well.

'There was a lot about love at first sight in that movie of yours I watched. Did you write any of it?'

'Yes.'

'Do you believe in it?'

'No. Well, I didn't. I am wrong on rare occasions,' I tell him with a smile. 'Look, it's been so long since I was in a real relationship, I don't even remember what they're like.'

'And yet I'm still willing to remind you,' he smiles, taking one of my hands from my lap and holding it in his. 'Are you happy in LA?' he asks. 'Truly happy?'

'Well, I thought I was. All I had there was work.'

'Had?' he asks curiously.

'I got fired,' I confess.

'When?'

'Yesterday. When I refused to bail on the wedding to go back to work.'

Leo squeezes my hand.

'You're a lovely girl, Mia Valentina.'

'Thanks, just don't tell anyone. I've got a reputation to keep in the dirt.'

We sit in silence for a few more minutes, with nothing but the sound of the sea and the noise of me tapping my shoes together to break the silence.

'So, what reasons have you got to go back to LA now?' he asks.

'Not many. I could start looking for another job – I'll need to, the money I have saved up won't last me long over there.'

'What about people? No one to go back for?'

'No one to go back for,' I echo.

'Look, don't think I'm trying to rush you into anything, because it's quite the opposite, but all I know is that you've got a house full of people in there who love you—'

I open my mouth to interrupt him, but he doesn't give me the chance.

'Even if they don't show it,' he adds. 'And there's someone sitting next to you who loves you, so why don't you move back to the UK for a bit? Find a job here, do a little to enrich our movie industry, you traitor.'

He laughs and I see that smile of his I love so much, and I don't know how I could ever say no to him again. No one has ever cared for me so much before.

'That might be a good idea, taking some time out to figure out my next move,' I tell him. It's not much of a commitment, but it won't hurt to give it a go. I was thinking how I'd miss everyone when I went back; it might be nice to get involved again with the family, especially now we're all on better terms.

'There's no pressure from me,' he tells me. 'We'll just see how it goes.'

I nod my head.

'And you never know,' he starts, 'maybe next summer it will be us getting married on the beach.'

I narrow my eyes at him, and he struggles to keep a straight face, dissolving into laughter once again.

'You had me going for a second,' I laugh, pushing him back onto the sand and climbing on top of him. The second we start kissing, I know that I have made exactly the right choice. Is it love? I don't know, but it certainly feels like it. As Leo sits up and wraps his arms around me, I finally feel like I want to jump off a building, because I don't doubt for a second that he would catch me in his big, fireman arms.

***

After kissing on the beach for what feels like hours, like a couple of teens in the middle of a holiday romance, the rest of the party head outside to join us.

'Have you two figured it out?' my sister asks me.

'We have,' I tell her. 'And I've got some news. I'm thinking of moving back home for a while.'

'What?' she screeches. 'That's amazing!'

'I'm just going to apologise to Dan,' Leo excuses himself.

'So, are you two going to make a go of it?' Belle asks.

'I don't know.' I can't help but smile widely. 'But this just feels right.'

'But what about work?'

This is the part where I could tell her that I lost my job, and that the straw that broke the camel's back was sticking around for her wedding, but she seems so happy and she would feel so bad if she found out.

'I can find work here,' I tell her with a smile.

'Mia, I am so pleased for you.'

Belle grabs me and hugs me and I swear, despite my turbulent time here, I don't think my family have ever been so affectionate towards me.

'Likewise,' I tell her.

'Are you ready to dance?' she asks me.

Everyone is out on the beach for a bit of a disco. Now that the sun is starting to set, lanterns are being lit and there's a band getting ready to start playing on the patio.

'I am.'

'Can I go and tell everyone your news?' she asks excitedly.

'Sure,' I reply.

With that, my sister rushes off to tell everyone that I'll be moving back home, and now I really, really feel like I've made the right decision.

Chapter 51

The band is in full swing, it's getting dark and the beach looks gorgeous, lit up with pretty lanterns and abuzz with people dancing. On the surface everything looks perfect, but if you look closer you'll see that a few of the lanterns have gone out, almost everyone has sand on their outfit and the song the band is currently playing is missing a bass line, because I saw Josh and Max unplug him, and he hasn't realised yet.

That's life though, isn't it? In movies everything looks perfect, but in life you don't have a cinematographer giving you flattering lighting and angles, you don't have a script supervisor making sure that everything looks right and makes sense, you don't have a hair and makeup team to make sure you always look beautiful without a hair out of place and you don't have a director telling you what to do. Life is hard and people are going to mess up, but going about your days in a little protective bubble (even if said bubble is a swanky LA lad pad) and never letting anyone in, is no way to live life. You've got to take chances and risk getting hurt – even if it means putting yourself out there without the rest of the crew to back you up. Although now that I've decided to move back home for a while, it looks like I'm going to have quite the crew supporting me. My gran keeps tabs and makes helpful suggestions on the way I look, Belle has been doing a great job of making sure things make sense and as for my director ... well, Leo seems to be doing a pretty good job there.

Everyone is on their feet, enjoying the music, and as I dance with Leo, I don't think I could feel happier. Add being a great mover to his vast list of skills – although I suppose I already knew that one, just for different reasons.

Just when I think life is as close to movie perfection as it's ever going to get, Leo pulls me close and over his shoulder I notice a figure approaching the party – it's Chris the lifeguard.

'Back in a minute,' I whisper into Leo's ear.

'No worries,' he replies, 'I promised Meg I'd dance with her.'

I watch Leo run over to my cousin, who is short even for a thirteen-year-old, and grab her, lifting her up in the air.

'Hey stranger,' I say as I shuffle over to Chris, greeting him just outside the lit area so we're less likely to be seen. I can't help but notice he's wearing his lifeguard shorts – perhaps he thinks they're a deal-breaker for me. 'I didn't think I'd see you again.'

'Well, your dad invited me, didn't he? That night I saved your life,' he reminds me.

'Ah, yes, fond memories of that night,' I reply sarcastically.

'Anyway, weddings aren't really my scene. I just thought I'd swing by, see if you wanted to ditch this lot, maybe go finish what we keep trying to start?'

He wiggles his eyebrows as he grabs me by the tutu, pulling me close.

I glance back towards the party and watch as Leo dances with Meg, holding her up in the air so she is the same height as him, and the words leave my lips before I even have time to give it much thought.

'Sorry,' I reply. 'I'm taken.'

Acknowledgements

Thanks so much to Sophia, George and the rest of the team at HQ for all of their hard work on my books. You're doing such a fantastic job.

Thank you to my lovely readers for taking the time to read and review my books. It means so much to me.

Finally, thank you to my incredible family (Joe, Joey, James, Kim, Pino, Aud & Darcy) for all of their support – I couldn't do it without you.

Fallen in love with *Always a Bridesmaid*?

Discover *Truth or Date*!

Another uplifting and laugh-out-loud romantic comedy from Portia MacIntosh.

Continue reading for a sneak preview of *Truth or Date* …

Chapter 1

'You look good in red,' Nick tells me, stifling a laugh.

Were I not so happy to have just tied the knot with the love of my life, I would've climbed the nearest palm tree, removed the biggest coconut I could find and thrown it at my darling hubby because, as much as I love him, I hate it when he's right. Last week as we shopped for the few last bits for our honeymoon, I dragged Nick into Hollister where I saw this beautiful cream sundress. I knew that it would be perfect for our trip to Hawaii, but Nick didn't seem convinced. He just doesn't buy into fashion; he's one of those guys who just doesn't get it, whereas I'm the kind of girl who would swap a kidney for an Hermès bag. It wasn't so much the price Nick took issue with (although he did say it was a lot of money for very little material), what he worried about most was the fact the dress was cream.

'You'll spill,' he told me as I admired it on its hanger.

'Fuck off,' I replied.

'You will,' he insisted. 'You're the messiest girl in the world.'

Of course, this just made me want the dress all the more, so I bought it and here we are, the first day of our honeymoon and I've spilled my Lava Flow cocktail all the way down the front. Just like Nick said I would.

Nick retrieves the chunk of pineapple that garnished my drink from my cleavage and pops it in his mouth.

'I told you you'd spill on it.' He chuckles. 'It's a miracle you didn't spill on your wedding dress.'

'That's because I *couldn't* eat in it,' I admit, although it wasn't because I didn't want to. 'If I so much as inhaled too deeply, it felt like it might burst open – and flashing my boobs on my wedding day is just the kind of *Carry On* moment you expect of me. None of the glossy wedding mags prepare you for the fact that your wedding dress will be the most uncomfortable thing you'll ever wear.'

'Yeah, they don't warn you that the first thing your new bride will do when she gets to the honeymoon suite will be hurry off her dress before pillaging the minibar either.'

I scoop some of the cocktail slush from my chest and flick it at Nick's bare stomach. He just laughs, lying back on the sand to catch some rays.

'Throw it in the sea,' he suggests. 'Back to its natural habitat. I'll bet it has missed the sound of the waves in the shop – so stupid.'

'Leave Hollister out of this,' I snap, jokily.

I peel off my dress, lie down on the sand next to Nick and rest my head gently on his bicep.

'I'll tan weird if you cuddle me.' He laughs, the sweltering heat from the Hawaiian sun beaming down on us.

'You'll get over it,' I reply.

Lying here with the man of my dreams, with nothing but the peaceful sound of the ocean filling my ears and the delicious smell of strawberries filling my nostrils, I sigh and smile to myself. I am so disgustingly happy.

Unable to resist him a second longer, I climb on top of Nick, leaning forwards to kiss him passionately. He places his hands on my hips before running them slowly up my body. I part our lips, but only so I can moan softly at his touch.

'I love you, Nick,' I tell him.

'I love you too, Ruby,' he replies. 'Ruby ... Ruby ... Ruby ...'

Nick's voice grows louder, louder still and then more aggressive. It sounds like he's pissed off, come to think of it.

'Ruby,' he shouts. 'Wake up.'

I jolt awake suddenly, sitting upright.

'What the hell?' he asks, angrily.

I glance around for a second, taking in my surroundings ... I'm not in Hawaii at all, I'm in my living room. I'm not wearing a bikini, I'm in my underwear. I'm not lying on a beach, I'm on top of Ben, a guy I've been seeing for a couple of weeks. Oh, and Nick isn't my husband, he's my flatmate. My boring, stuck-up, joyless flatmate that I can't stand. And I was just having a sex dream about him – eww! I feel my cheeks flush with shame – not because he's caught me semi-naked with a bloke, but because I was dreaming about *him*. That I was in love with him, that I'd married him ... *I was about to have sex with him!*

'What time is it?' I ask him, rubbing my tired eyes, only to cover my hands in black eye make-up.

'It's 7 a.m.,' he tells me, his eyes shooting laser beams of judgement at me as he glares. Luckily for me I'm used to Nick looking down his nose at me, and anyway, the sheer volume of body glitter I'm wearing can easily deflect even the strongest laser.

'What day is it?' I ask.

Nick shakes his head and sighs. 'Friday. It's Friday, Ruby.'

'Oh fuck, I'm at work in an hour,' I reply as I massage my temples, my hangover from last night now in full force.

As Nick stands over me, eating a bowl of Weetabix like he does every morning after he gets back from the gym, about to head out to his proper serious job, I can feel him judging me. It's not my fault he doesn't know how to have fun, is it?

'So this is your online dating weirdo. How are things going?' he asks, nodding towards the heavily tattooed, muscular man that I'm using as a bed. I take a moment too long to answer. 'That badly?'

'All good,' I reply, unconvincingly. I've been dating Ben for about three weeks now, and things aren't exactly going that well. Last night was our third date, and despite every girly magazine I could get my hands on assuring me that date three was when the magic happened, the magic did not happen last night. Still, from the way Nick is looking at me right now, I doubt he believes that. In Nick's head I'm his chaotic flatmate who seemingly ploughs through internet dates, when in reality that's not the case – I wish I were getting even one per cent of the action Nick thought I was.

Nick fakes a gasp.

'Are you telling me that you hooked up with a guy you met via your phone and it's not a fairy-tale romance?' he asks sarcastically.

I cast my mind back to our date last night. As much as I don't want to give Nick the satisfaction of being right, the need to tell someone feels greater.

'Things have been going well, it's just … I met up with him yesterday and he told me he was taking me to a family party,' I start.

'Weird,' Nick chimes in. 'You've only been on a couple of dates with him, kid.'

'I know, and weirder still: what he didn't tell me was that it was a wake.'

'A wake?' Nick echoes loudly in disbelief, and in a much higher pitch than his voice usually is.

'I'm awake, I'm awake,' Ben says, panicked as he jumps to his feet. He does so without having realised I was on top of him, causing me to fall back onto the sofa. As he glances between an angry-looking Nick, and me in my underwear, he puts two and two together – coming up with wrong answer.

'Look, calm down, nothing happened, OK? I didn't sleep with your girlfriend,' Ben babbles, stressing it in such a way that makes it sound like this is an excuse he has to make often.

'Oh, charming,' I say, annoyed that Ben thinks I'm the kind of girl who would have a boyfriend and still date around, but he isn't listening.

'She's not my girlfriend, she's my roommate,' Nick corrects him. I watch as Ben expresses visible relief.

'Well, in that case, good to meet you. I'm Jonathan,' he chirps, offering Nick a hand to shake. Nick doesn't oblige.

'Your name is Jonathan? I've spent three dates calling you Ben,' I blurt out.

'Yeah, I thought that was like a cute nickname or something,' he says and laughs.

I giggle, puzzled, but what I see as a hilarious story for social media, Nick is completely unimpressed by.

'I just don't get you, Ruby Wood,' Nick says angrily, pointlessly using my full name like a pissed-off parent. 'What are you doing with your life?'

'What are you, my fucking dad? Why can't you just be cool?' I ask him, sounding like a teenager whose dad just confiscated her cigarettes – incidentally, something Nick has done with me before. In the end it was just easier to quit smoking than it was to put up with his complaints and his borderline OCD smell-removal techniques.

'I've got to get to work,' Nick tells us. He heads to the kitchen, rinses his bowl and spoon, places them in the dishwasher and then leaves without so much as a 'see you later'.

Jonathan – not Ben – and I are sitting on the sofa next to each other awkwardly.

'So your roommate seems fun,' Jonathan says sarcastically.

'He really is like my dad or my granddad or something,' I reply, irritated, still sounding like a teenager.

'You should move out,' he tells me, like maybe that hadn't crossed my mind.

'There's no way I can find a flat this central for this cheap,' I tell him honestly. 'Nick comes from a super-rich family, but he won't take any money from them, so he reckons he can't afford to move either. If either of us should move out, it should be him, don't you think?'

'Yeah, maybe,' Jonathan replies, followed by an awkward silence.

I wonder how I managed to call him by the wrong name for so long. I suppose that's app dating for you – it's like fishing with multiple lines. I guess as I reeled this one in, I mixed up his name with a different fish.

'Listen, Ruby, we've had fun right?'

I think for moment. No. No we haven't. On our first date he suggested we go to the cinema – a rookie error, because it involves sitting in silence for two hours – and on the second we went to a bar and got drunk. Oh, and then the wake date. Jonathan is a good-looking dude, but he's a bit weird. There's something almost tortured about his personality, like he's got some issues he needs to work through. Don't we all, though? Still, he does have his good qualities too, so I'm happy to see where this goes. I'm not going to ditch the guy just because he took me to a family funeral without telling me.

'We have,' I lie with a warm smile.

'Well, I think we should call it a day,' he tells me.

I feel my smile drop. 'What?'

'I just … I think we're moving in different directions.'

'Oh my God, seriously? Are you really giving me the old lines? Is it not me, is it you?'

Jonathan grabs my hand.

'It *is* me,' he assures me, giving my hand a reassuring squeeze.

'You're damn fucking right it's you,' I reply.

Jonathan drops my hand and jumps to his feet, wrestling his clothes on as he talks, his tone suddenly becoming significantly less friendly.

'OK, cards on the table, when we got back last night I thought I might get lucky, but you didn't even want to sleep with me,' he explains.

'Dude, we'd just got back from *your dad's wake* – that you didn't even tell me we were going to.'

Oh, did I not mention that it was his dad's funeral? I suppose

I didn't want to give Nick too much ammunition for when he teases me about this every day until one of us moves out.

'Yeah, well don't you think I needed some comfort after that?'

'So I'm supposed to bang you out of sheer sympathy?'

'Well, it would've been nice,' he replies, like it's a fairly reasonable expectation.

'You're disgusting. Get out,' I demand.

Jonathan puts on his shoes and heads for the door, slamming it behind him.

Lying back on the sofa, I massage my temples for a moment. My head is banging, and I've got to be at work in an hour. Is getting dumped a good enough reason to call in sick?

'Awkward,' I say to myself. 'So, so awkward.' Not only what just happened with Jonathan, but my dream about Nick too. Not only do Nick and I not get on, but we're like enemies, both driving the other crazy, but neither of us is in a position to move out. The fact we're stuck with one another only makes us hate each other even more.

I glance around the floor for my outfit from last night, only to find that Nick has folded my dress and placed it neatly over the back of the sofa. I grab it, shaking my head at his anal neatness as I meaningfully and defiantly unfold it. All communal areas of the house must be neat and tidy to a military standard. Sir, yes, sir.

Tossing my clothes through my bedroom doorway, I head straight for the shower. I know that I'm running late, but after an uncomfortable night on the sofa cuddled up to a sweaty, emotional wreck of a man, there's no way I can go to work without washing some of yesterday's failed date off of me. I'm literally going to wash Jonathan out of my hair – well, his sweat and tears at least.

I turn on the shower, cranking up the hot water to make the bathroom nice and steamy while I brush my teeth. I've got that fuzzy-mouth feeling you're left with after too many sugary alcoholic drinks. Typically, I'm out of toothpaste, but that's what flatmates are for, right? Borrowing things from.

I can see from Nick's toothpaste tube that he's used approximately 1/8 so far, with the used 1/8 neatly folded over a few times, thus giving the appearance of a perfectly full, slightly smaller tool. Does he really have that much spare time on his hands? Really? In another act of defiance, I not only use his toothpaste, but I squeeze from the middle of the tube, leaving behind a big, fingertip-shaped dent in it.

Finally stepping into the hot shower feels glorious. I can feel my bad date washing off me. Sure, I'm annoyed at how he behaved, but mostly I'm just annoyed to have another bad date on my romantic CV. Hardly seems worth putting Jonathan down, for a mere three weeks, but they always say it's better to put jobs down that you didn't have for long/got fired from, rather than have big, unaccounted-for gaps in your employment, right?

I grab my delicious-smelling piña-colada-scented shower gel and rub it all over my body. I love the smell of it because it reminds me of my two favourite things: cocktails and the beach. Which reminds me, I'm not only washing away Jonathan, I need to scrub myself clean of that sex dream about Nick. Nick Hall! I can't believe it.

I think to myself as I shampoo my hair. I'll admit that the first time I met Nick here in this flat, the first thing I noticed about him was how sexy he was. A sexy doctor, no less – that's like every girl's fantasy. Sharing this small space didn't suit us though, and it's amazing how quickly you can go off a person when they start to grate on you. One thing I can definitely put on my CV is that I'm not shallow, because not even Nick's chiselled good looks, bulging biceps or romance-novel-worthy profession can sway how I feel about him.

So why the hell did I dream that about him today? It can't mean anything, can it? All that stuff about dreams meaning things has got to be a load of bollocks.

I shut off the water, and shut my dream about Nick out of my mind.

Once in the messy confines of my bedroom – where I am free to express my unorthodox organisational skills as I see fit – I grab a dress from the large pile of clothing on my bedroom floor – the division of my floordrobe, which I have dubbed Mount Clothesmore – and search for my make-up bag because today my face is going to need everything it has to offer. If I don't get a move on, I'm going to be late for work, but it's better to be late than ugly, right?

Dear Reader,

We hope you enjoyed reading this book. If you did, we'd be so appreciative if you left a review. It really helps us and the author to bring more books like this to you.

Here at HQ Digital we are dedicated to publishing fiction that will keep you turning the pages into the early hours. Don't want to miss a thing? To find out more about our books, promotions, discover exclusive content and enter competitions you can keep in touch in the following ways:

JOIN OUR COMMUNITY:

Sign up to our new email newsletter: http://smarturl.it/SignUpHQ

Read our new blog www.hqstories.co.uk

X https://twitter.com/HQStories
f www.facebook.com/HQStories

BUDDING WRITER?

We're also looking for authors to join the HQ Digital family!
Find out more here:

https://www.hqstories.co.uk/want-to-write-for-us/

Thanks for reading, from the HQ Digital team